"You want to consult me about a goldfish?"

Perry Mason couldn't believe his ears. Prospective clients had come to see him about many things but never an affair as seemingly silly as this.

He didn't even have time to tell Harrington Faulkner that he wouldn't take the case before a process server slapped on a summons and complaint for $100,000.

During the evening a golddigger got Faulkner to write a check for $5,000.

Before two days had passed there was a murder.

And both Perry Mason and Della Street were in danger of being convicted as accessories.

THE CASE OF THE GOLDDIGGER'S PURSE
was originally published by
William Morrow & Company, Inc.

THE CASE OF THE
GOLDDIGGER'S PURSE
ERLE STANLEY
GARDNER

PUBLISHED BY POCKET BOOKS NEW YORK

THE CASE OF THE GOLDDIGGER'S PURSE

William Morrow edition published May, 1945

A *Pocket Book* edition

1st printing............May, 1951
14th printing.........March, 1970

This *Pocket Book* edition includes every word
contained in the original, higher-priced edition. It is printed
from brand-new plates made from completely reset, clear, easy-to-read
type. *Pocket Book* editions are published by Pocket Books, a division
of Simon & Schuster, Inc., 630 Fifth Avenue, New York, N.Y. 10020.
Trademarks registered in the United States and other countries.

L

Standard Book Number: 671-75526-9.
Printed in the U.S.A.

Cast of Characters

THE CASE OF THE
GOLDDIGGER'S PURSE

1

Perry Mason, seated at the restaurant table, looked up at the tense, nervous face of the man who had deserted his spectacular companion to accost him.

"You said you wanted to consult me about a goldfish?" Mason repeated blankly. His smile was almost incredulous.

"Yes."

Mason shook his head. "I'm afraid you'd find my fees were a little too high . . ."

"I don't care how high your fees are. I can afford to pay any amount within reason, and I will."

Mason's tone contained quiet finality. "I'm sorry, but I've just finished with a rather exacting case. I have neither the time nor the inclination to bother with goldfish. I . . ."

A tall, dignified gentleman gravely approached the table, said to the man who was regarding Mason with an expression of puzzled futility, "Harrington Faulkner?"

"Yes," the man said with the close-clipped finality of one accustomed to authority. "I'm engaged now, however, as you can see. I . . ."

The newcomer's hand made a quick motion to his breast pocket. There was a brief flash of paper as he pushed a folded oblong into Faulkner's hand.

"Copy of summons, and complaint, case of Carson

versus Faulkner. Defamation of character, a hundred thousand dollars. Here's the original summons—directing your attention to the signature of the clerk and the seal of the court. No need to get sore about it. It's all in the line of work. If I didn't serve it somebody else would. See your lawyer. You have ten days to answer. If the other fellow isn't entitled to anything he can't get it. If he is, it's your hard luck. I'm just the man who serves the papers. No good getting mad. Thank you. Good night."

The words rattled along with such staccato rapidity that they sounded like a sudden, unexpected burst of hail on a metal roof.

The process server turned with quick, self-effacing grace, and merged himself into a group of diners who were just leaving the restaurant.

Faulkner, acting like a man who is in the middle of a bad dream and is being swept helplessly along by the events of his nightmare, pushed the papers down into a side pocket, turned without a word, walked back to his table and rejoined his companion.

Mason watched him thoughtfully.

The waiter hovered over the table. Mason smiled reassuringly at Della Street, his secretary, then turned to Paul Drake, the private detective who had entered a few minutes before.

"Joining us, Paul?"

"A big coffee and a slab of mince pie is all I want," Drake said.

Mason gave the waiter their orders. "What do you make of the girl?" he asked Della Street as the waiter withdrew.

"You mean the one with Faulkner?"

"Yes."

Della Street laughed. "If he keeps playing around with her he'll have another summons served on him."

Drake leaned forward so that he could look past the corner of the booth. "I'll take a look at that myself," he

2

announced, and then after a moment said, "Oh, oh. *That's* a dish!"

Mason's eyes thoughtfully studied the pair. "Incongruous enough," he said.

"Notice the getup," Drake went on. "The skin-fitting dress, the long, long eyelashes, the burgundy fingernails. Looking in those eyes, he's already forgotten about the summons in his side pocket. Bet he doesn't read it until . . . Looks as though he's coming back, Perry."

Abruptly the man pushed back his chair, arose with no word to his companion, marched determinedly back to Mason's table. "Mr. Mason," he said, speaking with the crisp, deliberate articulation of a man determined to make his point, "it has just occurred to me that you may have received an entirely erroneous impression of the nature of the case about which I was trying to consult you. I think perhaps when I mentioned that it concerned a goldfish, you naturally considered the case one of minor importance. It isn't. The goldfish in question is a very fine specimen of the Veiltail Moor Telescope. The case also concerns a crooked partner, a secret formula for controlling gill disease, and a golddigger."

Mason regarded the anxious face of the man who was standing beside the table and tried not to grin. "A goldfish *and* a golddigger," he said. "After all, perhaps we'd better hear about it. Suppose you draw up a chair and tell me about it."

The man's face showed sudden satisfaction. "Then you'll take my case and . . ."

"I mean I'm willing to listen and that's all," Mason said. "This is Della Street, my secretary, and Paul Drake, head of the Drake Detective Agency, who quite frequently assists me in gathering facts. Won't you invite your companion to come over and join us, and we may as well . . ."

"Oh, she's all right. Let her sit there."

"She won't mind?" Mason asked.

Faulkner shook his head.

"Who is she?" Mason asked.

Without changing his tone in the least, Faulkner said, "She's the golddigger."

Drake said warningly, "You leave that baby alone at that table and you won't find her alone when you get back."

Faulkner said fervently, "I'd give a thousand dollars to the man who would take her off my hands."

Drake said laughingly, "Done for five hundred. It's cheap at half the price."

Faulkner regarded him with unhumorous appraisal, drew up a chair. The young woman he had left sitting at the table merely glanced over at him, then opened her purse, held up a mirror and started checking her make-up with the careful appraisal of a good merchant inspecting his stock-in-trade.

2

Mason said to Faulkner, "You haven't even read the papers that process server handed you."

Faulkner made a gesture of dismissal. "I don't have to. It's just part of a campaign to annoy me."

"What's he suing for?"

"A hundred thousand dollars, the man who served the papers said."

Mason said, "You're not interested enough to read them?"

"I'm not interested in anything Elmer Carson does to annoy me."

"Tell me about the goldfish," Mason said.

Faulkner said, "The Veiltail Moor Telescope is a prized goldfish. The uninitiated would hardly consider him a goldfish. He isn't gold. He's black."

"All over?" Mason asked.

"Even the eyes."

"What's a Telescope fish?" Drake asked.

"A species of goldfish that has been developed by breeding. They're called Telescopes because the eyes protrude from the sockets, sometimes as much as a quarter of an inch."

"Isn't that rather—unprepossessing?" Della Street asked.

"It might be to the uninitiated. Some people have called the Veiltail Moor Telescope the Fish of Death. Pure superstition. Just the way people react to the black color."

"I don't think I'd like them," Della Street said.

"Some people don't," Faulkner agreed, as though the subject held no particular interest. "Waiter, will you please bring my order over to this table?"

"Yes, sir. And the lady's order?"

"Serve it to her over there."

Mason said, "After all, Faulkner, I'm not certain I like that method of handling the situation. Regardless of what the girl is, you're dining with her, and . . ."

"That's all right. She won't mind. She isn't the least bit interested in what I'm going to talk about."

"What is she interested in?" Mason asked.

"Cash."

"What's her name?"

"Sally Madison."

"And she is putting the bite on you?" Mason asked.

"I'll say she is."

"Yet you take her out to dinner?"

"Oh, certainly."

"And walk away and leave her?" Della Street asked.

"I want to discuss business. She wouldn't be interested. She understands the situation thoroughly. There's no need of any concern about her."

Drake glanced at Perry Mason. The waiter brought him his mince pie and coffee, shrimp cocktails to Della Street and Mason and consommé to Harrington Faulkner.

Over at the table Faulkner had vacated, Sally Madison completed her make-up, sat with a carefully cultivated expression of demure rectitude frozen on her face. She seemed to have no further interest in Harrington Faulkner or the party he had joined.

"You don't seem to have any hard feelings," Mason said.

"Oh, I don't," Faulkner hastily disclaimed. "She's a very nice young woman—as golddiggers go."

Mason said, "If *you're* not going to read that complaint and summons, suppose you let me glance through it."

Faulkner passed it across the table.

Mason unfolded the papers, glanced through them, said, "It seems that this Elmer Carson says that you've repeatedly accused him of tampering with your goldfish; that the accusation is false and has been made with malice; that Carson wants ten thousand dollars as actual damages and ninety thousand dollars by way of punitive damages."

Faulkner seemed to have only a detached interest in the claims made against him by Elmer Carson. "You can't believe a word he says," he explained.

"Just who is he?"

"He was my partner."

"In the goldfish business?"

"Good heavens, no. The goldfish is just my own hobby. We have a real-estate business. It's incorporated. We each own one third of the stock and the balance is held by Genevieve Faulkner."

"Your wife?"

6

Faulkner cleared his throat, said with some embarrassment, "My former wife. I was divorced five years ago."

"And you and Carson aren't getting along?"

"No. For some reason there's been a sudden change in him. I've made Carson an ultimatum. He can submit a buy-or-sell offer. He's jockeying around to get the best price available. Those are minor matters, Mr. Mason. I can handle them. I want to see you about protecting my fish."

"Not about the slander suit?"

"No, no. That's all right. I have ten days on that. Lots can happen in ten days."

"Not about the golddigger?"

"No. She's all right. I'm not worried about her."

"Just about the goldfish?"

"That's right. Only, you understand, Mr. Mason, the partner and the golddigger enter into it."

"Why the concern about the goldfish?"

"Mr. Mason, I've raised this particular strain of Veil-tail Moor Telescopes and I'm proud of them. You have no idea of the thought and labor that have gone into developing this particular fish, and now they're threatened with extinction by gill disease, and that disease has been deliberately introduced into my aquarium by Elmer Carson."

"He says in his complaint," Mason said, "that you accuse him of deliberately trying to kill your fish, and it's for that he's asking damages."

"Well, he did it all right."

"Can you," Mason asked, "prove it?"

"Probably not," Faulkner admitted glumly.

"In that event," Mason told him, "you might be stuck for a large sum by way of damages."

"I suppose so," Faulkner admitted readily enough, as though the matter held no immediate interest for him.

"You don't seem particularly worried about it," Mason said.

"There's no use crossing bridges like that before you come to them," Faulkner said. "I'm in enough trouble already. Perhaps, however, I haven't made my position entirely clear. The things Carson does to annoy *me* don't mean a thing to me. I am interested right now in saving my fish. Carson knows they are dying. In fact, it is because of him that they are dying. He knows that I want to remove them for treatment. So he has filed a suit, claiming the fish are the property of the corporation and not my individual property. That is, he claims the fish are affixed to the partnership real property and that I have threatened to and will, unless restrained, tear out the tank and remove the fish and tank from the premises. Because this constitutes a severance of the real property, he has flim-flammed a judge into giving him a temporary restraining order. . . . And hang it, Mason, he's right. The confounded tank *is* affixed to the property . . . I want you to beat that restraining order. I want to establish title to the fish and the tank as my own individual property. I want that restraining order smashed and smashed hard and quick, and I think you're the man to do it."

Mason glanced across to the girl at the table Faulkner had left. She seemed to be taking no interest in the conversation. A look of synthetic, motionless innocence was frozen on her face as painting is glazed on a china cup.

"You're married?" Mason asked Faulkner. "I mean you've remarried since your divorce?"

"Oh, yes."

"When did you start playing around with Sally Madison?"

Faulkner's face showed a brief flicker of surprise. "Playing around with Sally Madison?" he repeated almost incredulously. "Good heavens, *I'm* not playing around with her."

"I thought you said she was a golddigger."

"She is."

8

"And that she was putting the bite on you?"

"Indeed she is."

Mason said, "I'm afraid you're not clarifying the situation very much," and then, reaching a sudden decision, added, "if you people will excuse me, and there's no objection on the part of Mr. Faulkner, I think I'll go talk to the golddigger and get her ideas on the case."

Waiting only for Della Street's nod and not so much as glancing at Faulkner, Mason left the table and crossed over to where Sally Madison was seated.

"Good evening," he said. "My name is Mason. I'm a lawyer."

Long lashes swept upward, dark eyes regarded the lawyer with the unabashed frankness of a speculator looking over a piece of property. "Yes, I know. You're Perry Mason, the lawyer."

"May I sit down?"

"Please do."

Mason drew up a chair.

"I think," he said, "I'm going to like this case."

"I hope you do. Mr. Faulkner needs a good lawyer."

"But," Mason pointed out, "if I agreed to represent Mr. Faulkner, it might conflict with your interest."

"Yes, I suppose so."

"It might, therefore, cut down the amount of money you'd receive."

"Oh, I think not," she said with all the assurance of a person who occupies an impregnable position.

Mason glanced quizzically at her. "How much," he asked, "do you want out of Mr. Faulkner?"

"Today it's five thousand dollars."

Mason smiled. "Why the accent on today? What was it yesterday?"

"Four thousand."

"And the day before?"

"Three."

"And what will it be tomorrow?"

"I don't know. I think he'll give me the five thousand tonight."

Mason studied the expressionless countenance, heavy with make-up. His eyes showed he was taking a keen interest in the entire affair. "Faulkner says you're a golddigger."

"Yes, he *would* think so."

"Are you?"

"Perhaps. I really don't know. Probably I am. But if Mr. Faulkner wants to throw brickbats around, let him tell you about himself. He's a tight-fisted, miserly, over-bearing— Oh, what's the use! You wouldn't understand."

Mason laughed outright. "I'm trying," he said, "to make heads or tails out of this case. So far I don't seem to be having very much success. Now will you *please* tell me what it's all about?"

She said, "My connection with it is very simple. I want money out of Harrington Faulkner."

"And just why do you think Faulkner should give you money?"

"He wants his goldfish to get well, doesn't he?"

"Apparently, but I'm afraid I don't see the connection."

For the first time since Mason had seated himself, some expression struggled through the glazed make-up of her face. "Mr. Mason, did you ever see someone whom you loved sick with tuberculosis?"

Mason's eyes were puzzled. He shook his head. "Go on," he said.

"Harrington Faulkner has money. So much money that he'd never miss five thousand dollars. He's spent thousands of dollars on his hobby. Heaven knows how much he's spent on these black goldfish alone. Not only is he rich but he's *stinking* rich, and he hasn't the faintest idea of how to enjoy his money or how to spend it so it would do him or anyone else any good. He'll just keep on piling it up until some day he'll die and that granite-hearted wife of his will fall heir to it. He's a miser except on his goldfish. And in the meantime Tom Gridley has T.B. The doctor says he needs absolute rest, freedom from worry, complete relaxation. How much chance does Tom stand of getting any of that while he's working at twenty-seven dollars a week, nine hours a day, in a pet store which is damp and smelly. . . . He hasn't had a chance to get out in the sunlight except a few brief snatches he can get on Sundays. That, of course, isn't enough even to help.

"Mr. Faulkner goes into spasms because a few black goldfish are dying of gill disease, but he'd watch Tom die of T.B. and simply ignore the whole thing as being none of his concern."

"Go on," Mason said.

"That's all there is to it."

"But what," Mason asked, "does Tom Gridley have to do with Harrington Faulkner?"

"Didn't he tell you?"

"No."

She sighed with exasperation. "That's what he went over there to tell you about."

Mason said, "Perhaps it's my fault. I got off on the wrong tangent. I thought *you* were trying to blackmail him."

"I am," she said with calm candor.

"But apparently not the way I thought," Mason explained.

She said, "Do you know anything about goldfish, Mr. Mason?"

"Not a darn thing," Mason admitted.

"Neither do I," she said, "but Tom knows all about them. The goldfish that are Mr. Faulkner's most prized possession have some sort of a gill disease and Tom has a treatment that will cure it. The only other treatment is a copper sulphate treatment that quite frequently proves fatal to the fish, and is of doubtful value as far as the

11

disease is concerned. Sometimes it works and sometimes it doesn't."

"Tell me about Tom's treatment."

"It's a secret, but I can tell you this much. In place of being a harsh treatment that shocks the fish, it's a gentle treatment that is thoroughly beneficial. Of course, one of the problems of treating fish by putting things in the water is that the remedy has to be thoroughly mixed with the water, and then, the minute you let it settle, it is apt to concentrate in the wrong places. If the remedy is heavier than water it will settle to the bottom, or if it's lighter it will rise to the top."

"And how does Tom get away from that?" Mason asked, interested.

"I can tell you that much. He paints the remedy he uses on a plastic panel which is inserted into the fish tank and then the panels are changed at certain intervals."

"And it works?" Mason asked.

"I'll say it works. It worked with Mr. Faulkner's fish."

"But I thought they were still sick."

"They are."

"Then it wouldn't seem that the remedy worked."

"Oh, but it does. You see, Tom wanted to go ahead and cure the fish entirely, but I wouldn't let him. I gave Mr. Faulkner just enough of the remedy to keep them from dying, and then I told him that if he wanted to finance Tom in the invention we'd let him have a half interest in it and he could put it on the market. Tom's one of these simple souls who trusts everyone. He's a chemist and is always experimenting with remedies. He worked out one remedy for distemper and simply *gave* it to David Rawlins, the man who was running the pet shop. Rawlins just said 'Thank you,' and didn't even give Tom a raise. Of course, you can't blame him very much because I can understand *his* problem. He doesn't have a large volume of business and there isn't a whole lot of money to be made out of pets unless you have a *huge* place, but he works Tom terribly hard and . . . Well, after all, the man's making some money out of this invention of Tom's for distemper."

"Those two the only things Tom's invented?" Mason asked.

"No, no, he's done other things but somebody always gyps him out of them . . . Well, this time I decided things would be different. I am going to take charge of the thing myself. Mr. Faulkner could give Tom five thousand outright and then pay him a royalty to boot. I'm willing to let the five thousand be considered as an advance payment against one half of the royalties, but *only* against one half."

"I don't suppose there are a great number of goldfish fanciers in the country," Mason said.

"Oh, but I think there are. I think that *lots* of people collect them as a hobby."

"But do you think there's enough gill disease to enable Mr. Faulkner to break even on an investment of that size?"

"I don't know, and I don't care. All I'm interested in is seeing that Tom gets a chance to go out into the country, some place where there's sunshine and fresh air. He's got to go where he can take life easy for a while. If he does, they tell me he can be cured absolutely. If he doesn't, things will go from bad to worse until finally it will be too late. I'm giving Mr. Faulkner an opportunity to cure those prize fish of his and to have a remedy that will enable him to build up his strain without danger of future infection, and that's worth a lot to him. When you consider what he's spent on them, I'm letting him off cheap."

Mason smiled. "But you're boosting the ante on him one thousand dollars a day?"

"Yes, I am."

"Why?"

"He's trying to blackmail me. He says Tom worked out his invention while he was working for Rawlins and

13

that, therefore, the invention belongs to Rawlins and unless Tom cures his fish, then Mr. Faulkner will buy an interest in Rawlins' store and sue Tom for his invention. Mr. Faulkner is a hard man, and I'm dealing with him in the only way he'll understand—the hard way."

"And just what is Tom Gridley to you?" Mason asked.

She met his eyes steadily. "My boy friend."

Mason chuckled. "Well," he said, "it's no wonder Faulkner thinks you're a golddigger. I thought from the way he talked that he'd been making passes at you and that you were holding him up."

Her eyes flickered somewhat scornfully over to where Harrington Faulkner was sitting, stiffly uncomfortable, at the table. "Mr. Faulkner," she announced with cold finality, "never made passes at anyone," and then, after a moment, qualified by adding, "except a goldfish."

Mason smiled. "The man's married?"

"That's what I mean. A goldfish."

"His wife?"

"Yes."

The waiter appeared with food on a tray. "Shall I serve you at this table?" he inquired of Mason.

Mason looked over to where Harrington Faulkner had turned to regard proceedings at the other table, apparently with anxiety. "If you don't mind," he said to Sally Madison, "I'll return to my table, and send Mr. Faulkner back to join you. I don't think I'll take his case."

"You don't need to send *him* back," Sally Madison said. "Tell him to send over his check for five thousand bucks, and tell him from me that I'm going to wait here until I get it, or until his damn black goldfish turn belly up."

"I'll tell him," Mason promised, and, excusing himself, returned to his own table.

Faulkner glanced at him questioningly.

Mason nodded. "I don't know just what you want," he

14

said, "but I'll at least look into the matter—after I've had something to eat."

"We could talk right here," Faulkner said.

Mason's nod indicated Sally Madison sitting alone at the other table. "After I've had something to eat," he repeated, "and I take it you didn't want me to try and work out any terms with Miss Madison, because, if you did, I'm not interested."

Faulkner said, "Sally Madison's proposition amounts to blackmail."

"I dare say it does," Mason agreed calmly. "There's a lot of blackmail in the world."

Faulkner said bitterly, "I suppose she's played upon your sympathies. After all, her face and her figure are her biggest asset, and how well she knows it!" And then he added even more bitterly, "Personally, I don't see what people can see in that type."

Mason merely grinned. "Personally," he announced, "I have never collected goldfish."

3

A thick pea-soup fog had settled down upon the streets of the city until it seemed that Mason's automobile was swimming slowly through a sea of watered milk. The windshield wipers were busily beating a monotonous rhythm of cold protest against the clammy surface of the windshield. Some fifty feet ahead, the red taillight of Harrington Faulkner's automobile served as a guiding beacon.

"He's a slow driver," Della Street said.

"An advantage in weather of this kind," Mason agreed.

Drake laughed. "Bet the guy never took a chance in his life. He's a cold-blooded, meticulous bird with an ice-water personality. I almost died when I saw him kick through over there at the table with that golddigger. How much did she nick him for, Perry?"

"I don't know."

"Judging from the expression on his face when he took out his checkbook," Della said, "it must have been just about what the girl asked for. *She* certainly didn't waste any time once she got her hands on the check. She didn't even wait to finish her dinner."

"No," Mason said, "she didn't make any bones about it. Her interest in Harrington Faulkner was purely financial."

"And when we get out to his house, just what are we supposed to do?" Drake wanted to know.

Mason grinned. "I'll bite, Paul, but he feels that he has to show us the location of the goldfish tank before we can understand his problem. It seems that's an important phase of the case as far as he's concerned, and when he gets an idea, he gets it all the way. As I gather it, Faulkner and his wife live in a large duplex house. One side is their living quarters and the other is where Faulkner and his partner, Elmer Carson, have their office. Apparently, Faulkner has various goldfish tanks scattered around the place and this particular pair of Veiltail Moors that is the cause of all the excitement is in part of the building that was used as an office. For some reason, Faulkner wants us to see the tank and the fish, and he has to have things done just so or not at all. It's just the way he's made."

Drake said, "Faulkner's a self-contained little cuss. You'd think it would take more than an ordinary jolt to send him running to a lawyer, all steamed up. What I mean is, he's the sort you'd expect to find making an appointment two days in advance and keeping that appointment to the exact second."

Mason said, "He evidently thinks more of that pair of Veiltail Moors than he does of his right eye. However, we'll get the details when we get out to his house. My own idea is there's something on his mind other than these fish and the affair with his partner, but I'm not going to stick my neck out until I see what's in the offing."

The taillight of the car ahead veered abruptly to the right. Mason piloted his car around the corner. They drove down a side street, pulled to a stop in front of a house which showed in misty outlines through the fog. Mason, Della Street and Paul Drake jumped out of the automobile, watched Harrington Faulkner carefully lock the ignition of his car, then lock the car door, following which he walked completely around the automobile, trying each of the doors to make sure it was locked. He even tried the trunk to make sure that it too was firmly bolted. Then he moved over to join them.

Having joined them, he took a leather key container from his pocket, carefully slid the zipper around the edges, took out a key and said in the precise tones of a lecturer explaining something to an audience in which he had only an impersonal interest, "Now, Mr. Mason, you will notice that there are two outer doors to this house, the one on the left bears the sign 'FAULKNER AND CARSON, INCORPORATED, REALTORS.' The door on the right is the door to my house."

"Where does Elmer Carson live?" Mason asked.

"A few blocks down the street."

"I notice," Mason pointed out, "that the house is dark."

"Yes," Faulkner said tonelessly, "my wife evidently isn't home."

"Now the particular fish about which you are mainly concerned," Mason went on, "are the black Veiltail

17

Moors which are in the tank or aquarium that is in the office?"

"That's right, and Elmer Carson claims the tank is an office fixture and that the fish are a part of the office furnishings. He's secured a restraining order keeping me from moving any fixture or even tampering with them."

"The fish were raised entirely by you?"

"Correct."

"Carson made no financial contribution?"

"None whatever. The fish were raised from a strain which I developed. However, the tank, Mr. Mason, *was* billed to the corporation as an article of office furniture, and it is so fastened to the building that it probably would be considered a fixture. It is, you understand, an oblong tank some three feet by two feet and four feet deep. There was a recess in the wall of the building, a place which was occupied by a china closet and which certainly added nothing to our office. I suggested that this closet could be removed and an aquarium inserted in the space. This was done with Carson's approval and co-operation. When the bills came in, without thinking, I okayed them as an office expense, and, unfortunately, they were so carried on our books and in our income tax report. The tank is undoubtedly affixed to the building, and the building is owned by the corporation."

"The entire building?" Mason asked.

"Yes. I have taken a lease on the other side of it where I live."

"Then how did it happen that you put such valuable fish in the tank that was a part of the office?"

"Well, you see, Mr. Mason, it's rather a long story. Originally, I put in a water garden in the bottom of the tank, a device to aerate the water and an assortment of some two dozen various types of interesting goldfish—the Fringetail, the Chinese Telescope, some Japanese Comets, some Nymphs and some Autumn Brocades. Then I developed these Veiltail Moor Telescopes, and suddenly

18

found that other fish in another tank in which they were kept had developed something which looked suspiciously like gill fever, or rather a gill disease, since the fish really had passed the gill-fever stage. I wanted some place to move these Moors at once where I could have them under observation; and, without thinking of the possible legal complications, I cleaned out the other fish and inserted these Veiltail Moors in the office tank. Almost immediately my troubles commenced. The fish developed disease and Elmer Carson suddenly blew up and demanded that I pay him an exorbitant price for his interest in the business. He went to court and got a restraining order preventing me from moving that fish tank away from the premises, on the ground that it was a fixture. I simply can't understand what caused his sudden change of attitude, the bitter animosity with which he regards me. It happened almost overnight and followed an attempt on my life."

"An attempt on your life!" Mason exclaimed.

"Exactly."

"What happened?"

"Someone tried to shoot me. But after all, gentlemen, this is hardly the place to discuss these matters. Let's go on in and— Hello, what's this?"

"Seems to be a car stopping in front of the place," Mason said.

The automobile which had pulled in to the curb disgorged two passengers, a man and a woman. As the figures materialized through the fog, Faulkner said, "It's that Madison girl and her boy friend. This is a great time for *them* to be getting here! I gave her a key to the place. They should have been here thirty minutes ago. She started out fast enough. Didn't even wait to finish her dinner. I suppose it's that boy who held her up."

Mason lowered his voice and talked rapidly. "Look here, Faulkner, that *tank* may be a fixture and therefore a part of the building which can't be moved, but the fish

19

certainly aren't a fixture. They're swimming around in the tank. Get a bucket or a net and lift those fish out and leave the tank in place—then you can fight out the restraining order with Elmer Carson."

"By George, you've got something there!" Faulkner exclaimed. "Those fish are . . ." He broke off abruptly to turn to the couple who were hurrying up the walk. "Well, well," he said testily. "What was holding *you* up?"

The slender, somewhat bony-shouldered young man with Sally Madison said, "I'm sorry, Mr. Faulkner, but the boss had a case of gill disease to treat and I had to coat a tank so he'd have a place to . . ."

"Wait a minute, wait a minute," Faulkner interrupted. "Do you mean to say you're passing out the secret of this remedy right and left? Don't you realize I just paid for an interest in that invention? You can't tell a soul . . ."

"No, no," Sally Madison interposed hastily and soothingly, "he isn't *telling* anyone, Mr. Faulkner. The remedy is a secret, but you know Tom's been experimenting with it there at the pet shop and of course Rawlins knew what he was doing and— Well, you know how it is. But no one knows the secret formula, except Tom. It will be turned over to you and . . ."

"I don't like it," Faulkner snapped. "I don't like it at all. That's not the way to do business. How do we know that Rawlins isn't faking the whole business? He'll get hold of the material Tom is using to coat those panels and have it analyzed and then where will my investment be? I tell you I don't like it."

Faulkner angrily inserted a key in the lock of the door, snapped back the catch, flung the door open, reached inside, switched on a light and marched truculently into the room.

Sally Madison placed a hand on Mason's arm, said proudly, "This is Tom, Mr. Mason."

Mason grinned, said, "How are you, Tom?" and extended his hand, which was wrapped in the grip of long, bony fingers.

Gridley said, "I'm glad to know you, Mr. Mason. I've heard so much about you that . . ."

He was interrupted by an exclamation from Harrington Faulkner. "Who's been in here? What's happened? Call the police!"

Mason pushed through the doorway and followed the direction of Harrington Faulkner's angry eyes.

The tank which had been inserted in place of the china closet had been ripped from its fastenings and moved out to the extreme edge of a built-in sideboard. A chair had been placed in front of the sideboard, making a convenient step upon which some person had evidently stood. Water was splashed about on the waxed hardwood floor, and lying on the floor beside the chair was an ordinary long-handled silver soup ladle. To the handle of this ladle a four-foot section of broomstick had been attached so as to form a rude but effective extension.

The bottom of the goldfish tank contained an inch or two of small pebbles and sea shells with a few plants that stretched green shoots up toward the surface of the water. There was no sign of life in the tank.

"My fish!" Faulkner exclaimed, grasping the edges of the tank with his hands, pressing his face to within a few inches of the glass sides of the tank. "What's happened to the fish? Where are they?"

"They seem to have disappeared," Mason said dryly.

"I've been robbed!" Faulkner exclaimed. "It's a low-down dastardly attempt by Elmer Carson to . . ."

"Careful now," Mason warned.

"Careful!" Faulkner exploded. "Why should I be careful? You can see what's happened with your own eyes. It's as plain as the nose on your face. He's removed the fish from the tank and intends to use that as a club to make me come to his terms. . . . Hang it, it's just the same as kidnaping. I don't intend to stand for this. He's

21

gone too far now. I'm going to have him arrested! I'm going to get the police on the job and we'll settle this thing right here and right now."

Faulkner darted over to the telephone, snatched up the receiver, dialed Operator, and screeched into the mouthpiece, "Get me police headquarters quick! I want to report a burglary."

Mason moved over to the telephone. "Look here, Faulkner," he warned, "be careful what you say. You can call the police, tell them your story and let *them* reach any conclusions they want, but don't go making accusations and don't mention names. From a collector's standpoint those fish of yours are probably of considerable value, but so far as the police are concerned, they're just two more goldfish you . . ."

Faulkner motioned Mason to silence, said into the telephone in a voice that was tremulous with emotion, "I want police on the job right away. This is Harrington Faulkner. I've been robbed. My most priceless possession. . . . Get the best detectives on the force out here right away."

Mason moved back to join the others. "Let's get out," he said quietly. "If the police take this thing seriously they'll want to take fingerprints."

"Suppose they don't take it seriously?" Drake asked.

Mason shrugged his shoulders.

Over at the telephone, Harrington Faulkner repeated his name, gave the address and hung up. "The police say to get everyone out of the room." He fairly screeched in his excitement. "They told me . . ."

"I know, I know," Mason interpolated soothingly. "I've just told everyone to get out and leave the place as it is."

"You can come next door," Faulkner said. "That's where I live. We'll wait there for the police."

Faulkner ushered them out to the porch, across to the other door of the duplex house which he opened, and switched on lights. "My wife is out," he explained, "but if you'll just wait here. . . . Make yourselves right at home, please. Just be seated. The police say it will only be a few minutes before they have a radio car out here."

"How about the door to the other side of the house?" Mason asked. "You'd better see that it's locked and that no one gets in until the police arrive."

"There's a spring lock on it. It locks when you pull the door shut."

"You're certain that the door was locked when you arrived?" Mason asked.

"Yes, yes. You saw me insert the key and open the door," Faulkner said impatiently. "The door was locked and the lock hadn't been tampered with."

"How about the windows?" Drake asked. "Did you notice whether *they* were locked?"

"*I* noticed," Mason said as Faulkner scowled in an effort to concentrate. "All the windows in that room at least were locked. How many rooms are in the place, Faulkner?"

"Four. That room is our executive office where we have our desks. Then there's another room which we use as a filing room. We fitted up the kitchen so there's a little bar and an electric icebox. We can buy a customer a drink if the occasion seems appropriate. I'll go and look through those other rooms and see if I can find where anything's been disturbed. But I'm certain I'll find everything in order. The man who stole those fish opened the front door with a key and walked right in. He knew exactly where to go, what to get and just what he was doing."

"Better not go in there until the police come," Mason warned. "They might not like it."

The sound of a siren cut through the foggy darkness outside and throbbed ominously. Faulkner jumped up, ran to the front door and stood on the porch, waiting for the police car.

"Going in?" Drake asked Mason.

Mason shook his head, said, "We stick right here."

Tom Gridley moved uneasily. "I left a couple of plastic panels out in my car," he said. "They were painted and all ready to insert in the tank. I . . ."

"Your car locked?" Mason asked.

"No, that's the point, it isn't."

"Better go out and lock it then. Wait until after the police get in. I take it you're taking every precaution to keep your formula secret?"

Tom Gridley nodded. "I shouldn't have even told Rawlins I had a remedy."

Authoritative voices sounded from the outside. Harrington Faulkner by this time had regained control of his emotions and his voice was once more precise in its articulation. Steps moved across the porch. The door to the other house opened and closed.

Mason nodded to Gridley. "Better take advantage of this opportunity to run out and lock your car," he said.

Paul Drake grinned across at Mason. "The great goldfish case!"

Mason chuckled. "Serves me right for letting my curiosity run away with me."

"Wait until the police find out *you're* here," Drake said gleefully.

"And you," Mason retorted. "Particularly when they report the call to the press room."

The grin faded from Drake's face. "Hang it, I feel sort of sheepish."

"There's no reason why you should," Sally Madison said. "These goldfish mean as much to Mr. Faulkner as though they were members of his family. It's just the same as if he had had a son kidnaped. Is that someone coming?"

They listened, heard the sound of a car, then quick steps, and a moment later the front door opened.

The woman who stood on the threshold was a blonde somewhere in the middle thirties and making a valiant

24

attempt to preserve a figure which had begun to fill out. The curves were still attractive, but were becoming ample, and there was a girdled smoothness about the fit of her skirt, a conscious elevation of the corners of the mouth, a determined effort at holding the chin high—all of which combined to give an effect of static immobility. The woman seemed somehow to have robbed herself of all her natural spontaneity in an attempt to stay the hand of time. Her every move seemed to have been rehearsed in front of a mirror.

Sally Madison said almost under her breath, "Mrs. Faulkner!"

Mason and Drake jumped to their feet. Mason moved forward. "Permit me to introduce myself, Mrs. Faulkner. I'm Perry Mason. I came out here at the request of your husband who seems to have encountered some trouble in the real estate office next door. This is Miss Street, my secretary, and Miss Madison. And may I present Mr. Paul Drake, head of the Drake Detective Agency."

Mrs. Faulkner swept on into the room. From the doorway a somewhat embarrassed Tom Gridley stood uncertainly as though debating whether to enter or to turn and seek refuge in the car.

"And," Mason observed, swinging around to include Gridley in his introduction, "Mr. Thomas Gridley."

Mrs. Faulkner's voice was well-modulated. It had a slow, almost drawling quality that was deep-throated and seductive. "Do make yourselves right at home," she said. "My husband has been very much upset lately and I'm glad that he has finally consulted a prominent attorney. I have been suggesting that he do so for some time. Do be seated, please, and I'll get you a drink."

"Perhaps," Della Street suggested, "I could be of some help."

Mrs. Faulkner turned wary, appraising blue eyes upon Mason's secretary, regarded her for a moment, then her

25

face softened into a smile. "Why yes," she said graciously, "if you'd like to. It would be very nice."

Della Street followed Mrs. Faulkner out through the dining room into the kitchen.

Sally Madison turned to Mason. "See what I mean?" she asked cryptically, and then added parenthetically, "Goldfish."

Tom Gridley moved over to Sally Madison, said apologetically, "Of course, I *could* have kept Rawlins waiting on coating those other panels until after I'd put these panels in Faulkner's tank. I suppose I should have insisted."

"Don't be silly. It wouldn't have made a particle of difference. We'd have come dashing out here, and then *we'd* have been the ones to have found the tank empty. He'd have managed to blame us for that somehow, for . . . Say, you don't suppose the old buzzard's going to get technical about that check, now that his goldfish have been stolen?"

Gridley said, "I don't see any reason why he should. That formula is a safe and sure cure for gill disease. They've never had anything before that could come anywhere near touching it. Why, I can cure any case within forty-eight hours—well, make it seventy-two hours to be on the safe side, but . . ."

"Never mind, dear," Sally Madison said, as though cautioning him to silence. "These people aren't particularly interested in goldfish."

Paul Drake caught Mason's eye, closed his own eye in a slow wink.

Mrs. Faulkner and Della Street returned from the kitchen with glasses, ice cubes, scotch and soda. Mrs. Faulkner poured drinks, Della Street served them. Then Mrs. Faulkner seated herself across the room from Mason. She crossed well-curved legs and saw that the sweep of her skirt was just right across the knee. "I have," she said to Perry Mason with an artificial smile, "heard a lot about you. I hoped that someday I'd meet you. I've read about all your cases—followed them with a great deal of interest."

"Thank you," Mason said, and had just started to say something else when the front door was pushed open and Harrington Faulkner, white with rage, said in a voice indignation had made harsh and rasping, "Do you know what they told me? They told me that there's no law against kidnaping fish! They said that if I could *prove* outside thieves got into the place it would be burglary, but since Elmer Carson owns a half interest in the place and has the right to come and go as he pleases, that if *he* wanted to enter the place and take my goldfish, the only thing I could do would be to start a civil suit for damages. And then one of the officers had the temerity to tell me that the damages wouldn't amount to much; that you could buy a whole flock of goldfish for half the amount I'd have to pay a lawyer to draw up the papers. The ignorance of the man is as annoying as it is unpardonable. A *flock* of fish! The ignoramus! You'd have thought he was talking about birds."

"Did you," Mason asked, "tell him that Elmer Carson was the one who had taken the fish?"

Faulkner's eyes shifted away from Mason's. "Well, of course I told him that I'd been having trouble with Carson and that Carson had a key. You see, whoever got in must have got in through the door."

"The windows all locked?" Mason asked.

"The windows were all locked. Someone had taken a screw driver or a chisel and pried open the kitchen door, but it was a clumsy job. As the officers pointed out, it had been done from the *inside,* and furthermore, the door on the screen porch was hooked shut. Whoever did it made a very clumsy attempt to make it seem that burglars had forced an entrance through the back door. No one would have been fooled by it. I don't know anything about burglary, but just as soon as I looked at the marks on the door even *I* could tell what had happened."

Mason said, "I warned you not to make any charges against Carson. In the first place, you're putting yourself in a dangerous position making accusations which you can't substantiate, and in the second place, I felt certain that once the police got the idea that it was a feud between two business associates, they'd wash their hands of the entire affair."

"Well, it's been done now," Faulkner said coldly, "and personally I don't think the way you suggested that I handle it was the proper way to have handled it. When you come right down to it, Mr. Mason, my interest in the matter lies in recovering my fish before it is too late. Those fish are very valuable. They mean as much to me as my own family. The fish are in a very critical condition and I want them back so I can treat them and save their lives. You're as bad as the police, with your damned don't-do-this and don't-do-that."

Faulkner's voice rose to a rasp of nervous tension. The man's calm seemed so completely shattered that he might have been on the verge of hysteria. "Can't any of you understand the importance of this? Don't you realize that those fish represent the crowning achievement of something that has been my hobby for years? You all sit there doing nothing, making no constructive suggestions. Those fish are sick. They may be dying right now, and no one lifts a finger to do anything about it. Not a finger! You just sit here guzzling my whisky while they die!"

Faulkner's wife didn't shift her position or even turn her head to look at her husband. She said, over her shoulder, as though speaking to a child, "That will do, Harrington. There's nothing anyone could have done. You called the police, and apparently you botched things all up with them. Perhaps if you'd have invited *them* in to have a drink with us they'd have been inclined to look at the situation in an entirely different manner."

The telephone rang. Faulkner went to it, picked up the receiver, rasped, "Hello . . . yes, this is he speaking."

For several seconds he listened to what was being said at the other end of the line. Then a triumphant smile spread over his face. "Then it's all right. The deal's closed," he said. "We can sign the papers as soon as you can get them drawn up. . . . Yes, I'll expect you to pay for them . . . all the details of transferring title."

He listened a moment more, then hung up.

Mason watched the man curiously as he marched from the telephone to stand in front of Sally Madison. "I hate to be held up," he announced in a rasping voice.

Sally Madison moved only her long eyelashes. "Yes?" she asked in a drawling voice.

"*You* tried to hold me up tonight," Faulkner went on, "and I warned you I was a bad man to fool with."

She blew out cigarette smoke, said nothing.

"So," Faulkner stated triumphantly, "I'm stopping payment on that check I gave you. I have just completed a deal that has been pending with David Rawlins by which I have purchased his business outright, including the fixtures, the good will, all formulae, and all inventions he or any of his employees have worked out."

Faulkner turned swiftly to Tom Gridley. "You're working for me now, young man."

Sally Madison kept the dismay out of her eyes, but her voice held a quaver, "You can't do that, Mr. Faulkner."

"I've already done it."

"Tom's invention doesn't go with Mr. Rawlins' business. Tom perfected that on his own time."

"Bosh. That's what they all say. We'll see what a judge has to say about *that*. And now, young woman, I'll trouble you to return that check I gave you earlier this evening. I've bought the entire business for less than half of the amount you were holding me up for."

Sally Madison shook her head doggedly. "You closed the deal. You paid for the formula."

"A formula you had no right to sell. I should have you arrested for obtaining money under false pretenses. As it is, you'll either give me back that check or I'll stop payment on it."

Tom Gridley said, "After all, Sally, it doesn't amount to so much. It's only . . ."

Faulkner turned to him. "Not amount to so much, young man! Is that any way to talk about . . ."

Mrs. Faulkner's voice showed interest as her husband suddenly became silent. "Go on, dear," she said. "Let's hear how much. I'm wondering just how much you paid her."

Faulkner scowled at her and said savagely, "If it's any of your business, it was five thousand dollars."

"Five thousand dollars!" Tom Gridley exclaimed. "Why I told Sally to sell it for . . ." Abruptly he caught Sally Madison's eyes and stopped speaking in the middle of the sentence.

Drake hurriedly gulped down his drink as he saw Perry Mason put down his glass, arise from his chair, cross over to Faulkner. "I think," Drake said in a low voice to Della Street, who was watching Mason with amused eyes, "this is where we came in—and it's damned good whisky. I hate to waste it."

Mason said to Faulkner, "I don't think we need to trouble you further, Mr. Faulkner. Your case doesn't interest me in the least, and there's no charge for the preliminary investigation."

Mrs. Faulkner said hastily, "Please don't judge him too harshly, Mr. Mason. He's just a bundle of nerves."

Mason bowed. "And I'd also be a bundle of nerves—if I had him for a client. Good night."

4

■

Mason, attired in pajamas and lounging robe, stretched out in a reclining chair, a floor lamp shedding soft radiance on the book in his hand. The telephone at his elbow rang sharply.

Only Paul Drake and Della Street had the number of this telephone. So Mason promptly closed his book, scooped the receiver to his ear and said, "Hello."

Drake's voice came over the wire. "Remember the golddigger, Perry?"

"The one in the restaurant the other night?"

"That's right."

"What about her?"

"She's having a fit trying to get in touch with you. She's begging me to give her your number."

"Where is she?"

"Right now she's on the other telephone."

"What does she want?"

"Darned if I know, but *she* seems to think it's terribly urgent."

"It's after ten o'clock, Paul."

"I know it, but she's begging with tears in her voice to be permitted to talk with you."

Mason said, "Won't tomorrow morning be all right?"

"She says not. It's something terribly important. She's made a sale with me, Perry, otherwise I wouldn't have called you."

"Get a number where I can call her," Mason said.

"I've already done that. Got a pencil handy?"

"Okay. What's the number?"

"Columbia six-nine-eight-four-three."

"Okay. Tell her to hang up and wait for a call from me. Where are you, at the office?"

"Yes. I looked in on my way to the apartment to see if there was anything important, and this call came in while I was here. She'd called twice before within a period of ten minutes."

Mason said, "Okay. Better stick around there for a while, Paul, in case it turns out to be something really important. I'll call you in case I need you. Stick around for an hour anyhow."

"Okay," Drake said, and hung up.

Mason waited a full minute, then dialed the number Drake had given him. Almost immediately he heard Sally Madison's throaty voice saying, "Hello—hello—this is Miss Madison. Oh, it's Mr. Mason! Thank you *so* much for calling, Mr. Mason! Something has happened that makes it terribly important I see you at once. I'll come any place you say. But I must see you, I simply must."

"What's it about?"

"We've found the goldfish."

"What goldfish?"

"The Veiltail Moor Telescopes."

"You mean the ones that were stolen?"

"Well . . . yes."

"Where are they?"

"A man has them."

"Have you notified Faulkner?"

"No."

"Why not do it?"

"Because . . . because of the circumstances. I don't think . . . I think I'd better talk with *you*, Mr. Mason."

"And it won't keep until tomorrow?"

"No. No. Oh, please, Mr. Mason. Please let me see you."

"Gridley with you?"

"No. I'm alone."

"All right. Come up," Mason said, and gave her the address of his apartment. "How long will it take you to get here?"

"Ten minutes."

"All right. I'll be waiting."

Mason hung up the telephone, dressed leisurely, and had just finished knotting his necktie when a ring sounded at the outer door of his apartment. He let Sally Madison in, said, "What's all the excitement?"

Her eyes were bright with animation and excitement, but her face still retained its glazed veneer of expressionless beauty. "You remember that Mr. Rawlins wanted a tank built . . ."

"Who's Rawlins?" Mason asked.

"The man Tom Gridley is working for. He owns the pet store."

"Oh yes, I remember the name now."

"Well, that man who had Tom fix up a tank for him was James L. Staunton. He's in the insurance business and no one seems to know very much about him. I mean that he hasn't ever done anything with goldfish as far as anyone knows. He telephoned in to Mr. Rawlins Wednesday night and told him he had some very valuable fish that had gill disease and he understood the Rawlins Pet Shop had a treatment that would cure it, and he was willing to pay any amount if Rawlins would treat these fish. He finally offered a hundred dollars if Mr. Rawlins would promise to give him whatever was necessary for the fish. Well, that was too much money for Rawlins to pass up, so he got hold of Tom and insisted that Tom put a couple of panels in a small tank before we went out to Mr. Faulkner's that night. That's what detained us. You remember I didn't even finish my dinner, but went tearing out to get hold of Tom the minute I got the check, because I didn't want Faulkner's fish to die on us."

Mason nodded silently as she paused in her rapid-fire statement long enough to take a quick breath.

"Well," she went on, "Mr. Rawlins himself delivered the tank and Staunton told him his wife was ill and he didn't want to have any noise—and that he'd take care of the fish himself if Mr. Rawlins would just tell him how to do it. So Rawlins told him there wasn't anything to it, just to fill the tank with water, transfer the fish, and that sometime the next morning Rawlins would send out another panel to be inserted in the tank. You're getting this straight, Mr. Mason?"

"Go ahead, I think I'm getting it okay."

"Well, Tom painted up some panels and Mr. Rawlins took the second panel out the next morning. Once more Staunton met him at the door, told him in a whisper that his wife had had a very bad night, and that it would be better if Rawlins didn't come in. So Rawlins told him that there was nothing complicated about the treatment—to just slip the old panel out of the tank and gently put the new one in. He asked Mr. Staunton about how the fish were, and Staunton said they seemed to be better. He took the panel and paid Mr. Rawlins fifty dollars on account, and Rawlins told him a new panel would have to be put in the tank thirty-six to forty-six hours later."

Once more she stopped, partially out of breath, partially in preparation for the dramatic climax to her story.

Mason nodded for her to proceed.

"Well, tonight I was down at the store. Tom had been home sick, and I was helping Mr. Rawlins. You see, Mr. Faulkner really did buy out the store and Rawlins was taking inventory, and because Tom was sick today he needed someone to help him. Mr. Faulkner had been there from a little after five o'clock until around seven-thirty, making a lot of trouble. He'd even done something terrible that Mr. Rawlins wouldn't tell me about. It had

34

upset Mr. Rawlins so that he'd quarreled—Rawlins said he'd tell me tomorrow—he'd taken something of Tom's. Well, all of this is just to explain why I promised to take out that treatment. You see, Mr. Rawlins was planning to go out to Staunton's house to put that last panel in the tank when Rawlins' wife called up and said there was a movie she wanted to see and wanted him to take her. When Mrs. Rawlins wants anything like that she doesn't want to be put off, and so Mr. Rawlins said he'd have to go and I told him I'd finish up, lock up the store and use my own car to take the panel out."

"And you did?" Mason asked.

"That's right. Mr. Rawlins was so nervous he was almost crazy. I finished the inventory and then just a short time ago took the panel out there. Mr. Staunton wasn't home, but his wife was there and I told her I was from the pet store and that I had a new panel to insert in the fish tank, that it would only take a minute or two to put it in. She was very gracious and told me to come right on in. She said her husband had the fish tank in his study. That he was out and wouldn't be back for awhile and that it would probably be better if I put the panel in, as she didn't want to take the responsibility."

"So you went on in with the panel?" Mason asked.

"That's right, and when I got in the study I found the tank contained a pair of *Veiltail Moor Telescopes!*"

"What did you do?"

"For a moment I was too flabbergasted to do anything."

"Where was Mrs. Staunton?"

"Standing right beside me. She'd shown me into the study and was waiting for me to change the panel."

"What did you do?"

"After a minute I just walked over to the tank, took the old panel out and slipped in the new one that was coated with Tom's remedy. Then I tried to start talking about the fish. You know, saying they were very beautiful, asking whether Mr. Staunton had any other fish or not, and how long he'd had these."

"What did his wife say?"

"She thought the fish were ugly, and said so. She told me that her husband picked them up somewhere, that he'd never dabbled around with fish before and didn't know anything about them. She said that some friend had given him these two and that they hadn't been well when he got them. That the friend was giving him specific instructions, telling him just what to do. She said that personally she'd have liked it a lot better if her husband had started out with just a couple of plain goldfish. That these were supposed to be extra fancy—that they gave her the creeps with their long, sweeping black fins and tails, their swivel eyes and the funereal color. She said that somehow they seemed symbolic of death. Well, of course, *that* wasn't anything new because the fish have long been called 'The Fish of Death,' due to some ancient superstition and the peculiar appearance they have."

"Then what?" Mason asked.

"Well, I hung around and talked with her for a minute and lied to her a little. I told her I'd been sick and that there'd been a lot of sickness at the store. I talked along those lines for a minute and then she told me that she had been sick last year but that she hadn't even had so much as a headache since then—that she had taken some cold shots a year ago and started taking vitamins steadily, and that the combination seemed to have done wonders for her."

"And then?" Mason asked.

"Then I realized what I was up against, and suddenly became afraid Mr. Staunton would come back and I'd run right slap into him. So I got out just as fast as I could. I've been terribly afraid that if he came home his wife would tell him what we were talking about, and about the questions I'd asked, and then he'd get rid of the fish, or do something."

36

"What makes you think they were Faulkner's fish?"

"Oh, I'm certain they were. They're the same size and description and they were suffering from gill disease, although they're pretty well cured now and, of course, Veiltail Moors, particularly Telescopes, are very rare and it's inconceivable a man would start out with two fish like that, particularly if they were sick. And then, of course, there's all those lies he told about his wife being sick. All the things he did to keep Mr. Rawlins from getting a look at the fish."

"You've told Tom about this?" Mason asked.

"No, I've told no one. I got out of the house and went to your office and tried to get the night janitor to tell me where I could get in touch with you. He wouldn't do it—said he didn't know and then I was almost frantic. I remembered your secretary's name was Della Street, but I couldn't find her listed in the telephone book. Then I remembered you'd said Mr. Drake was the head of the Drake Detective Agency, so I looked *him* up in the book and found the number of his office. I called there and the night operator told me Mr. Drake was out but that he usually looked in at the office before he went home at night and that if he came in within the next hour they'd have him call me if I'd leave my number. I left my number but I also kept calling because I was afraid they might forget to give him the message."

"And you haven't told anyone about this?"

"No. I didn't even tell Mr. Drake. I decided I wouldn't tell him unless I had to in order to reach you."

"You didn't tell Tom Gridley?"

"No."

"Why?"

"Because Tom's been terribly upset. He's started running a high temperature every afternoon. You see, Mr. Faulkner has been exerting lots of pressure."

"Did he stop payment on his check?"

"Not that exactly. He put it up to me in another way.

37

He told me that the minute I cashed that check he'd have me arrested for obtaining money under false pretenses. He claims Tom developed the invention on Rawlins' time and that the whole secret of the thing is a part of the business that he's bought."

"He really bought the business?"

"Oh yes. He paid Rawlins two thousand for the business, the stock and the good will, and made Rawlins agree to stay on and run it for a small salary. Rawlins hates him. I think everyone hates him, Mr. Mason. And yet the man is *so* self-righteous according to his own code. He thinks the law is the law, and business is business. I presume he really thinks that Tom is holding out on him, and that I was trying to hold him up—and I guess I was."

"Has he made any offer by way of settlement?"

"Oh yes."

"What?"

"Tom is to turn over his formula. I'm to surrender the five-thousand-dollar check. Tom is to agree to keep on working in the pet store for a year at his present salary and to turn over all subsequent treatments or inventions he may work out. In return for all that, Mr. Faulkner will pay Tom seven hundred and fifty dollars and keep paying him the same salary."

"Generous, isn't he?" Mason said. "No provision for Tom to take a layoff for treatment?"

"No. That's what makes me so angry. Another year in that pet store and Tom would be past all cure."

"Doesn't Faulkner take that into consideration?"

"Apparently not. He says Tom can get out in the sunshine on week ends, and that if Tom is too sick to work now, he doesn't need to accept the position. He says Tom's at liberty to quit work any time he wants to, that Tom's health is Tom's own personal problem and that it's nothing to Faulkner. Faulkner says that if he went through life worrying about the health of his employees, he wouldn't have any time left to devote to his own business. Oh, Mr. Mason, it's men like that who make the world such a hard place for other men to live and work!"

"So you didn't tell Faulkner about finding his fish?"

"No."

"And you don't want to?"

She met Mason's eyes. "I'm afraid he'd accuse us of having stolen them or something. I want *you* to handle this, Mr. Mason. And I feel that somehow you might—well, might turn some of Mr. Faulkner's weapons against him—perhaps do something for Tom."

Mason grinned, reached for his hat. "It took you long enough to say so," he observed. "Come on. Let's go."

"You don't think it's too late—to do something tonight?"

"It's never too late to learn," the lawyer said. "And we're at least going to learn something."

5

The night was cold and clear. Mason drove rapidly through the late after-theater traffic. Sally Madison ventured a suggestion. "Wouldn't it perhaps be better to just start some detectives watching Staunton's house so as to make sure he didn't move the fish? And then wait until tomorrow?"

Mason shook his head. "Let's find out where we stand. The thing really has me interested now."

Thereafter they drove in silence until Mason slowed down as he came in sight of a rather pretentious stucco house with a red tile roof and wide windows. "This should be the number," he said.

"This is the place," Sally Madison declared. "They're still up. You can see there's a light in that side window."

Mason slid the car in to the curb, switching off the ignition, and walked up the cement walk to the three stairs which led to a tiled porch.

"What are you going to say?" Sally Madison asked, excitement raising her voice to a higher pitch than usual.

"I don't know," Mason told her. "It'll depend on what happens. I always like to plan my campaign after I've sized up my man." He pressed a bell button at the side of the door, and a moment later the door was opened by a tall, rather distinguished-looking gentleman in the middle fifties.

"Mr. James L. Staunton?" Mason asked.

"That's right."

Mason said, "This is Sally Madison from the Rawlins Pet Store, and I am Perry Mason, a lawyer."

"Yes. Oh yes. I was sorry I wasn't in tonight when you called, Miss Madison. I wanted to tell you that the treatment you had given the fish proved to be a great success and I suppose you want the rest of your money. I have it here all ready for you."

Staunton gravely counted out fifty dollars and, trying to make his voice sound very casual, added, "If you'll just give me a receipt, Miss Madison."

Mason said, "I think the matter has gone a little bit past that point, Mr. Staunton."

"What do you mean?"

"I mean there's some question about the ownership of the fish which you have. Would you mind telling us where you got them?"

Staunton drew himself up with a dignity so rigid that it might have been a mask to hide fright. "I certainly would. I don't consider it any of your business."

"Suppose I should tell you those fish had been stolen?"

40

"*Were* they stolen?"

"I don't know," Mason admitted frankly. "But there are some rather suspicious circumstances."

"Are you making an accusation?"

"Not at all."

"Well, it sounded to me as though you were. I've heard of you and I know you're a very able lawyer, Mr. Mason, but it occurs to me you had better watch what you say. If you'll pardon the suggestion, I'm quite capable of running my own business and it might be well if you'd devote *your* attention to *your* business."

Mason grinned, took his cigarette case from his pocket. "Have one?" he asked.

"No," Staunton said curtly, and stepped back as though to slam the door shut.

Mason extended the cigarette case to Sally Madison, said casually to Staunton, "Miss Madison asked my advice. I was about to tell her that unless you had some satisfactory explanation, I considered it was her duty to report the matter to the police. That, of course, might prove embarrassing. But if you want it that way, it's all right with me."

Mason snapped a match into flame, held it to the tip of Sally Madison's cigarette, then to his own.

"That sounds very much like a threat," Staunton charged, apparently falling back on a repetition of his previous charge.

By this time, Mason was sure of his man. He blew smoke into Staunton's face and said, "It does, doesn't it?"

Staunton drew back in startled surprise at the lawyer's insolent assurance. "I don't like your manner, Mr. Mason, and I don't care to stand here and be insulted."

"That's right," Mason agreed. "But you've already missed your chance to do anything about it."

"What do you mean?"

"I mean that if you hadn't anything to conceal about those fish, you'd have told me to go to the devil five

41

minutes ago and slammed the door. You didn't have nerve enough to do it. You're curious as to what I know, and afraid of what I'm going to do next. You're standing there in a lather of indecision, wondering whether you dare take the chance of slamming the door, rushing inside, and telephoning the man who told you to take care of the fish for him."

Staunton said, "Mr. Mason, as a lawyer, you're doubtless aware that you're defaming my character."

"That's right. And as a lawyer, I know that the truth is a defense to slander. So make up your mind, Staunton, and make it up fast. Are you going to talk with me, or are you going to talk to the police?"

Staunton clung to the doorknob for some two or three seconds, then suddenly lost the dignified shell which had been interposed as an ineffectual armor against the lawyer's attack.

"Come in," he said.

Mason stood to one side for Sally Madison to precede him into the house.

From a living room on the right, a woman's voice called, "What is it, dear?"

"A business matter," Staunton called, and then added, "some insurance. I'll take them into the study."

Staunton opened a door and ushered his visitors into a room which had been fitted up as an office, with an old-fashioned roll-top desk, a safe, a table, a half dozen steel filing cabinets, and a secretarial desk. On top of the filing cabinets was an oblong glass container filled with water. Two fish swam lazily about in this container.

Mason moved across to look at the fish, almost as soon as Staunton had switched on the light.

"So these," Mason said, "are the Veiltail Moor Telescopes, sometimes referred to as 'The Fish of Death'."

Staunton said nothing.

Mason curiously regarded the dark fish, their long fins sweeping down in black veils, regarded the protruding eyes which were as black as the bodies of the fish. "Well," he announced, "as far as I'm concerned, anyone who wants my interest in them can have them. There certainly is something sinister about them."

"Won't you sit down?" Staunton ventured, somewhat dubiously.

Mason waited for Sally Madison to seat herself, then stretched himself comfortably in a chair. He grinned over at Staunton and said, "You can spare yourself a lot of trouble and nerve strain if you'll begin at the beginning and tell your story."

"Suppose you ask me what you want to know."

Mason jerked his thumb toward the telephone. "I've asked my question. If there's any more questioning to be done, it'll be done by the police."

"I don't fear the police. Suppose I should just call your bluff, Mr. Mason?"

"Go ahead."

"I have nothing to conceal, and I have committed no crime. I've received you at this unusually late hour because I know who you are and have a certain respect for your professional standing, but I'm not going to be insulted."

"Who gave you the fish?" Mason asked.

"That's a question I don't care to answer."

Mason took the cigarette from his mouth, casually moved his long legs, and walked over to the telephone, picked up the receiver, dialed Operator, and said, "Give me police headquarters, please."

Staunton said rapidly, "Wait a minute, Mr. Mason! You're going altogether too fast! If you make any accusations against me to the police you'll regret it."

Without looking around, still holding the receiver to his ear, Mason said over his shoulder, "Who gave you the fish, Staunton?"

"If you want to know," Staunton almost shouted in exasperation, "it was Harrington Faulkner!"

"I thought it might have been," Mason said, and dropped the receiver back into its cradle.

"So," Staunton went on defiantly, "the fish belong to Harrington Faulkner. He gave them to me to keep for him. I write a lot of insurance for the Faulkner-Carson Realty Company. I was glad to do Mr. Faulkner a favor. There's certainly no law against that, and I think you'll *now* appreciate the danger of your position in insinuating the fish were stolen and that I am acting in collusion with the thief."

Mason returned to his chair, crossed his long legs at the knees, grinned at the now indignant Staunton and said, "How were the fish brought to you—in the tank which is on the filing cases at the present time?"

"No. If Miss Madison is from the pet store, she'll know that's a treatment tank they furnished. It's an oblong tank made to accommodate the medicated panels which are slid down into the water."

"What sort of tank were they in when you got them?" Mason asked.

Staunton hesitated, then said, "After all, Mr. Mason, I don't see what that has to do with it."

"It might be considered significant."

"I don't think so."

Mason said, "I'll tell you this much. If Harrington Faulkner delivered those fish to you, he did so as part of a fraudulent scheme he was perpetrating, and as a part of that scheme he reported the theft of these fish to the police. Now the police aren't going to like that. So, if you have any connection with what happened, you had better get into the clear right now."

"I didn't have any connection with any fraudulent scheme. All I know is that Mr. Faulkner asked me to take charge of these fish."

"And brought them to you himself?"

"That's right."

"When?"

"Early Wednesday evening."

"About what time Wednesday?"

"I don't know exactly what time it was. It was rather early."

"Before dinner?"

"I think it was."

"And how were the fish brought to you? In what sort of a container?"

"That's the thing which I told you before was none of your business."

Mason once more got up, walked across to the telephone, picked up the receiver and started to dial Operator. There was a grim finality about his manner.

"In a bucket," Staunton said hastily.

Mason slowly, almost reluctantly, put the receiver back into its cradle. "What sort of a bucket?"

"An ordinary galvanized iron pail."

"And what did he tell you?"

"Told me to call the David Rawlins Pet Shop, tell them I had a couple of very valuable fish that were suffering from gill disease, for which I understood there was a new treatment furnished by the pet shop. I was to offer to pay them one hundred dollars for treatment of these fish. I did *just* that. That's all I know about it, Mr. Mason. *My* skirts are entirely clean."

"They aren't as clean as you claim," Mason said, still standing by the telephone, "and they don't cover you as much as you'd like. You forget about what you told the man from the pet shop?"

"What do you mean?"

"About your wife being sick and that she wasn't to be disturbed."

"I didn't want my wife to know anything about it."

"Why?"

"Because it was a matter of business, and I don't discuss business with her."

"But you lied to the man from the pet shop?"

45

"I don't like that word."

"Describe it by any word *you* like," Mason said, "but let's remember that you made a false statement to the man from the pet shop. You did that to keep him from coming in so that he wouldn't see the fish."

"I don't think that's a fair statement, Mr. Mason."

Mason grinned and said, "Think it over for awhile, Staunton. Think over how you're going to feel on the witness stand in front of a jury when I start giving you a cross-examination. You and your clean skirts!"

Mason stepped over to the window, jerked back the heavy drapes which covered the glass and stood with his back turned to the people in the room, his hands pushed down into his trouser pockets.

Staunton cleared his throat as though about to say something, then shifted his position uneasily in the swivel chair. The chair creaked slightly.

Mason didn't so much as turn around, but stood for some thirty seconds in utter silence, looking out at the section of sidewalk which was visible through the window, waiting while his very silence exerted a pressure.

Abruptly the lawyer turned. "I guess that's all," he said to the surprised Sally Madison. "I think we can go now."

A slightly bewildered Staunton followed them to the outer door. Twice he started to say something but each time choked off the sentence almost at the beginning.

Mason didn't look around or make any comment.

At the front door, Staunton stood for a few moments watching his departing visitors.

"Good night," he ventured somewhat quaveringly.

"We may see you again," Mason said ominously, and kept right on walking toward the parked car.

Staunton abruptly slammed the door shut.

Mason clasped his hand on Sally Madison's arm, pushed her over to the right across a strip of lawn and toward the stretch of sidewalk which had been visible from the window of Staunton's study.

"Let's watch him carefully," Mason said. "I purposely pulled the drapes to one side and left the telephone turned toward the window. We may be able to get some idea of the number that he dials by watching the motion of his hand. At least we can tell if it's a number similar to that of Harrington Faulkner."

They stood just outside of the oblong of light cast from the open window. From where they stood, they could clearly see the telephone and the fish in the tank on the top of the filing cases.

A shadow crossed the lighted oblong on the lawn, moved over toward the telephone, then stopped.

The watchers saw James Staunton's profile as he held his face close to the fish tank, watching the peculiar undulating motion of the black veils which hung down from the "Fish of Death."

For what might have been a matter of five minutes, Staunton regarded the fish as though held with a fascination that was almost hypnotic—then he slowly turned away, his shadow moved back across the oblong, and a moment later the lights were switched off and the room left in darkness.

"Do you suppose he knew we were watching?" Sally Madison asked.

Mason remained there watching and waiting for nearly five minutes, then he circled her with his arm, guided her toward the parked automobile.

"Did he?" she asked.

"What?" the lawyer asked, his voice showing his preoccupation.

"Know that we were watching."

"I don't think so."

"But you thought he was going to telephone?"

"Yes."

"Why didn't he?"

Mason said, "I'll be damned if I know."

"So what do we do now?" she asked.

"Now," Mason said, "we go to see Mr. Harrington Faulkner."

6

Mason escorted Sally Madison up the walk which led to Harrington Faulkner's duplex house. Both sides of the building were in the sedate midnight darkness of a respectable house in the residential district.

"They're asleep," Sally Madison whispered. "They've gone to bed."

"All right. We'll get them up."

"Oh, Mr. Mason. I wouldn't do that."

"Why not?"

"Faulkner will be furious."

"So what?"

"He can be very annoying and disagreeable when he's angry."

Mason said, "The man who handles his insurance has stated to both of us that Faulkner brought him those fish on Wednesday night. Some time after that, if this man's story is true, Faulkner made a great to do about finding the fish gone from the aquarium where they'd been placed. He called the police and made false statements to the police. Under the circumstances, he's hardly in a position to explode with righteous indignation."

Holding her arm, Mason could feel her shiver with apprehension. "You're—different," she said. "You don't let these people frighten you when they get angry. They absolutely *terrify* me."

"What are you afraid of?"

"I don't know. I just don't like anger and fights and scenes."

"You'll get accustomed to them before we go very much farther," Mason said, and jabbed his finger with insistence against the bell button.

They could hear the chimes sounding melodiously from the interior of the house. There followed an interval of some fifteen seconds while Mason and Sally Madison waited. Then Mason pressed his fingers several times against the button, causing the chimes to repeat their summons.

"That should wake them up," Sally Madison said, unconsciously keeping her voice lowered almost to a whisper.

"It should for a fact," Mason agreed, pushing the button twice more.

The last notes of the chimes were still sounding when the headlights of an automobile swung around the corner in a skidding turn. The car straightened, slowed abruptly as brakes were sharply applied, swerved into a right-angled turn, and headed up the driveway toward the garage. When the car was halfway up the driveway, the driver, apparently for the first time, saw Mason's car parked at the curb and the two figures on the porch.

Abruptly, the car slid to a halt. The door opened. A pair of well-curved legs flashed in a generous display, then Mrs. Faulkner slid out from the seat, across the running board to the ground, adjusting her skirts well after she had alighted.

"Yes?" she asked anxiously. "What is it, please? Oh, it's Mr. Mason and Miss Street. No, it isn't. It's *Miss Madison*. Isn't my husband home?"

"Apparently not," Mason said. "If he is, he's a sound sleeper."

"I guess he hasn't returned yet. He said he'd be out until quite late."

Mason said, "Perhaps we could wait for him."

"I warn you, Mr. Mason, he won't be in a good humor if he comes home and finds you waiting. Are you *quite* certain you want to see him tonight?"

"Quite certain—if it won't inconvenience you."

Mrs. Faulkner laughed melodiously, a laugh which seemed to have been practiced assiduously. She said, "Oh well, I'll let you in and if it's *that* important we'll have some drinks and wait for Harrington to come in. However, don't say I didn't warn you."

She inserted a key in the latch of the door, clicked back the lock, turned on lights in the hallway, and in the living room, and said, "Do come in and sit down. You're sure it isn't anything that you could tell me, and then let me tell Harrington in the morning?"

"No. We want to see him tonight. He should be coming in soon, shouldn't he?"

"Oh, I'm quite certain he'll be home within an hour. Do sit down, please. Pardon me a moment and I'll get myself organized."

She stepped from the room, taking off her coat as she went through the door.

They heard her moving around the bedroom. A door opened. There was a moment of motionless silence, and then her high-pitched, piercing scream knifed through the silence.

Sally Madison glanced inquiringly toward Mason, but the lawyer was already in motion. He crossed the room in four swift strides, jerked open the door of the bedroom and crossed the bedroom in time to see Mrs. Faulkner, her hands held over her face, stagger back from a bathroom which evidently communicated with another bedroom.

"He's . . . he's . . . in there!" she said, and wheeled blindly, then lurched into Mason's arms.

"Take it easy," Mason said, his fingers gently pulling her jeweled hands away from her eyes.

50

As his fingers touched her flesh, he realized that her hands were icy cold.

He supported her with one arm, moved toward the bathroom.

She pulled back. Mason released his hold, caught Sally Madison's eye and nodded. Sally Madison took Mrs. Faulkner's arm, gently piloted her toward the bed, said, "There, there! Take it easy."

Mrs. Faulkner moaned, slid down on the bed, her head on the pillow, legs trailing over the edge of the bed so that her feet were dangling halfway between the bed and the floor. Her hands were once more over her eyes. She kept saying, "Oh . . . oh . . . oh . . . !"

Mason moved to the bathroom door.

Harrington Faulkner lay motionless in death. His coat and shirt had been removed, leaving him attired in trousers and undershirt, and the front of the undershirt was mass of blood. Back of the head was an overturned table, and on the floor fragments of curved glass caught the rays of the bathroom light and reflected them. A thin layer of water which had seeped over the floor had carried blood in a crimson stain to the far corners of the bathroom. On the floor near the figure were perhaps a dozen motionless goldfish, but as Mason looked, one of these goldfish gave a tired, dispirited flap of its tail.

The bathtub was half full of water and in this water a lone goldfish swam energetically back and forth, as though in search of companionship.

Mason stooped to pick up the lone fish which had shown signs of life. Gently he lowered it into the water of the bathtub. The fish kicked about for a moment, then turned half on its side, floated to the top of the water and remained motionless, save for a slight motion of the gills.

Mason felt the touch of Sally Madison's body, turned to find her standing just behind him.

"Get out," Mason said.

"Is he . . . is he . . . ?"

Mason said, "Of course he is. Get out. Don't touch anything. Leave a fingerprint here and it may make trouble. What's his wife doing?"

"Throwing a fit on the bed."

"Hysterics?"

"Not that bad, just a wild fit of grief."

"Does it mean that much to her?"

"It's the shock."

"Was she in love with him?"

"She was a fool if she was. You never can tell. I thought she didn't have any emotion at all. She had me fooled."

Mason said, "You don't ever show much emotion yourself."

Her eyes regarded him thoughtfully. "What's the use?"

"There isn't any," Mason said. "Go back to Mrs. Faulkner. Get her out of the bedroom. Call the Drake Detective Agency. Tell Paul Drake to get down here just as quick as he can, then, after you have done that, call police headquarters, get Homicide and ask for Lieutenant Tragg. Tell him you're speaking for Perry Mason and that I have a murder to report."

"Anything else?"

"That's all. Don't touch anything in the room. Get Mrs. Faulkner out of the bedroom and into the living room, then keep her there."

Mason waited until Sally Madison had left the room, then, moving backward away from the bathtub a few inches at a time, he carefully studied every part of the room, taking great care, however, not to touch any object with his hands.

On the floor, slightly to one side of the body, was a pocket magnifying glass consisting of two lenses, each approximately an inch and a half in diameter, hinged to a hard rubber case so that they would fold back out of the way when not in use. Back against the wall, almost directly under the washstand, were three popular magazines of approximately nine by twelve inches.

Mason bent over to notice the dates on the magazines. The top one was a current magazine, the one underneath that was three months old, and the bottom one four months old. On the top magazine was a smear of ink about half an inch in width by three or four inches in length and slightly curved in shape, trailing off almost to a point as it approached the end of the three-inch smear.

On a glass shelf over the washstand in the bathroom were two sixteen-ounce bottles of peroxide of hydrogen, one of them almost empty, a shaving brush, a safety razor, to the edge of which soapy lather was still adhering, and a tube of shaving cream.

The man had apparently been shot in the left side over the heart and had died almost instantly. When he fell he had apparently upset the table on which the goldfish bowl had been placed. One of the curved segments of broken bowl still held about half a cup of water.

On the floor, beneath the body of one of the goldfish was a pocket checkbook, and near by, a fountain pen. The cap of the pen lay some two feet away. The checkbook was closed, and bloody water had seeped against the edges of the ch.... Mason noticed that about half of the checks in the book had been torn out, leaving the stubs of approximately half the checks in the front part of the book.

Faulkner had apparently been wearing his glasses when he was shot and the left lens had been broken, evidently when he had fallen, as the fragments of curved glass from that lens of the spectacles lay within an inch or two of the head. The right lens had not been injured and it reflected the bathroom light in the ceiling with a glitter which seemed oddly animate in the face of the death that tarnished the floor of the bathroom with its crimson stain.

Mason regarded the overturned table, stepping carefully backward and bending over to get a good look at it.

There were drops of water on this table, and a slight blob of ink, partially diluted with water.

Then Mason noticed something that had hitherto escaped him. A graniteware cooking pan of about two-quart capacity was in the bottom of the bathtub, lying on its side.

As Mason finished his careful inspection of the contents of the room, Sally Madison called to him from the bedroom. "Everything's been done, Mr. Mason. Mrs. Faulkner is waiting in the living room. Mr. Drake is on his way out here and I've notified the police."

"Lieutenant Tragg?" Mason asked.

"Lieutenant Tragg wasn't in, but Sergeant Dorset is on his way out."

Mason said, "That's a break," and then added, "for the murderer."

7

A siren, at first as muted as the sound of a persistent mosquito, grew in volume until as the police car approached the house it faded from a keen, high-pitched demand for the right-of-way to a low, throbbing protest, then lapsed into silence.

Heavy steps sounded on the porch and Mason opened the front door.

Sergeant Dorset said, "What the hell are *you* doing here?"

"Reception committee," Mason announced briefly. *"Do* come in."

Men pushed into the room, not bothering to remove their hats, gazing curiously at the two women: Sally Madison calm and collected, her face as expressionless as that of a doll, Mrs. Faulkner, her eyes red from crying, half sitting, half reclining on the davenport, emitting low, moaning sounds which were too regular to be sobs, too low in volume to be groans.

"Okay," Sergeant Dorset said to Mason, "what's the story *this* time?"

Mason smiled suavely. "No need to run a blood pressure, Sergeant. I didn't discover the body."

"Who did?"

Mason inclined his head toward the woman on the sofa.

"Who's she, the wife?"

"If you wish to be technically correct," Mason said, "and I'm certain you do, she's the widow."

Dorset faced Mrs. Faulkner, and by the simple process of tilting his hat toward the back of his head, gave her to understand that she was about to be interviewed. The other officers, having spilled through the house in a questing search for the body, congregated almost at once at the entrance to the bathroom.

Sergeant Dorset waited until Mrs. Faulkner glanced up. "Okay," he said.

Mrs. Faulkner said in a low voice, "I really did love him. We had our troubles, and at times he was terribly hard to get along with, but . . ."

"Let's get to that later," Dorset said. "How long ago did you find him?"

"Just a few minutes."

"How many? Five? Ten? Fifteen?"

"I don't think it's been ten minutes. Perhaps just a little more than five."

"We've been six minutes getting here."

"We called you as soon as I found him."

"How soon after you found him?"

"Right away."

"One minute? Two minutes? Three minutes?"

"Not as much as a minute."

"How'd you happen to find him?"

"I went into the bedroom and—and opened the door to the bathroom."

"Looking for him?"

"No. I had let Mr. Mason in and . . ."

"What was *he* doing here?"

"He was waiting at the door as I drove up. He wanted to see my husband."

Dorset seemed to glance sharply at Mason.

Mason nodded.

"We'll talk about that later," Sergeant Dorset said.

Mason smiled. "Miss Madison was with me, Sergeant, and had been with me for the last hour or two."

"Who's Miss Madison?"

Sally Madison smiled. "Me."

Sergeant Dorset looked her over. Almost unconsciously his hand strayed to his hat, removed it and placed it on a table. "Mason your lawyer?" he asked.

"No, not exactly."

"What do you mean by that?"

"Well, I hadn't fixed things up with him—you know, retained him, but I thought perhaps he could help me, thought he would, you know."

"Help you what?"

"Get Mr. Faulkner to finance Tom Gridley's invention."

"What invention?"

"It has to do with curing sick fish."

A voice from the bedroom called, "Hey, Sarge. Look in here. He's got a couple of goldfish swimming around in the bathtub."

"How many goldfish are swimming?" Mason asked.

"Two of 'em, Sarge."

Sergeant Dorset said angrily, "That wasn't me who asked you that last question. That was Mason."

"Oh," the voice said, and a broad-shouldered officer came to the door to stare belligerently at the lawyer. "I'm sorry."

Mrs. Faulkner said, "Please, I want to have someone come to stay with me. I can't bear to be here alone after all this. I—I think I'm going to be sick."

"Hold it, lady," the officer in the bedroom said. "You can't go in the bathroom."

"Why not?"

A certain delicacy caused the officer to keep silent.

"You mean you aren't going to . . . to move him?" Mrs. Faulkner asked.

"Not for a while. We've got to take pictures and get fingerprints and do lots of things."

"But I'm going to be sick. What . . . what shall I do?"

"Ain't there any other bathroom in the place?"

"No."

"Look," Dorset said, "why don't you go to a hotel for the night? Perhaps you can ring up some friend and . . ."

"Oh, I couldn't do that. I don't feel up to going to a hotel. I'm all upset. I . . . I'm nauseated . . . Besides, I don't think I could get a room in a hotel this hour of the night, just ringing up and telling them I wanted a room."

"Got some friend you could stay with?"

"No—not very well. She'd have to come over here. She and another girl share an apartment. There wouldn't be any room there for me."

"Who is she?"

"Adele Fairbanks."

"Okay. Ring her up."

"I . . . oh . . . !" Mrs. Faulkner clapped a hand over her mouth.

"Go out on the lawn," the officer in the doorway said.

Mrs. Faulkner dashed for the back porch. The men

heard the sound of retching, then the running of water in a set tub.

Sergeant Dorset said to the officer in the bedroom, "She's got a girl friend who'll be coming over. They'll be using the bathroom. Get busy on the fingerprints."

"They're taking 'em now, Sergeant, but the place is full of latents. You can't get 'em classified, photographed and all that by the time they're ready to move the stiff."

Sergeant Dorset reached a prompt decison. "Okay," he said, "lift 'em." Then he turned to Mason and said, "You can wait outside. We'll call you when we want you."

Mason said, "I'll tell you what you want to know now, and if you want any more information from me you can reach me at my office tomorrow."

Dorset hesitated, said, "Wait outside for ten or fifteen minutes anyway. Something may come up I want to ask you about."

Mason glanced at his watch. "Fifteen minutes. No longer."

"Okay."

Sally Madison got up from her chair as Mason started for the door.

"Hey, wait a minute," Sergeant Dorset said.

Sally Madison turned, smiling invitingly. "Yes, Sergeant."

Sergeant Dorset looked her over, glanced at the officer who was standing in the doorway. The officer closed his eye in a surreptitious wink.

"All right," Dorset said abruptly, "wait outside with Mr. Mason. But don't *you* go away." He strode to the door, jerked it open and said to a man in uniform who was on guard outside, "Mr. Mason's going to wait outside for fifteen minutes. If I want him within that time I'll call him. The girl is going to wait outside until I call her. She isn't to leave."

The officer nodded, said, "Fifteen minutes," and looked at his watch. Then he added, "A private dick's

58

out here. I wouldn't let him in. He says the lawyer called him."

Sergeant Dorset glanced over to where Paul Drake was leaning against the side of the porch, smoking a cigarette.

"Hello, Sergeant," Drake said.

"What are *you* doing here?" Dorset asked.

"Keeping the porch from falling over," Drake drawled.

"How did you come—in a car?"

"Yes."

"All right. Go on out and sit in it."

"You're *so* good to me," Drake said humorously.

Sergeant Dorset held the door open until Sally Madison and Perry Mason had moved out to the porch, then slammed it shut.

Mason jerked his head toward Paul Drake and moved off toward the place where he had left his automobile. Sally Madison hesitated a moment, then followed. Drake joined them at the curb.

"How'd it happen?" Drake asked.

"He was in the bathroom. Somebody shot him. One shot. Dead center. Through the heart. Death must have been instantaneous, but the medical examiner hasn't said anything yet."

"Did *you* find him, Perry?"

"No, the wife did."

"That's a break. How did it happen? Wasn't she home when you got here?"

"No. She drove up just as I was ringing the bell. You know, Paul, she seemed to be in one hell of a hurry. There was a peculiar smell to the exhaust fumes. Suppose you can get over and take a look at her car before the officers start questioning her and perhaps get the same idea I have?"

"What idea?"

"Oh, I don't know. It isn't definite enough to be an idea, but she certainly slammed that car around the corner and up into the driveway. I don't know what gave me the idea, Paul, other than the smell of the fumes from the exhaust—but I wondered if she'd driven the car a long ways, or whether she'd been parked around the corner somewhere. I remember there was something peculiar about the way the motor sounded, and I got the smell of all but raw gasoline when she slammed the car to a stop. How about taking a look at the choke?"

"Well," Drake said dubiously, "I can try."

"They can't hook you for trying," Mason said.

Drake moved away, starting toward the front porch. The officer grinned, shook his head and jerked his thumb. "Nothing doing, buddy," he said, and then added, "sorry."

Drake veered off to one side, made a few aimless motions, then strolled quite casually over toward the automobile Mrs. Faulkner had driven up to the house. Acting very much as though this were the automobile in which he had driven up, the detective settled down in the front seat and after a moment took a cigarette from his pocket and lit a match, delaying the application of the match to the end of the cigarette long enough to study the dashboard of the automobile.

"What do they mean by lifting fingerprints?" Sally Madison asked Mason.

"They dust objects with a special powder," Mason said, his eyes on Paul Drake. "That brings out what are known as latent fingerprints. Sometimes they use a black powder, sometimes a white powder, depending on the surface. Mostly when they lift fingerprints they use a black powder to bring out the latent, and then take a piece of adhesive, place it over the developed latent, rub it smoothly until every bit of powder has had a chance to adhere to the adhesive, and then pull off the adhesive. That definitely lifts the fingerprint from the object on which it was found."

"How long do fingerprints keep when they do that?"

"Indefinitely."

"How do they know where they took the prints from?"

Mason said, "You're asking a lot of questions."

"I'm curious."

"It all depends on the expert who's doing the job. Some of them make marks on the object from which the print was lifted, number the adhesive and put a corresponding number on the object. Some of them put the numbers in a notebook with a sketch or a description of the place from which the print was lifted."

"I thought they had fingerprint cameras and took photographs."

"Sometimes they do. Sometimes they don't. It all depends on who's doing it. Personally, I'd photograph all latents, even if the women *never* got the use of the bathroom."

Sally Madison looked at Mason curiously. "Why?"

"Because," Mason said, "if there were a lot of latents, the man's going to have a heck of a job keeping them all straight."

"I don't see the importance of that."

"You would if they found one of your fingerprints."

"What do you mean?"

"It might make a difference whether they found it on the doorknob or on the handle of the gun—a difference to you, anyway."

Paul Drake opened the door of the car Mrs. Faulkner had been driving, swung his feet around to the ground, stretched, yawned, slammed the door shut, and the red of his cigarette glowed in the darkness as he casually walked over to where Mason and Sally Madison were standing, talking.

"You played a hunch, Perry."

"What did you find?"

"Choke halfway out, motor temperature almost stone cold. Even making allowances for the fact that she's been here for twenty minutes or even half an hour, the motor wouldn't have cooled off that fast. It looks as though the car hadn't been driven more than a quarter of a mile. Perhaps less than that."

Sally Madison said, "She was coming fast enough when she slewed around that corner."

Mason flashed Paul Drake a warning glance.

The door of the house opened, and Sergeant Dorset stood framed in the illumination of the doorway. He said something to the officer who was guarding the entrance to the house. The officer walked out to the edge of the porch and in the manner of a bailiff calling a witness to the stand, intoned, "Sally Madison."

Mason grinned. "That's you, Sally."

"What shall I tell them?" she asked in sudden panic.

"Anything you want to hold back?" Mason asked.

"No—I don't suppose there is."

"If you think of anything you want to hold back," Mason told her, "hold it back, but don't lie about anything."

"But if I held anything back I'd have to lie."

"No you wouldn't, just keep your mouth shut. Now then, the minute the police get done with you, I want you to call this number. That's Della Street's apartment. Tell her you are coming out there. The two of you go to a hotel, register under your own names. Don't let anyone know where you are. In the morning have Della telephone me, somewhere around eight-thirty. Have breakfast sent up to your room. Don't go out and don't talk with anyone until I get there."

Mason handed her a slip of paper with Della Street's number written on it.

"What's the idea?" Sally Madison asked.

Mason said, "I want you to keep away from the reporters. They may try to interview you. I'm going to try to get five thousand bucks for you and Tom Gridley out of Faulkner's estate."

"Oh, Mr. Mason!"

"Don't say a word," Mason warned. "Don't let the

62

police or anyone else know where you're going. Don't even tell Tom Gridley. Keep out of circulation until I have a chance to see how the land lies."

"You mean you think there's a chance . . ."

"There may be. It will depend."

"On what?"

"On a lot of things."

Sergeant Dorset spoke sharply to the officer on the porch and the officer once more intoned in his best courtroom manner, "Salleeeeeee Madisonnnn," and then, lapsing into a less formal manner, bellowed down at the trio, "cut out that gabbing and get up here. The sergeant wants to see you."

Sally Madison walked rapidly up toward the porch, her heels echoing her rapid, nervous step.

Drake said to Mason, "What gave you the hunch that she was parked around the corner, Perry?"

Mason said, "It may not have been around the corner, Paul. I had a hunch the car might have been running on a cold motor, judging from the way the exhaust smelled. And then, of course, the possibility naturally occurred to me that she might have been waiting somewhere around the corner for an auspicious moment to make her appearance."

"Well, it's a possibility, all right," Drake said, "and you know what it means if it's true."

"I'm not certain that I do," Mason said thoughtfully. "And I'm not even going to think about it until I find out whether it's true, but it's an interesting fact to file away for future reference."

"Think Sergeant Dorset will get wise to it?" Drake asked.

"I doubt it. He's too much engrossed in following the routine procedure to think of any new lines. Lieutenant Tragg would have thought of it if he'd been here. He has brains, Paul . . . Dorset is all right but he came up the hard way, and he relies too much on the old browbeating methods. Tragg is smooth as silk and you never know where he's heading from the direction in which he's pointed. He . . ."

Once more the door of the house opened. Sergeant Dorset didn't wait this time to relay his message through the guard at the door. He called out, "Hey, you two, come up here. I want to talk with you."

Mason said in a low voice to Paul Drake, "If they try to put skids under you, Paul, get in your car, and drive around the corner. Scout the side streets just for luck, then after the newspaper boys show up, grab one with whom you're friendly, buy him a couple of drinks and see what you can pick up."

"I can't do that until after he's phoned his story in to his paper," Drake said.

"No one wants you to," Mason told him. "Just . . ."

"Any old time, any old time," Sergeant Dorset said sarcastically. "Just take your time, gentlemen, no need to be in a hurry. After all, you know, it's only a murder."

"Not a suicide?" Mason asked, climbing up the porch steps.

"What do you think he did with the gun, swallow it?" Dorset inquired.

"I didn't even know how he was killed."

"Too bad about you. What's Drake doing here?"

"Looking around."

"How'd you get here?" Dorset asked Drake suspiciously.

"I told Sally Madison to call him at the same time she called you."

"What's that?" Dorset demanded sharply. "*Who* called me?"

"Sally Madison."

"I thought it was the wife."

"No, the wife was getting ready to have hysterics. Sally Madison put through the call."

"What did you want Drake for?"

64

"Just to look around."

"What for?"

"To see what he could find out."

"Why? You're not representing anyone, are you?"

Mason said, "If you want to get technical, I wasn't paying Faulkner a social call at this hour of the night."

"What's this about a man named Staunton having those stolen goldfish?"

"He claims Faulkner gave them to him to keep."

"Faulkner reported to the police that they'd been stolen."

"I know he did."

"They say you were here when the radio officers got here the night the fish were stolen."

"That's right. Drake was here too."

"Well, what's your idea? Were they stolen or weren't they?"

Mason said, "I've never handled any goldfish, Sergeant."

"What's that got to do with it?"

"Nothing perhaps. Again, perhaps a lot."

"I don't get you."

"Ever stand on a chair and dip a soup ladle down into a four-foot goldfish tank, try to pick up a fish and then, sliding your hands along a four-foot extension handle, raise that fish to the surface, lift him out of a tank and put him into a bucket?"

Sergeant Dorset asked suspiciously, "What's that got to do with it?"

Mason said, "Perhaps nothing. Perhaps a lot. My own idea is, Sergeant, that the ceiling of the room in that real-estate office is about nine and one half feet from the floor, and I would say that the bottom of the fish tank was about three feet six inches from the floor. The tank itself is four feet deep."

"What the devil are you talking about?" Dorset asked.

"Measurements," Mason said.

"I don't see what that has to do with it."

"You asked me if I thought the fish had been stolen."

"Well."

Mason said, "The evidence that indicates they were stolen consists of a silver soup ladle, to the handle of which was tied a four-foot extension pole."

"Well, what's wrong with that? If you were going to reach to the bottom of a four-foot fish tank you'd need a four-foot pole, wouldn't you? Or does your master mind have some new angle on that?"

"Only," Mason said, "that if you were lifting a goldfish out of water which was within a half inch of the top of a four-foot tank and that tank was already three and a half feet from the floor, the surface of your water would then be seven feet five inches above the floor."

"So what?" Dorset asked, his voice showing that he was interested, despite his elaborate attempt to maintain a mask of skeptical sarcasm.

"So," Mason said, "you would lower your four-foot ladle into the tank, all right, because you could slip it in on an angle, but when you started lifting it out you'd have to keep it straight up and down in order to keep from spilling your fish. Now let's suppose your ceiling is nine and a half feet from the floor and the surface of the water is seven and a half feet from the floor, then when you've raised the ladle, with its four-foot extension handle, some two feet from the bottom of the tank, the top of your extension handle knocks against the ceiling. Then what are you going to do? If you tilt your pole on an angle so you can get the ladle out of the tank, your fish slips out of the ladle."

Dorset got the idea. He stood frowning portentously, said at length, "Then you don't think the fish were stolen."

Mason said, "I don't think they were lifted out of that tank with any soup ladle and I don't think that soup ladle with its four-foot extension was used in fish stealing."

Dorset said somewhat dubiously, "I don't get it," and then added rather quickly, as though trying to cover his confession, "shucks, there's nothing to it. You'd have held the soup ladle with one hand straight up and down. The end of the pole would have been up against the ceiling, all right, but you'd have reached down into the water with your other hand and pulled out the fish."

"Two feet of water?" Mason asked.

"Why not?"

Mason said, "Even supposing you'd lift the fish from the bottom of the tank up to within two feet of the surface. Do you think you could have reached down with your other hand, caught the fish in your fingers and lifted him to the surface? I don't, and, furthermore, Sergeant, if you want to try rolling up your sleeve and picking something out of two feet of water, you'll find that you're rolling your sleeve pretty high. Somewhere past the shoulder, I'd say."

Dorset thought that over, said, "Well, it's a nice point you're making, Mason. I'll go in there and make some measurements. You may be right."

"I'm not trying to sell you anything. You simply asked me what I thought about the fish being stolen, and I told you."

"When did that idea occur to you?"

"Almost as soon as I saw the room with the fish tank pulled out to the edge of the sideboard and the soup ladle with its extension handle lying on the floor."

"You didn't say anything about that to the officers who came out to investigate."

"The officers who came out to investigate didn't ask me anything about that."

Dorset thought that over, then abruptly changed the subject. "What's this about this guy Staunton having the fish?"

"He's got them."

"The same fish that were taken out of the tank?"

"Sally Madison thinks they're the same."

"You've talked with Staunton?"

"Yes."

"And he said Faulkner gave the fish to him?"

"That's right."

"What would be the idea in that?"

"I wouldn't know."

"But you heard Staunton state that Faulkner gave him those fish?"

"That's right."

"Did he say when?"

"Sometime in the evening of the day Faulkner reported them as having been stolen—last Wednesday, I believe it was. He wasn't too definite about the time."

Dorset was thinking that over when a taxicab swung around the corner and came to a stop. A woman jumped out without waiting for the cab driver to open the door. She handed him a bill, then ran up the walk, a small overnight bag clamped under her arm.

The officer on guard blocked the porch stairway. "You can't go in here."

"I'm Adele Fairbanks, a friend of Jane Faulkner. She telephoned me and told me to come . . ."

Sergeant Dorset said, "It's all right, you can go in. But don't try to get into the bedroom yet and don't go near the bathroom until we tell you you can. See if you can get Mrs. Faulkner to calm down. If she starts getting hysterical, we're going to have to call in a doctor."

Adele Fairbanks was in the late thirties. Her figure had very definitely filled out. Her hair was dark but not dark enough to be distinctive. She wore thick-lensed glasses and had a nervous mannerism of speech which caused her words to spurt out in groups of four or five at a time. She said, "Oh, it's simply terrible. . . . I just can't believe it. Of course, he was a peculiar man. . . . But to think of someone deliberately killing him . . . If it was deliberate,

68

Officer . . . it wasn't suicide, was it? No, it couldn't have been. . . . He had no reason to . . ."

"Go on inside," Dorset interrupted hastily. "See what you can do for Mrs. Faulkner."

As Adele Fairbanks eagerly popped through the door and into the house, Sergeant Dorset said to Mason, "This Staunton angle looks to be worth investigating. I'm going to take Sally Madison out there. I'd like to have you as witnesses because I want to be damn certain he doesn't change his story about Faulkner giving him those fish. If he does change it, then you'll be there to confront him with the admission he made earlier in the evening."

Mason shook his head. "I've got other things to do, Sergeant. Sally will be all the witness you need. I'm going places."

"And that," Dorset said to Paul Drake, "just about leaves you with no excuse to be sticking around *here* any more."

Drake said, "Okay, Sergeant," with a docility that was surprising, and immediately walked over to his car, opened the door and started the motor.

The officer who was guarding the porch said suspiciously, "Hey, Sarge. That ain't *his* car. His car is the one parked there in the driveway."

"How do you know?" Mason asked.

"How do I know?" the officer demanded. "How do I know anything? Didn't the guy go sit in that car and smoke a cigarette? Want me to stop him, Sergeant?"

Drake turned his car out from the curb toward the center of the road.

"That's his car," Mason said quietly to Dorset.

"Then what's that other car out there?" the officer demanded.

"To the best of my knowledge," Mason said, "that car belongs to the Faulkners. At least it's the car in which Mrs. Faulkner drove up to the house."

"Then what was that guy doing in it?"

69

Mason shrugged his shoulders.

Dorset said angrily to the officer, "What the hell did you suppose I was leaving you out here for?"

"Gosh, Sergeant, I thought it was his car all the time. He walked across to it just as though he owned it. Come to think of it, I guess that car was there when we got here, but . . ."

Dorset said angrily, "Give me your flashlight."

He took the flashlight and strode over toward the parked automobile. Mason started to follow him. Dorset turned angrily and said, **"You can stay right there. We've had enough interference in this case already."**

The officer on the porch, trying to cover up his previous blunder by a sudden increase in efficiency, announced belligerently, "And when the Sergeant says you stay there, Buddy, it means you stay *right there!* Don't take even another step toward that automobile."

Mason grinned, waited while Sergeant Dorset's flashlight made a complete exploration of the interior of the car which Mrs. Faulkner had been driving.

After several minutes of futile search, Sergeant Dorset rejoined Mason, said, "I don't see a thing in the car except a burnt match on the floor."

"Drake probably lit a cigarette," Mason said casually.

"Yes, I remember that. He did for a fact," the officer on guard admitted readily enough. "He walked over to the car just as though he'd been going to drive off, lit a cigarette and sat there and smoked for awhile."

"Probably he just wanted a place to sit down," Mason observed, yawning, "and thought that was a good place to take a load off his feet."

"So you thought he was going to drive off," Sergeant Dorset said sarcastically to the officer.

"Well, I sort of thought . . . well, you know . . ."

"And I suppose if he'd driven that car off you'd have stood there with your hands in your pockets while this guy got away with what may be an important piece of evidence."

In the embarrassed silence which followed, Mason said placatingly, "Well, Sergeant, we *all* make mistakes."

Dorset grunted, turned to the officer and said, "Jim, as soon as they get done with those fingerprints in the bedroom and bathroom, tell the boys I said to go over that automobile for fingerprints. Pay particular attention to the steering wheel and the gearshift lever. If they find any fingerprints, lift them and put them with the others."

Mason said dryly, "Yes, indeed, Sergeant, we *all* make mistakes."

Once more Sergeant Dorset merely grunted.

8

■

Mason had started his car motor and was just pulling away from the curb when he saw headlights behind him. The headlights blinked significantly, once, twice, three times. Then the car slowed almost to a crawl.

Mason drove rapidly for a block and a half, watching the headlights in his rearview mirror, then he pulled in to the curb and the car behind him promptly swung in to a position just behind Mason's automobile and stopped. Paul Drake slid out from behind the steering wheel and walked across to Mason's car, where he stood with one foot on the running board.

"Think I've found something, Perry."

"What?"

"The place where Mrs. Faulkner was parked, waiting for you to show up."

"Let's take a look," Mason said.

"Of course," Drake added apologetically, "I haven't a lot to go on. When someone parks a car on a paved roadway you don't leave many distinctive traces, particularly when you take into consideration the fact that hundreds of automobiles are parked every day."

"What did you find?" Mason interrupted.

"Well," Drake said, "when I gave that car the once-over I did everything I could in the short time I had available. I noticed the choke was out, almost as soon as I got in; and then I lit the match to light my cigarette, turned on the ignition, and that gave me a chance to look at the gasoline gauge and the temperature gauge. The gasoline gauge didn't tell me anything. The tank was half full of gas and that of course just doesn't mean a darn thing. The temperature gauge showed the motor was barely warmed up and that was all I could find from the gauges, but I thought I'd better take a look in the ash tray, so I pulled it out and the darn thing was empty. At the time, it didn't register with me. I just saw the ash tray was empty and let it go at that."

"You mean there wasn't a single thing in it?" Mason asked.

"Not so much as a burnt match."

"I don't get it," Mason said.

"I didn't get it at first, myself. It wasn't until I had driven away from Faulkner's house that the thing began to register with me. Ever sit in a parked automobile waiting for something to happen and being a little nervous—not knowing what to do with yourself?"

"I don't believe I have," Mason said. "Why?"

"Well, I have," Drake told him, "lots of times. It usually happens on a shadowing job when the man you're tailing goes into a house somewhere and you just have to stick around and wait, with nothing in particular to do. You begin to get fidgety, and after a while, you begin to play around with the dashboard. You don't care to turn on the radio because a parked car with a radio blaring out noise is too noticeable, so you just sit there and fiddle around."

"And empty the ash tray?" Mason asked, his voice showing keen interest.

"That's right. You'll do it nine times out of ten, if you sit there long enough. You start thinking of all the little chores there are around a car and the ash tray is one of the first things you think of. You take it out and dump it out of the window on the left-hand side of the car, being sure you've got it all clean."

"Go ahead," Mason said.

"So," Drake told him, "after I drove away from Faulkner's place, I started looking for some place where you could park an automobile and still see the entrance to the Faulkner house."

"Some place straight down the street?" Mason asked.

"I looked there at first," Drake said, "but didn't find anything, so I swung around the corner and found there's a place on the side street where you can look across a vacant lot and see the front of the Faulkner house, and also the driveway to the garage. Just about as far up the driveway as the point where Mrs. Faulkner parked the car. You're looking across a vacant lot and between two houses but you can see the place all right. And that's where I found a pile of cigarette stubs and some burnt matches."

"What brand of cigarettes, Paul?"

"Three or four. Some with lipstick, some without. Different kinds of matches, some paper matches, some wooden ones."

"Any identifying marks on the paper matches?"

"To tell you the truth, Perry, I didn't stay there long enough to look. As soon as I found the place, I beat it back to tip you off. I thought perhaps you'd like to look at it. You were just pulling away from the curb, so I blinked my lights and tagged along behind. I was afraid to pull up alongside because I didn't want the cop in charge to think I'd discovered something important within four or five minutes after I'd driven away from the place. Not that I think the idea would have registered with him, but it *might* have, you never can tell. Want me to go back and make a more detailed examination?"

Mason tilted back the brim of his hat, moved the tips of his fingers through the wavy hair on his temple. "Hang it, Paul, if you can see the house from the place where the ash tray was emptied, then anyone standing in the front of the house or on the driveway can look back and see the place where we would be looking the stuff over. Your flashlight would be something they couldn't overlook."

"I thought of that," Drake said.

"Tell you what you do, Paul. Go back and mark the place some way so you can identify it. After that, get a dustpan and brush, sweep up the whole outfit and drop it in a paper bag."

"You don't suppose Dorset will think that's concealing evidence, do you?"

"It's preserving evidence," Mason pointed out. "It's what the police would do if they happ___ __ __ __ nk of it."

"But suppose they happen to think of it and the stuff is gone?"

Mason said, "Let's look at it from the other angle, Paul. Suppose they *don't* happen to think of it, and a street-washing outfit comes along and sluices the stuff down into the sewer."

"Well," Drake said dubiously. "Of course, we *could* tell Sergeant Dorset."

"Dorset has taken Sally Madison out to Staunton's place. Don't be so damn conscientious, Paul. Get busy and get that stuff in a paper bag."

Drake hesitated. "Why should Mrs. Faulkner have been waiting there for you to drive up, and then come scorching around the corner as soon as she saw your car stop?"

Mason said, "It might mean she knew the body was in there on the floor and didn't want to be the one to discover it, all by herself. It must also mean that she knew Sally Madison and I were going to call at the house, and that in turn means that Staunton must have reached her on the telephone, almost immediately after we left his place."

"Where would he have telephoned her?"

"Probably at her house. She may have been there with the body on her hands and when she knew we were coming, she saw a chance to give herself a sort of alibi. You know, that she'd been absent all evening and arrived just about the same time we did. That brings us back to what must have happened out at Staunton's house. I pulled back the drapes on the window of Staunton's study so I could have a clear view of the telephone from outside the window. I thought he'd be certain to rush to the telephone and call the person who had given him the fish. All he did was switch out the lights in the study. That must mean there's another telephone in the house. Maybe an extension, maybe even a second line because he seems to do business from the house. I'm going to get a telephone book and look up the address of Faulkner's partner, Elmer Carson, and see if I can get there before the police do. You beat it up to your office, Paul, get a dustpan and a bag and sweep up that stuff from the ash tray. I'll drive up to the boulevard and cruise around until I find a restaurant or an all-night drugstore where I can get a telephone directory. Carson lives right around here somewhere. I remember Faulkner saying that while he leased one side of the duplex house from the corporation, Carson had a private residence a few blocks away."

"Okay," Drake said. "It'll take me fifteen or twenty minutes to get to the office, pick up the stuff and get back."

"That's okay. Dorset won't get back for half an hour, anyway; and the boys he's left in charge certainly won't think of scouting around the block and connecting up an empty ash tray in Jane Faulkner's car with a pile of cigarette stubs at the curb on a side street."

Drake said, "On my way," and walked back to his car.

Mason drove rapidly to the main boulevard, cruised along until he found an all-night lunch counter. He entered the place, had a cup of coffee, consulted the telephone directory and, to his chagrin, found that James L. Staunton had two telephones listed, one in his insurance office, one in his residence. Both at the same street address.

Mason then thumbed through the directory to find the residence of Elmer Carson and noted the address. It was exactly four blocks from Faulkner's residence.

Mason debated for a moment whether to call Carson on the telephone, then decided against it. He paid for his coffee, got in his automobile and drove to Carson's house. It was dark.

Mason parked his car, climbed to the porch and was ringing the bell for the third time when lights showed in the hallway. A man in pajamas, dressing gown and slippers was outlined for a moment against lights from an inner room. Then he closed the door, switched off lights in the hallway and, walking along the darkened passageway, reached a point where he could switch on the porch light.

Mason stood outlined in the brilliant illumination of the porch light, trying in vain to see through the curtained glass of the doorway into the darkened corridor.

From the inner darkness, a voice called out through the door, "What do you want?"

"I want to see Mr. Elmer Carson."

"This is a hell of a time to come punching doorbells."

"I'm sorry, but it's important."

"What's it about?"

Mason, conscious of the fact that his raised voice was audible for some distance, glanced somewhat apprehensively at the adjoining houses, and said, "Open the door and I'll tell you."

The man on the inside said, "Tell me and I'll open the door," and then added, "maybe."

"It's about Harrington Faulkner."

"What about him?"

"He's dead."

"Who are you?"

"My name's Mason—Perry Mason."

"The lawyer?"

"That's right."

The porch light clicked off. A light was switched on in the corridor. Mason heard the sound of a lock clicking back, then the door opened, and for the first time Mason had a good look at the man who was standing in the corridor. He was, Mason judged, around forty-two or three, a rather chunky individual inclined to baldness at the top and at the back. Such hair as he had had been left long so that it could be trained to cover the bald areas. Now that the man had been aroused from slumber, the long strands of hair hung incongruously down over the left ear almost even with the man's jawbone. It gave his face a peculiar one-sided appearance which was hardly conducive to the dignity which he tried to assume. His mouth was firm and straight. A close-clipped mustache was just beginning to turn gray. He was a man who wouldn't quit easily and wouldn't frighten at all.

Carson raised rather prominent blue eyes to Mason, said curtly, "Come in and sit down."

"You're Elmer Carson?" Mason asked.

"That's right."

Carson moved around to close the front door, then ushered Mason into a well-kept living room, scrupulously clean, save for a tray containing cigarette stubs, a champagne cork and two empty champagne glasses.

"Sit down," Carson invited, gathering the bathrobe around him. "When did Faulkner die?"

"Frankly, I don't know," Mason said. "Sometime tonight."

"*How* did he die?"

"That also I don't know. But rather a hurried inspection of the body leads me to believe that he was shot."

"Suicide?"

"I don't believe the police think so."

"You mean murder?"

"Apparently so."

"Well," Carson said, "there were certainly enough people who hated his guts."

"Including you?" Mason asked.

The blue eyes met Mason's without flinching. "Including me," Carson said calmly.

"Why did you hate him?"

"Lots of reasons. I don't see any necessity to go into them. What did you want with me?"

Mason said, "I thought perhaps you could help me ascertain the time of death."

"How?"

"How long," Mason asked, "would a goldfish live out of water?"

"Hell, I don't know. I'm sick and tired to death of hearing about goldfish or seeing goldfish."

Mason said, "Yet apparently you spent some money on a lawsuit trying to keep a couple of goldfish in your office."

Carson grinned. "When you start fighting a man, you hit his most vulnerable spot."

"And his goldfish hobby was Faulkner's most vulnerable spot?"

"It was the only one he had."

"Why were you hitting at him?"

"Various reasons. What's the length of time goldfish

could live out of water got to do with the time Harrington Faulkner was bumped off?"

Mason said, "When I looked at the body, there were some goldfish on the floor, one of them gave a feeble flick of its tail. I picked it up and put it in the bathtub. It started to turn belly up, but I understand a few minutes later it had come to life and was swimming around."

"When *you* looked at the body?" Carson asked.

"I wasn't the first to discover it," Mason told him.

"Who was the first?"

"His wife."

"How long ago?"

"Perhaps half an hour, perhaps a little longer."

"You were with his wife?"

"When we entered the house, yes."

The blue eyes blinked a couple of times rapidly. Carson started to say something, then apparently either changed his mind or hesitated while he searched his thoughts for some suitable phraseology. Abruptly he added, "Where had his wife been?"

"I don't know."

Carson said, "Someone tried to kill him last week. Did you know that?"

"I'd heard of it."

"Who told you?"

"Harrington Faulkner."

"His wife say anything about that to you?"

"No."

Carson said, "There's something strange about that whole affair. According to Faulkner's story, he was driving along in his automobile and someone took a shot at him. He claims he heard the report of the gun and that a bullet went whizzing past him and embedded itself in the upholstery of the automobile. That's the story he told the police, but at the time he never said a word to me or to Miss Stanley."

"Who's Miss Stanley?" Mason asked.

79

"The stenographer in our office."

"Suppose you tell me just what happened."

"Well, he came driving up to the office and parked his car out in front of the place. I noticed him take out his knife and start digging at the upholstery in the back of the front seat, but I didn't think anything of it at the time."

"Then what happened?"

"I saw him go into his house—you know, the other side of the duplex. He was in there for about five minutes. He must have telephoned the police from there. Then he came over to the office and, except for the fact that he was unusually nervous and irritable, you wouldn't have known anything had happened. There was some mail on his desk. He picked it up and read it, took the letters over to Miss Stanley's desk and stood beside her while he dictated some replies directly to the typewriter. She noticed that his hand was shaking, but aside from that, he seemed perfectly normal."

"Then what happened?" Mason asked.

Carson said, "As it turned out, Faulkner put the bullet down on Miss Stanley's desk when he signed one of the letters she'd written for him, and then she'd placed the carbon copy of the letter over the bullet. But she didn't notice it at the time and neither did Faulkner."

"You mean that Faulkner couldn't find the bullet when the police arrived?" Mason asked, his voice showing his keen interest.

"Exactly."

"What happened?"

"Well, there was quite a scene. The first thing that we knew about any shooting was a good twenty minutes after Faulkner came in. Then a car pulled up outside, and a couple of officers came pushing into the office and Faulkner spilled this story about having been driving along the road, hearing a shot, and then hearing something smack into the seat cushions within an inch or two

80

of his body. He said he'd dug out the bullet, and the police asked where the bullet was. Then the fireworks started. Faulkner looked around for the bullet and couldn't find it. He said he'd left it on the top of his desk and finally as good as accused me of having stolen it."

"And what did you do?"

"As it happened," Carson said, "I hadn't moved from my desk, from the time Faulkner came in until the police arrived, and Miss Stanley could vouch for that. However, as soon as I saw what Faulkner was driving at, I insisted the police search me, and search my desk."

"Did they?"

"I'll say they did. They took me into the bathroom, took off all my clothes and made a thorough search. They didn't seem too enthusiastic about it, but I insisted they make a thorough job of it. I think by that time they had Faulkner pretty well sized up as an irascible old crank. And Miss Stanley was hopping mad. She wanted them to bring out a matron to search her. The police didn't take it that seriously. Miss Stanley was so angry she darn near took off her clothes right there in the office. She was white-faced with rage."

"But the bullet was on her desk?" Mason asked.

"That's right. She found it there late that afternoon when she was cleaning up her desk, getting ready to go home. She has a habit of piling carbon copies of stuff on the back of her desk during the day, and then doing all her filing at four-thirty. It was about quarter of five when she found the bullet. Faulkner called the police back again, and when they came, they told Faulkner quite a few things."

"Such as what?"

"They told him that the next time anybody shot at him, he should stop at the first telephone he came to and notify the police at once, not wait until he got to his home and not go digging out any bullets. They said that if the bullet had been left in the car the police could have dug it out and used it as evidence. Then they might have been able to identify the gun from which it had been fired. They told him that the minute *he* dug that bullet out, it ceased to be evidence."

"How did Faulkner take it?"

"He was pretty much chagrined over finding the bullet right where he'd left it, after making all that fuss and excitement."

Mason studied Carson for several thoughtful seconds. "All right, Carson," he said, "now I'll ask you the question you've been hoping I wouldn't ask."

"What's that?" Carson asked, avoiding his eyes.

Mason said, "Why did Faulkner drive to his house before he notified the police?"

Carson said, "I suppose he was frightened and afraid to stop."

Mason grinned.

"Oh well," Carson said impatiently, "your guess is as good as mine, but I suppose he wanted to see if his wife was home."

"Was she?"

"I understand she was. She'd been quite nervous the night before and hadn't been able to sleep. About three o'clock in the morning she'd taken a big dose of sleeping medicine, and she was still asleep when the officers went in."

"The officers went over there?"

"Yes."

"Why?"

"Faulkner didn't make too good an impression with the officers. I think they thought he might have fired the shot himself."

"Why?"

"Heaven knows. Faulkner was a deep one. Understand, Mason, I'm not making any accusations or any insinuations. All I know is that after a while the officers wanted to know if Faulkner had a gun, and when he said he did have one, the officers told him they'd go over and take a look at it."

"He showed it to them?"

"I presume so. I didn't go over with them. They were gone ten or fifteen minutes."

"When was this?"

"A week ago."

"What time?"

"Around ten o'clock in the morning."

"What caliber is Faulkner's gun?"

"A thirty-eight, I believe. I think that's what he told the police."

"And what caliber was the bullet that Faulkner dug out of the upholstery?"

"A forty-five."

"How did Faulkner and his wife get along?"

"I wouldn't know."

"Could you make a guess?"

"I couldn't even do that. I've heard him talk to her over the phone and use about the same tone he'd use to a disobedient dog, but Mrs. Faulkner kept her feelings to herself."

"There had been bad blood between you and Faulkner before this?"

"Not bad blood, exactly—a little difference of opinion here and there, and some friction, but we were getting along with some outward semblance of harmony."

"And after this?"

"After this I blew up. I told him either to buy or sell."

"You were going to sell out to him . . . to his estate, I mean?"

"I may. I don't know. I'd never have sold out to that old buzzard at the price *he* wanted to pay. If you want to know something about him in a business deal, ask Wilfred Dixon."

"Who's he?"

"He looks after the interests of the first Mrs. Faulkner—Genevieve Faulkner."

"What interests?"

"Her share in the realty company."

"How much?"

"One third. That was her settlement when the divorce went through. At that time Faulkner owned two thirds of the stock and I owned a third. He got dragged into divorce court and the judge nicked him for a half of the stock he owned and gave it to the wife. Faulkner's been scared to death of divorces ever since that experience."

Mason said, "If you hated him that much, why didn't you and the first Mrs. Faulkner get together and pool your stock and freeze him out? I'm asking just as a matter of curiosity."

Carson said frankly, "Because I couldn't. The stock was all pooled. That was a part of the divorce business. The judge worked out a pooling agreement by which the management was left equally in the hands of Faulkner and myself. Mrs. Faulkner—that is Genevieve Faulkner, the first wife—couldn't have any say in the management of the company unless she first appealed to the court. And neither Faulkner nor I could increase the expenses of the company past a certain point, and we couldn't raise salaries. The judge also pointed out that any time the dividends on the stock fell below a certain point he'd reopen the alimony end of it and take another bite if he had to. He certainly had Faulkner scared white."

"The stock's been profitable?" Mason asked.

"I'll say it has. You see, we didn't handle things on a commission basis alone. We had some deals by which we took title in our own name and built houses and sold them. We've done some pretty big things in our day."

"Faulkner's ideas or yours?"

"Both. When it came to making money, old Harrington Faulkner had the nose of a buzzard. He could smell a potential profit a mile away. He had the courage to back

84

up his judgment with cold hard cash and he had plenty of operating capital. He should have. Lord knows he never gave his wife anything, and he never spent anything himself, except on those damned goldfish of his. He'd really loosen up the purse strings on those, but when it came to parting with money for anything else he was like the bark on a log."

"And Dixon?" Mason asked. "Was he appointed by the court?"

"No. Genevieve Faulkner hired him."

"Faulkner was wealthy?" Mason asked.

"He had quite a bit of money, yes."

"You wouldn't know it from looking around his house," Mason said.

Carson nodded. "He'd spend money for his goldfish and that was all. As far as the duplex was concerned, I think Mrs. Faulkner liked it that way. After all, there were just the two of them and she could keep up this small duplex by having a maid come in a couple of days a week, but Faulkner certainly counted every penny he spent. In some ways he was a damned old miser. Honestly, Mr. Mason, the man would lie awake nights trying to work out some scheme by which he could trim you in a business deal. By that, I mean that in case you owned something Faulkner wanted to buy, he'd manage to get you in some kind of a jackpot where you'd lose your eyeteeth. He . . ."

The doorbell rang a strident summons, followed almost immediately by heavy pounding of knuckles and a rattling of the doorknob.

Mason said, "That sounds like the police."

"Excuse me," Carson said, and started for the door.

"It's okay," Mason told him. "I'm leaving. There's nothing more I can do here."

Mason was a step behind Carson when the latter opened the door. Lieutenant Tragg, backed by two plain-clothes officers, said to Mason, "I thought that was your car out front. You certainly do get around."

Mason stretched, yawned, and said, "Believe it or not, Lieutenant, my only interest in the case is over a couple of goldfish that really aren't goldfish at all."

Lieutenant Tragg was as tall as Mason. He had the forehead of a thinker, a well-shaped nose and a mouth which held plenty of determination but had a tendency to curve upward at the corners, as though the man could smile easily.

"Quite all right, Counselor. Quite all right," he said, and then added, "your interest in goldfish seems to be somewhat urgent."

"Frankly," Mason told him, "I would like to chisel some money out of Harrington Faulkner's estate. In case you don't know it, at the time of his death a young woman named Sally Madison was holding his check for five thousand dollars."

Tragg's eyes studied Mason with keen appraisal. "We know all about it. A check dated last Wednesday for five thousand dollars, payable to Thomas Gridley. And have you perhaps talked with Thomas Gridley lately?"

Mason shook his head.

There was a hint of a sardonic smile playing around the corners of Tragg's mouth. "Well, as you've remarked, Counselor, it's late, and I take it you're going home and go to bed. I don't suppose there's anything in connection with your interest in the case that will cause you to lose any sleep."

"Not a thing," Mason assured him cheerfully. "Good night, Lieutenant."

"And good-by," Tragg said, entering Carson's house, followed by the two officers, who promptly kicked the door shut.

9

■

Perry Mason struggled up through an engulfing sea of warm languor which seemed to make it impossible for him to move. Fatigue kept lulling him back to the blissful inertia of slumber; the strident ringing of the telephone bell insisted upon pulling him back to consciousness.

More than half asleep, he groped for the telephone.

"Hello," he said, his tongue thick.

Della Street's voice at the other end of the line knifed his brain to consciousness. "Chief, can you get over here right away?"

Mason sat bolt upright in the bed, every sense alert.

"Where?" he asked.

"The Kellinger Hotel on Sixth Street."

Mason's sleep-swollen eyes glanced at the luminous dial of his wrist watch, then he realized there was enough daylight filtering through the windows of his apartment to rob the hands of their luminosity. "As quick as I can make it, Della," he promised, and then added, "just how urgent is it?"

"I'm afraid it's terribly urgent."

"Is Sally Madison with you?"

"Yes. We're in six-thirteen. Don't stop at the desk. Come right up. Don't knock. The door will be unlocked. I'll . . ."

The receiver at the other end of the line was suddenly

slipped into place in the middle of the sentence, cutting off Della Street's words as neatly as though the wire had been severed with a knife.

Perry Mason rolled out of bed. Out of his pajamas, he was groping for clothes even before he switched on the lights in his apartment. Two minutes later he was struggling into a topcoat as he ran down the hall.

The Hotel Kellinger was a relatively unpretentious hotel which evidently catered largely to permanent guests. Mason parked his car and entered the lobby, where a somewhat sleepy night clerk looked up in a casual survey which changed to a frown of thoughtful inspection.

"I already have my key," Mason said hastily, and then added somewhat sheepishly, "darn near missed out on a night's sleep."

The elevator was an automatic. Mason noticed there were seven floors in the hotel. As a precaution, in case the doubtful scrutiny on the part of the clerk below should have ripened into skepticism, Mason punched the button which took the elevator to the fifth floor, and then, walking down the corridor, wasted precious seconds locating the stairway. During that time he heard the automatic mechanism of the elevator whirl into activity.

Mason ran up the uncarpeted stairs, located the room he wanted on the sixth floor and gently tried the knob of the door. The door was unlocked. He swung it open noiselessly.

Della Street, attired in a housecoat and slippers, held a warning finger to her lips and motioned toward the room behind her, then pointed to the twin bed near the window.

Sally Madison lay on her back, one arm flung out from under the covers, her fingers limp and relaxed. The girl's glossy dark hair streamed out over the pillow. The absence of shoulder straps and the curving contours which were visible indicated that she was sleeping nude. Her alligator-skin purse, which had evidently been placed under the pillow, had fallen to the floor and opened, partially spilling its contents.

Della Street's insistent finger pointed to the purse.

Mason bent over to get a look at the articles which were illuminated by a bedside lamp which had apparently been lowered from its normal position on a small table between the two beds to a point on the floor, where the light would not shine in Sally Madison's eyes.

He saw a roll of bills fastened together with an elastic band. The denomination of the outer bill was visible and showed that it was for fifty dollars. Back of the roll of bills there was the dull gleam of blued steel, where the barrel of a revolver caught and reflected the rays of the electric light.

Della Street glanced inquiringly at Mason. When she saw that the lawyer had fully appreciated the significance of the contents of the purse, she raised her eyebrows in silent inquiry.

Mason looked around the room, searching for some place where he could talk.

Della Street beckoned him around the foot of the bed and opened the door of the bathroom. She switched on the light, and, when Mason had entered, closed the door behind him.

The lawyer seated himself on the edge of the bathtub, and Della Street started talking in a whisper. "She clung to that purse like grim death. I wanted to get her some night things but she said she'd sleep in the raw. She got out of her clothes in nothing flat, was careful to put the purse under her pillow and then lay there watching me while I undressed. I switched out the lights and got into bed. Apparently she couldn't sleep at first. I heard her twisting and turning."

"Any sobs?" Mason asked.

Della shook her head.

"When did she get to sleep?"

"I don't know. I went to sleep first, although I had

intended to stay awake and make sure she was asleep and all right before I closed my eyes."

"When did you see the purse?"

"About five minutes before I telephoned you. Before she went to sleep she must have squirmed around so that the purse had worked over to a position near the edge of the bed—then when she turned in her sleep the purse fell out. I heard the jar and I was nervous enough so that I wakened suddenly and almost jumped out of my skin."

"Did you know what had wakened you?"

"Not right away, but I turned on the light. Sally was lying there sound asleep, just about as you see her now, but she was twitching restlessly and her lips were moving. The words she was uttering were all mumbled together so you couldn't distinguish anything. I could only hear some confused sounds.

"As soon as I turned on the light, I realized what had happened, and, without thinking, reached down to pick up the purse. First, I saw the rolls of bills and started to put them back in the purse. Then the tips of my fingers touched something cold and metallic. I immediately lowered the light to the floor so I could see what it was all about. At that time the purse was lying just as you see it now, and I left the light right there on the floor by the purse.

"Chief, I was just sick. I didn't know *what* to do. I didn't dare to leave her alone and go down to the lobby. Finally I took a chance on telephoning you because I knew that was all there was for me to do."

"Just what did you do?" Mason asked. "I mean how did you place the call?"

She said, "It was almost thirty seconds before I could get anyone to answer at the hotel switchboard, then I kept my voice just as low as possible and asked for an outside line. But the man downstairs told me all numbers had to go out through the hotel switchboard. And I saw then there was no dial on the telephone. I'd been so rattled I hadn't noticed that before. So I gave him your unlisted number. It was the only thing I could have done under the circumstances."

Mason nodded gravely.

"It seemed like an age before you answered," she went on. "And then I started talking to you, keeping my eye on Sally Madison all the while, so I could hang up in case she started to wake up."

"Is that why you were cut off in the middle of a sentence?"

"Yes. I saw her move restlessly and her eyelids fluttered. So I didn't dare to keep on talking. I slipped the receiver back into place and put my head back on the pillow so in case she opened her eyes I could pretend to be asleep—although, of course, the purse on the floor and the light by the purse would have been a giveaway. If she wakened, I was going to call for a showdown, but if I could postpone it until you got here I thought it would be better to play it that way. Well, she rolled her head around a bit and said something in that mumbled voice of a person talking in her sleep, and then she heaved a long sigh and seemed to relax."

Mason rose from his seat on the edge of the bathtub, pushed his hands deep into his coat pockets, said, "We're in a jam, Della."

Della Street nodded.

"She's supposed to be broke," Mason said. "If she has a roll of bills like that she must have got them from Mrs. Faulkner. I guess I played right into her hands. I wanted to be alone there in Faulkner's bathroom so I could take a good look at all the evidence. I didn't want her checking up on what I was doing, so I told her to take Mrs. Faulkner out into the living room and kid her out of her hysterics. I guess while she was out there, she must have put the bite on Mrs. Faulkner. That means she must have uncovered some evidence that escaped me. Or else, Mrs. Faulkner propositioned her to ditch the gun, and the golddigger ran true to form and wanted some heavy dough. In any event it leaves *us* in a mess.

"You can see what's going to happen now. I thought we were getting her out of circulation so the newspaper reporters wouldn't get hold of her, and so we could do something about building up a claim against the estate of Faulkner without having her spill any beans before we knew the lay of the land. That's what comes of being big-hearted and trying to help a guy who has T.B. and a golddigging girl friend.

"You've registered under your own name and under her name. If that gun happens to be the one with which the murder was committed, you can realize what a spot we're in. Both of us. What did she tell you when she telephoned?"

"She said you had told her to get in touch with me and had given her my number; that I was to take her to a hotel, stay with her and fix it so that no one would know anything about where she was until you got ready to let them find out."

Mason nodded. "That's exactly what I told her to do."

Della Street said, "I was asleep and the telephone kept ringing. It wakened me out of a sound slumber and I guess I was a little groggy. Sally Madison gave me your message, and one of the first thoughts that flashed through my mind was where I could find a hotel. I told her to call me back in about ten minutes, and then I got busy on the telephone and called half a dozen hotels. I finally found there was a room with twin beds here at the Kellinger."

Mason slitted his eyes in concentration. "Then she called you back in fifteen minutes?"

"I guess so. I didn't notice the exact time. I had started to dress as soon as I located the room. I was rushing around and I didn't notice the time."

"And you told her to meet you here?"

"That's right. I told her to come directly to the hotel,

and if she got here first to wait for me in the lobby; if I got here first, I'd wait for her in the lobby."

"Which was the first one here?"

"I was."

"How long did you wait?"

"I'd say about ten minutes."

"She came in a taxi?"

"Yes."

"What kind?"

"It was a yellow cab."

"Notice anything strange about the way she carried her purse?"

"Not a thing. She got out of the cab and . . . Wait a minute, Chief, I *do* remember that she had a bill all ready in her hand. She didn't have to take it out of the purse. She handed it to the cab driver and didn't get any change. I remember that."

"Probably a dollar bill," Mason said. "That would mean she had about an eighty-cent ride on the meter, and gave a twenty-cent tip."

Della Street, searching her memory, said, "I remember the cab driver looked at the bill—looked at it in a peculiar sort of way, then grinned, and said something, put it in his pocket and drove off. Then Sally Madison entered the lobby and we went directly to the room."

"You'd already registered?"

"Yes."

"Then Sally didn't have any occasion to open her purse from the time you first saw her until she got into bed and tucked it under her pillow?"

"That's right. I remember thinking at the time that she should take more care of her skin, but she just got out of her clothes and climbed into bed."

Mason said, "Of course she didn't want you to have any opportunity to see what was in the purse. All right, Della, there's only one thing to do. We've got to get that gun out of the purse."

"Why?"

Mason said, "Because it's got your fingerprints on it."

"Oh, oh!" Della Street exclaimed in dismay. "I hadn't thought of *that.*"

"After we get your fingerprints off of it," Mason said, "we're going to wake Sally Madison up and ask her some questions. What we do after that depends on the answers, but probably we're going to tell her to go back to her apartment, act just as though nothing had happened, and under no circumstances say anything to anyone about having spent the night here."

"Think she'll do it?"

"You can't tell. She may. The probabilities are they'll pick her up before noon. Then if they ask a lot of questions, she'll probably drag us into the mess. *But if your fingerprints aren't on that gun,* we don't have to tell anyone that we knew what was in her purse. We were simply keeping her out of the way of the newspaper reporters. She was going to be our client in a civil action we were about to bring against the Faulkner Estate in order to collect five thousand dollars for her boy friend."

Della Street nodded.

"But," Mason went on, "if your fingerprints are found on that gun, then we're in an awful mess."

"But when you take my fingerprints off the gun, won't you automatically remove all fingerprints that are on it?"

Mason nodded. "That's one of the things we've got to do, Della."

"Doesn't that constitute tampering with evidence or something of the sort?"

Mason said, "We don't even know that it's evidence, Della. It may or may not be the gun with which Harrington Faulkner was killed. Okay, here we go."

Mason opened the bathroom door, paused for a whispered word of caution to Della Street, and had taken one step toward the bed where Sally Madison was sleeping, when knuckles pounded loudly on the door of the room.

Mason stopped in dismay.

"Open up!" a voice called. "Open up in there," and knuckles once more banged on the panels of the door.

The noise aroused Sally Madison. With a half-articulate exclamation, she sat up in bed, threw one leg out from under the covers, then in the dim light of the room saw Perry Mason standing motionless by the doorway.

"Oh!" she exclaimed. "I didn't know *you* were here," and promptly grabbed the covers up to her chin and pulled her leg back into the bed.

"I just came," Mason said.

She smiled.

"I didn't hear you come."

"I wanted to make sure everything was all right."

"What's happening? Who's at the door?"

Mason said to Della Street, "Open it, Della."

Della Street opened the door.

The night clerk said, "You can't pull that stuff here."

"What stuff?" Della Street asked.

The man said, "Don't pull that line on me. Your boy friend went up to the fifth floor with the elevator, then sneaked up the stairs to the sixth floor. He thought he was being smart. I happened to remember that you'd put through a call from this room and thought I'd give it the once-over. I was listening outside the door. I heard the bathroom door open and heard you two whispering. This isn't the sort of a place you girls think it is. Get your things together and get out."

Mason said, "You're making a mistake, Buddy."

"Oh, no, I'm not. *You're* the one that's making the mistake."

Mason's hand slid enticingly down into his right-hand trouser pocket. "All right," he said, laughing, "perhaps I'm the one that's made the mistake, but it's getting daylight and it isn't going to hurt the hotel any if the girls

95

check out after breakfast." Mason pulled out a roll of bills, peeled a ten-dollar bill from the roll, held it between his first and second fingers so the night clerk could get a good look at the denomination.

The man didn't even lower his eyes. "No you don't," he said. "That sort of stuff doesn't go here."

Mason glanced over to where Sally Madison was holding the sheet up under her chin. He noticed that she had taken advantage of the diversion to retrieve her purse from its position on the floor. It was now safely tucked out of sight.

Mason pushed the bills back into his pocket, took out his card case, produced one of his cards. "I'm Perry Mason, the lawyer," he said. "This is Della Street. She's my secretary."

The clerk said doggedly, "She'd have to be your wife to let you get by with this, and that's final. We're trying to run a decent place here. We've had trouble with the police before, and I'm not going to take any chances on having any more."

Mason said angrily, "All right. We'll get out."

"You can wait down in the lobby," the clerk told him.

Mason shook his head. "If we're going to be put out, I'll stay here and help the girls pack."

"Oh no you won't."

"Oh yes I will."

The clerk said, "Then *I'll* stay." He jerked his head at the girls. "Get your clothes on."

Sally Madison said, "You'll have to get out while I get something on. I'm sleeping in the raw."

The night clerk said to Mason, "Come on. Let's go down to the lobby."

Mason shook his head.

Della Street flashed an inquiring glance at Mason.

The lawyer's right eye slowly closed in a wink.

Almost imperceptibly, Della Street motioned her head toward the door.

Mason shook his head.

Della Street said suddenly, "Well, I'm not going to be put out of here at this hour of the morning. *I* haven't done anything wrong. It's bad enough to be disturbed in a night's sleep without getting put out of a second-rate hotel because your boss wants to give you some orders. *I'm* going back to bed. If you don't like it, call the police and see what they have to say about it."

Della Street pulled back the covers, kicked off her slippers and jumped into bed. Surreptitiously, she glanced at Mason.

Mason gave her an almost imperceptible nod of encouragement.

The clerk said gloomily, "I'm sorry but it won't work. I suppose if we hadn't had any trouble before this you could bluff us out, but the way it is right now, you either get out or I call the police. Make up your mind which you want."

"Call the police," Mason said.

The clerk said, "Okay, if you want it that way, that's the way you'll have it." He walked over to the telephone, picked it up, held the receiver to his ear, said, "Police headquarters," and then after a moment, "this is the night clerk at the Kellinger Hotel on Sixth Street. We've got some disorderly tenants in Room 613. I've tried to put them out and they won't go. Send a car around right away, will you? I'll be up here in the room. . . . That's right. The Kellinger Hotel, and the room number is six-thirteen."

The clerk slammed the receiver back into place, said, "I'm keeping my nose clean. Let me give you folks a friendly tip. You'll just about have time to take a powder before the police get here. Take my advice and beat it."

Perry Mason settled himself comfortably on the foot of Della Street's bed. He took a notebook from his pocket and scribbled a note to Della Street. "Remember that the telephones are only connected through the downstairs switchboard. My best guess is it's a bluff. Stick it out."

Mason tore the page from his notebook, handed it to Della.

She read it, smiled, and settled back against the pillow.

Sally Madison said, "Well, *I'm* going to get out. You two can do whatever you want to," and without more ado she jumped out of bed, snatched her clothes from the chair and ran into the little dressing room.

Mason casually leaned over and raised the pillow on her bed.

She had taken her purse with her.

Mason took a cigarette case from his pocket, handed Della Street a cigarette, took one himself. They lit up, and Mason once more settled back comfortably. From the little dressing room, came the sounds of Sally Madison hurriedly dressing.

Mason waited for nearly two minutes, then said to the clerk, "Okay, you win. Better get dressed, Della."

Della Street slid out of the bed, adjusting the housecoat around her. She picked up her overnight bag, entered the dressing room and said to Sally Madison, "Okay, Sally, I'm going with you."

"You're not going with me," Sally Madison said, the sound of her shod foot hitting the floor. "Personally, I don't like cops. As far as I'm concerned, you stuck around just a little bit too long. I'm on my way."

She had dressed herself with the facility of a lightning-change artist and now she stepped out from the dressing room ready for the street. Her hair was the only thing about her that bore witness to her hasty toilet.

"Wait a minute," Mason said. "We're all going."

Sally Madison, clutching the purse under her arm with the tenacity of a football player holding an intercepted pass, said, "I'm sorry, Mr. Mason, but I'm not waiting for anyone."

Mason played his trump card. "Don't let him bluff

you," he said. "There isn't any dial on that telephone. It would have to be connected through the downstairs switchboard before he could call anyone. He was just pretending to call the police."

The clerk, in a dispirited voice, said, "Don't think I haven't had to go through with this before. The minute I decided you were in six-thirteen, I plugged the line from this room through the switchboard to an outside line. I did that before I came up. Don't ever kid yourself that telephone wasn't connected."

Something in the man's manner carried conviction.

Mason said, "Okay, Della, do the best you can. I'm leaving you to take the rap. I'm going with Sally. Come on, Sally."

Sally eyed him with disfavor. "Wouldn't it be better if I went alone?"

"No," Mason said, and piloted her to the door.

The clerk hesitated a moment, deciding what to do.

Mason said to Della Street, "When the officers come, tell them that the clerk was trying to annoy you with his attentions."

The clerk promptly got up from his chair and followed Mason and Sally Madison out into the corridor. "I'll take you down in the elevator," he said.

"No need," Mason told him. "We'd rather use the stairs."

"Speak for yourself," Sally Madison told Mason in something of a panic. "I'm going down in the elevator. It's quicker."

They entered the elevator. The clerk removed the catch which had been holding the door open, and pressed the button for the lobby. "The bill's six dollars," he said.

Mason gravely took a five-dollar bill, a one-dollar bill, and a twenty-five-cent piece from his pocket, handed them to the clerk.

"What's the two-bits for?"

"A tip for checking out," Mason said.

The clerk calmly pocketed the twenty-five-cent piece, held the six dollars in his left hand. "No hard feelings," he said as he opened the door of the elevator on the lobby floor. "We have to keep the joint clean or we'll be closed up."

Mason took Sally Madison's arm. "You and I are due for a little talk," he said.

She didn't even look at him, but quickened her step until she was almost running across the lobby. They were halfway to the door when it was pushed open and a uniformed officer from a radio car said, "What's the trouble?"

Mason tried to edge past him. The man blocked the door, looked over Mason's shoulder to the clerk.

"Couple of girls in six-thirteen," the clerk said wearily. "They violated the rules of the hotel, receiving company in their room. I asked them to get out."

"This one of the girls?"

"That's right."

"Where's the other one?"

"Getting dressed."

"Who was the company?"

The clerk jerked his thumb toward Mason. The officer grinned at Mason, said, "We don't want you, but since I'm here, I think I'll ask a few questions of the girls."

Mason gravely produced a card. "The fault," he said, "lies with the hotel. My secretary was spending the night with Miss Madison, who is my client. I'm representing her in rather an important piece of litigation. I called to get some information."

The officer seemed duly impressed by Mason's card. "Then why didn't you tell that to the clerk and save us a trip?"

"I tried to," Mason said self-righteously.

"It's an old gag," the clerk said wearily. "You'd be surprised how many times I've heard that stuff. They're all secretaries."

"But this man is Perry Mason, the lawyer. Haven't you ever heard of him?"

"Nope."

The officer said, "I'll just check up on this thing, Mr. Mason. I guess it's all right, but seeing the call's been made, I've got to make a report on it, and I'd better make a check, and—let's take a look at the register."

Sally Madison started to push past him to the door.

"No you don't, Sister," the officer said, "not yet. Don't be in such a hurry. Wait five minutes and it'll all be cleared up and you can go get yourself some breakfast, or go back to your room, whichever you want. Let's just take a look at the register."

The clerk showed the officer where Della Street had signed.

"This Sally Madison your secretary?" the officer asked.

"No. Della Street is."

The elevator made noise in the shaft.

"She's up in the room?" the officer asked.

"That's right," Mason said.

The clerk said somewhat querulously, "I'm doing just what the Vice Squad told me to. They said that we could either get a house dick who would be acceptable to the Vice Squad, or we'd have to report every violation of rules in regard to visitors. I had a hunch not to let these two girls in in the first place. I'm going to be sore if I follow instructions and then you show up and pour a bucket of whitewash over 'em."

"What time did they check in?"

"About half past two this morning."

"Half past two!" the officer said, and gave Mason the benefit of a frowning scrutiny.

Mason said suavely, "That's why I wanted my secretary to keep Miss Madison with her tonight. It was late when we finished working on the case, and . . ."

The elevator rattled to a stop. Della Street, carrying

101

her overnight bag, stepped out, then stopped as she saw the trio at the desk.

"This is the other one," the clerk said.

The officer said to Della Street, "You're Mr. Mason's secretary?"

"That's right."

"I suppose you have something in your purse—social security card, or something of that sort."

Della Street said brightly, "*And* a driving license, a key to Mr. Mason's office, and a few other things."

"I'd better take a look," the officer said apologetically.

Della Street took out a small inner purse, showed him her driving license and her social security number.

The officer nodded to the night clerk. "Okay," he said. "You did all right under the circumstances. I'll report it. But you don't need to put these girls out. Let them go back to the room."

"I'm on my way," Sally Madison announced definitely. "I've had all the sleep I want, and right now I'm hungry."

Della Street looked to Mason for a signal.

Mason said, "I'm sorry your rest was disturbed, Sally. Drop into my office some time before noon."

"Thank you, I will," she said.

The officer, plainly impressed by her face and figure, said, "Sorry you were put to all this trouble, Miss. There isn't any restaurant near here. Perhaps we could give you a lift down to where there's a restaurant that's open."

"Oh no, thank you," Sally Madison told him, turning on her charm. "I *always* like to walk in the morning. It's the way I keep my figure."

"Well," the officer said approvingly, "you sure make a good job of it."

Mason and Della Street stood watching Sally Madison walk briskly across the lobby and out through the door. The officer, watching the lines of the golddigger's figure with evident approval, turned back to Mason only after the door was closed on Sally Madison. "Well, Mr. Mason, I'm sorry this happened, but it's just one of those things."

"Yes," Mason said, "it is. I don't suppose I could buy you a cup of coffee?"

"No thanks, we're on patrol. We'll be going. My partner's out in the car."

Mason moved his hand significantly toward his pocket. The officer grinned and shook his head, said, "Thanks all the same," and walked out.

The clerk said to Mason, "The room's all paid for. Go on back up if you want to."

Mason grinned. "Just the two of us?"

"Just the two of you," the clerk said dispiritedly. *"My* nose is clean. Stay as long as you want to—up until three o'clock this afternoon. That's checking-out time. Stay longer than that and you'll get charged for the room— *double."*

Mason relieved Della Street of her overnight bag. "We'll go now," he said. "My car is outside."

10

■

Mason and Della Street sat in a little all-night restaurant where the coffee was good. The ham was thin but had an excellent flavor and the eggs were cooked to golden perfection.

"Do you think we're in the clear?" Della Street asked.

"I think so," Mason said.

"You mean she'll get rid of the gun?"

Mason nodded.

"What makes you think she's going to do that?"

Mason said, "She was so anxious to get away. She certainly had something in mind. It doesn't take more than six guesses, you know."

"Didn't she have an opportunity to get rid of the gun last night?"

"Perhaps not," Mason said. "Remember that Sergeant Dorset took her out to see James Staunton. Did she tell you anything about the result of that interview?"

"Yes. Staunton insisted that Faulkner had brought him the fish. What's more, he brought out a written statement to prove it."

"The deuce he did!"

"That's what *she* said."

"A statement signed by Faulkner?"

"Yes."

"What was done with the statement?"

"Sergeant Dorset took it. He gave Staunton a receipt for it."

Mason said, "Staunton didn't tell *me* about having any written statement from Faulkner. What was in it?"

"Something to the effect that Faulkner had turned over these two particular fish to Staunton. That he wanted Staunton to care for them and secure treatment for them; that he absolved Staunton of all responsibility in case anything should happen to the fish, either death from natural causes or theft or sabotage."

"It was Faulkner's signature?"

"Staunton insisted that it was, and apparently there was nothing about it to arouse Sergeant Dorset's suspicions. He took the statement at its face value. Of course, I'm going by what Sally told me."

Mason said, "Now why do you suppose Staunton didn't produce that statement when *I* questioned him?"

"Probably because he felt your questioning wasn't official."

"I suppose so. But I thought I had him pretty well frightened."

"But if Faulkner himself took those fish out of the tank, what was the reason for the soup ladle and the four-foot extension on the handle?" Della Street asked.

Mason said, "I've already pointed that out to Sergeant Dorset. The ladle couldn't have been used to take the fish out of the tank."

"Why not?"

"In the first place," Mason said, "the surface of the water in the tank was about seven and a half feet from the floor, and I don't think the ceiling of the room was over nine and a half feet high. It's one of those low-ceilinged bungalow rooms. Now take a four-foot handle on a soup ladle, try to bring it out of the tank, and you've got two feet of handle that remain in the tank after the *top* of the handle is against the ceiling."

"But you can tilt the ladle, can't you? That is, you can take it out on an angle."

"Exactly," Mason said, "and when you do that, you lose your fish."

Della Street nodded, then frowned. She gave the problem thoughtful consideration.

"What's more," Mason went on, "I don't think you could lift a fish out of a tank with a soup ladle. I don't think the fish would stay in one position long enough to let you get him out. I think it would take something bigger than a soup ladle. Of course, I'm making allowances for the fact that these fish weren't as active as they might have been. But even so, I doubt if it could be done."

"Then what *was* the ladle used for? Was it just a blind?"

Mason said, "It could have been a blind. It could have been something else."

"Such as what?" Della asked.

"It could have been a device to get something out of the tank other than fish."

"What do you mean?"

Mason said, "Someone took a shot at Faulkner last week. At any rate he claims they did. The bullet missed him and embedded itself in the upholstery of the car. Of course, that bullet was valuable evidence. Police have worked out the science of ballistical detection now so that they can tell a great deal about the weapon which fired any particular bullet. And they can examine a bullet under a microscope and tell absolutely whether or not it was fired from any given gun."

"And what does all this have to do with the goldfish tank?" Della Street asked.

Mason grinned. "It goes back to something Elmer Carson told me. He was in the office when Faulkner came in carrying the bullet with him."

"The one he'd dug out of the car?"

"That's right. He'd recovered the bullet from where it had embedded itself in the upholstery, and he'd notified the police, although he didn't tell anyone in the real-estate office about it."

"And what happened?"

"The police came there and then Faulkner couldn't find the bullet."

"Oh, oh," Della said.

"Now Carson points out that he never left his seat at his office desk, and the stenographer there, a Miss Stanley, apparently corroborated his statement. However, police searched him, also his desk."

"So then what?"

"So then later on, along in the evening, when Miss Stanley was cleaning up her desk, she found *a* bullet under some paper on her desk."

"You mean it wasn't the same bullet?"

"I don't know," Mason said. "I don't think anyone else knows. It was simply a bullet. Everyone acted on the assumption that it was the same bullet Faulkner had brought in earlier in the day and had then misplaced. But as nearly as I can tell, there were no identifying marks on the bullet, so that it could not definitely be said to be the same one."

"I don't see just what you're getting at," Della Street said.

Mason said, "Faulkner thought that he had placed the bullet on the top of his desk when he came in. Then he'd gone over to dictate some correspondence, standing by Miss Stanley's desk."

"He must have been a pretty cool customer," Della Street said. "If someone shot at me, I don't think I'd dig out the bullet and then start dictating correspondence."

Mason said, "As I gather it, Miss Stanley noticed that his hand was shaking a little, but, aside from that, there were no other evidences of emotion."

Della Street looked at her employer as though trying to peer behind his eyes and penetrate his thoughts. "Personally I would have said that Faulkner was excitable. If someone had actually shot at him I'd think he would have been as nervous as a kitchen cockroach when a light is suddenly turned on."

"He was rather a complex character," Mason said. "Remember that night when the process server served the papers on him in Carson's suit for defamation of character?"

"Yes, I remember the occasion quite distinctly."

"Remember that he didn't get the least bit nervous. Didn't even read the papers, but pushed them down in his side pocket and kept his attention concentrated on the business of the moment—which was to get me to protect his precious goldfish by beating the temporary restraining order preventing him from moving the goldfish tank?"

Della Street nodded. "That's right. He took the service of those papers right in his stride. They seemed to constitute only a minor irritation."

"Despite the fact that the suit was for a hundred thousand dollars," Mason pointed out.

"You're getting at something, Chief. What is it?"

Mason said, "I'm simply sitting here sipping coffee and putting two-and-two together, trying to find out if perhaps someone may not have actually taken a shot at Faulkner while he was riding along in his automobile."

Della Street said, "But Faulkner hardly impressed me as a man who would have forgotten where he placed that bullet after he'd dug it out. That doesn't seem to be in keeping with his character."

"It wasn't," Mason conceded readily enough.

"Chief, what *are* you getting at?"

Mason said, "Let's consider another possibility, Della. A person seated at an adjoining desk, as Carson was, could have reached over to Faulkner's desk, picked up the bullet Faulkner had left on the desk and hidden it where it would never have been discovered."

"You mean without leaving his desk?"

"Yes."

"But I thought you said they searched Carson and searched his desk."

"They did."

"I don't see . . . oh! Now I get it! You mean he could have tossed it into the goldfish tank?"

"Exactly," Mason said. "The goldfish tank was right back of Carson's desk; was wide enough at the top so he could have tossed the bullet over his shoulder and been almost certain of having it light inside the tank, and then it would drop down to the bottom and be a relatively inconspicuous object among the pebbles and gravel at the bottom of the tank."

Della Street's eyes were sparkling with interest now. "Then when Faulkner thought attempts were being made to steal his goldfish . . . you mean it was actually someone trying to get the bullet back out of the tank?"

"Exactly," Mason said, "and the soup ladle would

108

have been an excellent instrument to have dredged down to the bottom of the tank, scooped up the bullet and eased it back out again. If someone had been reaching for the goldfish it wouldn't have been necessary to have tied a four-foot extension to the handle of the soup ladle. The goldfish would have been swimming around in the water, and by waiting for a favorable opportunity, they could have been fished out with a container that had a handle not over two feet in length."

"Then Carson must have been the one who shot at him and . . ."

"Not so fast," Mason said. "Carson had been in his office all that morning. Remember, Miss Stanley will give him an alibi. Or so Carson says, and he would hardly dare to falsify that, because he must know the circumstances incident to that first shooting are now to receive a lot of police attention."

"Then for some reason Carson was trying to confuse the issues."

"Trying to protect the person who had fired the shot, or the person *who he thought had fired the shot.*"

"You mean they may not have been the same?"

"It's a possibility."

"Would that account for the sudden animosity which developed between Carson and Faulkner?"

"The animosity had been there for some time. The thing that flared suddenly into existence was Carson's *open* hostility."

"And what did that have to do with it?"

Mason grinned and said, "Put yourself in Carson's position. He'd tossed a bullet into a fish tank. He'd evidently acted on the spur of the moment, looking for the best possible place of concealment. It was a simple matter to toss the bullet in, but it was a difficult matter to get the bullet out. Particularly when you remember that Faulkner was living in the other side of the duplex house and that he was suspicious of Carson and would have promptly rushed over to see what Carson was doing if Carson came to the office outside of office hours."

Della Street nodded.

"You can't reach down to the bottom of a four-foot fish tank," Mason said, "and pull out a lead bullet without making some rather elaborate preparations. And it was at this time that Carson suddenly realized Faulkner was concerned about the health of the goldfish and was planning to remove the entire tank to some place where the fish could be given treatment."

"But wouldn't Carson have been in a position to profit by that? Wouldn't he have stood more chance of getting the bullet if the tank had been moved?"

"Probably not. And you must also remember that he was running the risk of having the bullet discovered as soon as the tank was moved. Of course, once that bullet was discovered, it wouldn't take very much of a detective to piece together what must have happened, and Carson would find himself in quite a spot."

"I'd say he was in a spot anyway," Della Street said.

"He was," Mason told her. "And so it became necessary for him to take steps to prevent the goldfish tank from being removed from the office. *That* was the reason for his sudden flare-up of hostility and the filing of his initial action against Faulkner, the action which resulted in a temporary restraining order preventing Faulkner from removing the fish tank. Of course, Carson might have been left without a leg to stand on when he finally got into court, but that didn't bother him. He knew that by filing the action against Faulkner he could at least delay things until he had a chance to get that bullet out of the tank."

"That certainly sounds logical," Della Street admitted, "and would account for some of the things Carson did."

"And," Mason went on, "in order to make the filing of that injunction suit seem logical, Carson had to play the part all the way along the line. Otherwise, his sudden

110

concern over the goldfish tank would have been so conspicuous that it might have aroused suspicion."

"So that accounts for his action for defamation of character?"

"Exactly."

"But what about the earlier attempts to steal the goldfish?"

"There weren't any. Carson had probably managed to get access to the fish tank for some rather limited period. At that time, he probably tried various methods of extracting the bullet and found that he was up against a tougher problem than he had anticipated. The size of the tank, the weight of the tank, and its position, made it something of a job to get that bullet out of the tank."

"And I suppose that the forty-five bullet which was subsequently found on Miss Stanley's desk was simply another bullet that had been deliberately planted."

"So it would seem," Mason said. "You will note that Miss Stanley vouched for the fact that Carson had not left the office *before* the police arrived, and that he had been seated at his desk during all of the time which had elapsed between Faulkner's entrance and the arrival of the police, but it's logical to assume that between the arrival of the police and the discovery of the bullet, Carson must have gone out—perhaps several times. He certainly must have gone out for lunch. He could easily have picked up another bullet then."

Della Street showed her excitement. "Chief, you've got it all figured out. It must have happened in exactly that way. And if it did, then Carson must have been the one who killed Faulkner and . . ."

"Take it easy, Della," Mason cautioned. "Remember that all I have at present is a beautiful theory, a logical theory, but nevertheless, *only* a theory. And remember that *we're in a jam.*"

"How do you mean?"

"Sally Madison had a gun in her purse. Let's hope

she's smart enough to either hide that gun where it won't be discovered, or to wipe all the fingerprints off of it, or to do both. In the event she doesn't, and if it should prove to be the murder gun, the police will find fingerprints on it and sooner or later they're pretty apt to discover they're *your* fingerprints. Then we're up against a serious charge. It will be a simple matter for the police to prove that we took Sally Madison out of circulation during a crucial period in the investigation. And if we try to plead innocence, or pretend that we didn't know she had the murder weapon in her purse, we will be confronted with your fingerprints on the gun. So, taken by and large, we're up against it *if* Sally Madison is caught before she gets rid of that gun."

"Chief, couldn't you have telephoned the police as soon as we'd found out that she had a gun in her purse?"

"We could have," Mason said, "and in the light of subsequent events, we undoubtedly should have. However, the police would have been skeptical, and at the time, it seemed like a better bet to wipe your fingerprints off the gun, wash our hands of Sally Madison, and step out of the case. The peculiar combination of circumstances which made that night clerk enter the room and decide to stay there couldn't very well have been foreseen."

"So what do we do now?" Della Street asked.

Mason said, "We keep our fingers crossed and . . ."

Abruptly, Mason lowered his coffee cup to the saucer. "Damn!" he said.

"What is it, Chief?"

"Don't look startled and don't act guilty," Mason warned. "Leave the talking to me. Lieutenant Tragg has just entered the restaurant and is headed this way, and if you think Tragg isn't the last person in the world I want to talk to just now, you've got another think coming."

Della Street's face changed color. "Chief, *you* keep out of it. Let *me* take the rap. After all, *I'm* the one whose fingerprints are on the gun. They can't prove that *you* knew anything . . ."

Mason abruptly raised his head to look over Della Street's shoulder and said, with every semblance of surprise, "Well, well, well! Our old friend, Lieutenant Tragg! What brings you out here so early in the morning?"

Tragg placed his hat on a vacant chair, drew up another one and calmly seated himself. "What brings *you* here?"

"Hunger," Mason said, smiling.

"Is this your regular breakfast place?" Tragg asked.

"I think we'll adopt it," Mason told him. "The menu isn't large, but it's attractive. You'll find the coffee excellent, and the eggs are well cooked. I don't know about you, Lieutenant, but I particularly detest eggs that are fried in a pan so hot that a crust forms on the bottom of the eggs. Now, you take the fried eggs here, and they're thoroughly delicious."

"Exactly," Tragg said, and to the man behind the counter called out, "Ham and eggs, and a big cup of coffee now, and another cup of coffee when you serve the eggs."

Tragg shifted his position slightly, smiled at Mason and said, "And now, Counselor, since you've exhausted the subject of fried eggs, suppose we talk about murders."

"Oh, but I haven't exhausted the subject of eggs," Mason protested. "A great deal depends on cooking them at just the right temperature. Now, the yolk of a fried egg should be thoroughly warm all the way through, not cooked almost solid at the bottom but runny on top. Nor should . . ."

"I agree with you entirely," Tragg interrupted. "That also depends entirely on the temperature of the frying pan. But what do you think about Faulkner's murder?"

"I never think about murders, Lieutenant, unless I'm paid to do so. And in the event I'm paid for my thoughts,

113

I try to give only my client the benefit of them. Now you are in a different position . . ."

"Quite right," Tragg interposed calmly, reaching for the sugar as the waiter served his first cup of coffee. "I am paid by the taxpayers to think about murders at all times, and, thinking about murder, I somehow find my thoughts turning to a certain Miss Sally Madison. What can you tell me about her?"

"A rather attractive young woman," Mason said. "She seems to be devoted to her present boy friend who works in a pet store. Doubtless she has had other boy friends to whom she has been devoted, but I think that her present affair with Tom Gridley is, perhaps, more apt to result in matrimony."

"Something of a golddigger, I understand," Tragg observed.

Mason's face showed surprise. "Who told you that?"

"Oh, I get around. Is she a client of yours?"

"Now there again," Mason said smiling, "you are asking a difficult question. That is, the question is easy; it's the answer that's difficult."

"You might try answering it either yes or no," Tragg said.

"It isn't that easy. She hasn't as yet definitely retained me to represent her interests. But on the other hand, I think she desires to do so, and I am investigating the facts."

"Think you'll represent her?"

"I'm sure I can't say. The case she presents is far from being an easy one."

"So I would gather."

"You see," Mason went on, "as the agent of her boy friend, Tom Gridley, she may or may not have reached a contract with Harrington Faulkner. A contract involves a meeting of the minds, and a meeting of the minds in turn depends upon . . ."

Tragg held up his hand. "Please," he begged.

114

Mason raised his eyebrows in apparent surprise.

Tragg said, "You're unusually loquacious this morning, Counselor. And a man who can deliver such an extemporaneous dissertation upon the art of frying eggs could doubtless talk almost indefinitely on the law of contracts. And so, if you'll pardon me, I think I'll talk to your charming secretary."

Tragg turned to Della Street and asked, "Where did you spend the night last night, Miss Street?"

Della smiled sweetly. "That question, of course, Lieutenant, involved an assumption that the night is, or was, an indivisible unit. Now, as a matter of fact, a night is really divided into two periods. First, the period before midnight, which I believe was legally yesterday, and the period after midnight, which is today."

Tragg grinned, said to Perry Mason, "She's an apt pupil, Counselor. I doubt if you could have stalled for time any better if you had stepped in and answered the question for her."

"I doubt if I could have done as well," Mason admitted cheerfully.

"Now," Tragg said, suddenly losing his smile and becoming grimly official in his manner, "suppose we quit talking about fried eggs and contracts and the legal subdivisions of the period of darkness, and suppose, Miss Street, you tell me exactly where you were from ten o'clock last night until the present time, omitting nothing—and that's an official question."

"Is there any reason why she should have to answer that question?" Mason asked. "Even conceding that it *is* a legal question."

Tragg's face was as hard as granite. "Yes. In the event I get the run-around it will be an important factor in determining whether any connection Miss Street may have had with what transpired was accidental or deliberate."

Della Street said brightly, "Well, of course . . ."

"Take it easy, Della," Mason warned.

She glanced at him and at what she saw in his eyes the expression of animation fled from her features.

"I'm still waiting for an answer to my question," Lieutenant Tragg said harshly.

"Don't you think you should be fair with Miss Street?" Mason asked.

Tragg didn't take his eyes from Della's face. He said, "Your interruptions all go on the debit side of the ledger as far as I'm concerned, Mason. Miss Street, *where did you spend the night?*"

Mason interposed suavely, "Of course, Lieutenant, you're not a mind reader. The fact that you came to *this* restaurant means that you knew we were in the neighborhood. There are logically only two sources from which you could have acquired that information. One of them is that you received over the radio a report from a patrol car stating that it had been called to the Kellinger Hotel, where a complaint had been made that two young women were receiving a male guest as a visitor in violation of the rules of the hotel, and the police had been called to eject the tenants. You thereupon acted upon the assumption that you would, perhaps, find the parties who had been ejected in a near-by all-night restaurant, and by the simple process of cruising around, located us here."

Tragg started to say something, but Mason, slightly raising his voice, kept the conversational lead. "The other assumption is that you picked up Sally Madison on the street a few moments ago and questioned her. In which event you learned from her that we were in the vicinity. And if you questioned her, you doubtless made a rather complete job of it."

Mason's warning glance at Della Street conveyed the impression to her that in such event Lieutenant Tragg had doubtless examined the purse and by this time was fully familiar with its contents.

Tragg was still looking at Della Street. "Now that

116

you've been properly coached, Miss Street, *where did you spend the night?*"

"I spent part of it at my apartment. The rest of it at the Kellinger Hotel."

"How did you happen to go to the Kellinger Hotel?"

"Sally Madison called me on the telephone and told me Mr. Mason wished me to take her to some hotel."

"Did she say why?"

Della Street said quite innocently, "I can't remember quite definitely whether *she* told me why or whether I subsequently learned why from Mr. Mason. He wanted me to get her out of . . ."

"Out of circulation," Tragg prompted as Della Street's voice suddenly trailed away into silence.

"Out of the way of newspaper reporters," Della Street finished, smiling sweetly at Lieutenant Tragg.

"What time was this?" Tragg asked.

"That Sally Madison called me?"

"Yes."

Della Street said, "I really couldn't say. I don't think I looked at my watch, but doubtless the Kellinger Hotel can tell you approximately what time we arrived."

"What I am asking you now," Tragg said, "is what time you received this call from Sally Madison."

"I'm sure I can't say."

"Now then," Tragg said, "we're getting to the important part. Watch your answers carefully, because a great deal is going to depend on what you say. Did you notice anything unusual about Sally Madison?"

"Oh, yes," Della Street told him quickly.

Tragg's voice was grim and harsh. "What?" he asked, and the single word was as harshly explosive as the cracking of a whip.

Mason's eyes warned Della Street.

"Why," she said, "the girl slept in the nude." She smiled at Lieutenant Tragg and then went on rapidly, "That's rather unusual, you know, Lieutenant . . . I mean

117

she simply stripped her clothes off and jumped into bed. Ordinarily a young woman as beautiful as Sally Madison takes much more care of her personal appearance before retiring. She'll put creams and lotions on her face and usually . . ."

"That isn't what I meant," Tragg said.

"Of course," Mason interposed, "you've interrupted Della, Lieutenant. If you had let her keep on talking, she might have told you exactly what you had in mind."

"If I'd let her keep on talking," Tragg said, "she'd have been here until noon describing Sally Madison's bedtime habits. The question is, Miss Street, did you or did you not notice anything unusual about Sally Madison or did she make any confession or admission to you?"

"Remember, Lieutenant," Mason said, "that as a potential client, anything Sally Madison may have said was a privileged communication and as Della Street is my secretary, she can't be questioned concerning that."

"I think I understand that rule," Tragg conceded. "And it applies to anything that was necessarily said in connection with the matter on which Sally Madison was consulting you. Now I take it that matter related exclusively to a claim she had against the estate of Harrington Faulkner. I now want to know definitely, once and for all, whether Della Street noticed anything unusual or significant in connection with Sally Madison. Did you or did you not, Miss Street?"

Della Street said, "Of course, Lieutenant, I had only met the girl a day or two ago, and so I don't know what is usual about her. Therefore, when you ask me if I noticed anything unusual, it's hard to tell . . ."

"All this stalling around," Tragg said, "causes me to reach a very definite conclusion in my own mind. Miss Street, how did it happen Perry Mason came up to call on you at the hour of five o'clock in the morning?"

"Was it five o'clock?" Della Street asked, with some

118

show of surprise. "I'm certain that I didn't look at my watch, Lieutenant. I merely . . ."

Mason said, "There again, of course, the records of the Hotel Kellinger will be of some assistance to you, Lieutenant."

Tragg said, "Despite your repeated warnings to Della Street that she isn't to conceal any information which I can subsequently ascertain by interviewing the clerk at the Kellinger Hotel, I want to know whether you noticed anything unusual in connection with Sally Madison, anything in connection with her wearing apparel, what she had on, what she had with her, what she did, or what she said."

Mason said, "I'm quite certain, Lieutenant, that if Miss Street had noticed anything such as you have mentioned that was sufficiently unusual to be of any importance, she would have told me, so you can ask your question of me."

"I don't have to. I'm asking Miss Street. Miss Street, why did you call Perry Mason and ask him to come to the hotel?"

Della Street's eyes were suddenly hard and defiant. "That is none of your business."

"Do you mean that?"

"Yes."

"You know my business is rather inclusive," Tragg said, "particularly insofar as murders are concerned."

Della Street clamped her lips together in a tight line.

Abruptly, Tragg said, "All right, you two have sparred around here trying to find out how much I know. The very fact that you've been sparring for time convinces me that you do know the thing I wanted to find out. As Perry Mason so aptly pointed out, you could gamble with either one of two alternatives. One was that I'd received a report from the officers who answered the call to the Kellinger Hotel, and had cruised the neighborhood simply on the off chance of picking you up. The other was that I had first picked up Sally Madison and questioned her. You stalled for time, hoping that the first alternative was the correct one. You're wrong. I'd picked up the report from the officers when it came in as a routine radio report. I'd been up all night, waiting for a break in the case. That radio report looked like the break I'd been waiting for. I dashed out and picked up Sally Madison on the street. In her purse she had two thousand dollars in cash, the possession of which she couldn't explain. She also had a thirty-eight caliber, double-action revolver which had recently been fired, and which bears every evidence of having been the weapon with which Harrington Faulkner was murdered. Now then, Perry Mason and Della Street, if I can prove that either one of you knew of the contents of that purse, I'm going to stick you as being accessories after the fact. I gave you every opportunity to report to me and to communicate any significant information connected with the murder of Harrington Faulkner. You chose not to do so. And, so help me, Mason, if I can prove that you knew that gun was in Sally Madison's purse, I'm going to nail you to the cross."

Abruptly, Lieutenant Tragg pushed back his chair, said to the puzzled waiter, "Never mind the ham and eggs. I'll pay the check now."

And Tragg slammed money down on the counter and walked out.

Della Street's eyes, sick with dismay, caught those of Perry Mason. "Oh, Chief," she said, "I should have told him! I'm sick all over."

The lines of Mason's face could have been carved from stone. He said, "It's okay, kid. There were two possible alternatives. We took a chance and we lost. Now we'll carry on from there. It seems to be our unlucky day. We're in it together, and it's a sweet mess."

11

■

Perry Mason, Della Street and Paul Drake sat in Mason's office, grouped around Mason's big desk.

Mason finished his account of the events of the past few hours, and said, "So you see, Paul, we're in a jam."

Drake whistled softly. "I'll say you're in a jam. Why didn't you toss the jane overboard as soon as you saw that rod and call the cops?"

"Because I was afraid they wouldn't have believed us in the first place, and, in the second place I hated to throw her to the wolves without knowing what it was all about. I wanted to hear her side of the story first. And, if you want to know, I thought we could sneak out of it and get away with it."

Drake nodded, said, "Yes, it was a good gamble all right, only you seem to have lost with every throw of the dice."

"We did indeed," Mason said.

"Just where does that leave you now?"

Mason said, "If they can pin some part in the murder on Sally Madison, it leaves us right out on the end of the limb. If they can't, we'll probably squeeze out. What have you found out about the facts of the murder, Paul?"

Drake said, "They're putting an official hush-hush on the thing, but I can tell you this much—the medical examiner made a bad slip. The young deputy coroner who went out there was green, and Sergeant Dorset was helping to ball things up. The police have fixed the time of death within a very short time, but, as I understand it, the autopsy surgeon neglected to do the one thing that would have given the cops a perfect case."

Mason said, "That's good."

"I can tell you something else, Perry, that doesn't look so good."

"What?"

"This chap that works in the pet shop, Tom Gridley, seems to have been out there and got a check for one thousand dollars, and that check may have been about the last thing that Faulkner ever wrote."

"How do they figure that out, Paul?"

"There was a checkbook lying on the floor. The last stub in it had been partially filled out. It was a check for one thousand dollars, and Faulkner had been writing on that stub when all of a sudden his pen simply quit writing, but he had written 'Tom' and then the letters 'G-r-i.' Quite evidently he'd been intending to write 'Tom Gridley.' There was a fountain pen found on the floor."

Mason thought that over for a moment, said, "What did Tom Gridley say about it, Paul?"

"No one knows. The police swooped down on him as soon as they found that stub in the checkbook, and Gridley has been out of circulation ever since."

"When do the police think the murder was committed?"

"Right around eight-fifteen. Say between eight-fifteen and eight-thirty. Faulkner was to have attended a meeting of goldfish experts. He was to have been there at eight-thirty. About ten minutes past eight he telephoned and said that he'd been delayed by a business matter which had detained him longer than he'd expected; that he was just shaving and was going to jump in a hot bath, that as soon as he'd finished he'd be right over, but that he would be perhaps a few minutes late. He also said he'd have to leave probably at nine-thirty, as he had a business appointment for that hour. And then, right in the middle of the conversation, he said to someone who had evidently entered the room while he was telephoning, 'How did *you* get in here? I don't want to see you, and if and when I do want to see you, I'll send for you.' The person at the other end of the line could hear the mumble of some voices, and then Faulkner said, apparently very irritated, 'Well, I'm not going to discuss it tonight. Damn it, either get out or I'll throw you out. All right, if you want it that way, here it is,' and then abruptly he slammed the telephone receiver into place right in the middle of the conversation.

"These people who were having the meeting wanted to be sure to have Faulkner there. They wanted to get some money out of him. They called him back at eight-twenty-five and no one answered the telephone, so they concluded Faulkner was on his way. They waited another five or ten minutes, then when he hadn't shown up, tried to get him again. Then they went ahead with the meeting. Now, obviously, Faulkner had been dressing and getting ready to go to that meeting. There was a razor on the glass shelf in the bathroom with lather and whiskers still adhering to the blade, and Faulkner was freshly shaved when the body was discovered. Putting all that together, the police are absolutely positive that while Faulkner was telephoning, some visitor walked in unexpectedly, some visitor who hadn't rung a doorbell, but had simply walked in. Faulkner resented his coming, and decided to throw him out physically. That's when he slammed up the telephone and started toward the intruder. The police think that's just about when the shot was fired."

"And the autopsy surgeon?" Mason asked.

"Apparently the autopsy surgeon was asleep at the switch. When the cops got there, it didn't appear to be particularly important to fix the time of death right down to a minute, and there was more work done in connection with photographing the position of the body, getting fingerprints and trying to reconstruct the physical evidence than in getting to work with body temperatures and all that sort of stuff. The detectives think it was a blunder on the part of the medical department and there's some feeling about it. Taking the body's temperature right at the time the police first arrived would have given them some fine corroborations. As it is, they have to rely on deductions."

Mason said, "Yes, I can see where that would make for considerable complications. It looks as though the police might be right. What's their theory about the overturned goldfish bowl?"

"Well," Drake said, "the goldfish *could* have been in a bowl on that overturned table, and Faulkner could have upset the whole works when the shot was fired and he fell down dead."

Mason nodded.

"Or," Drake went on, "someone could have been in the room some time after the murder was committed and upset the goldfish bowl either accidentally or on purpose."

"Any theories about that someone?"

"It could have been Mrs. Faulkner, who didn't like the looks of the thing, upset the goldfish bowl, either accidentally or on purpose, then got in her car and went around the corner to wait for you to show up."

"But how could she have known that I was coming?"

"As nearly as I can tell," Drake said, "it's the way you doped it out last night, Perry. Staunton must have given her a ring."

"In other words, she was in the house. She had already discovered the body. She had upset the goldfish bowl. Staunton rang up on the telephone. He wanted to talk with Faulkner. She told him Faulkner couldn't be reached at the present moment; was there any message she could take, and Staunton told her that Sally Madison and I were on our way out there."

Mason got up from behind his desk, started pacing the floor restlessly. "That, of course, presupposes the fact, Paul, that there was some inducement used to make Staunton keep his mouth shut. I mean about that telephone conversation. If Faulkner died at around eight-fifteen or eight-thirty, Staunton must have learned by this time from the police or the papers that Mrs. Faulkner was there in the house with her dead husband. . . . Hang it, Paul, what are we sticking around here talking for? Why don't we get in touch with Staunton and see what he has to say when we really start pouring it on him."

Drake didn't move from his chair. "Don't be silly, Perry."

"You mean the police have sewed him up?"

"Tighter than a drum. He won't get back into circulation until after he's made a complete written statement and sworn to it. By that time, he'll have sewed himself up in a sack. He won't dare to make any statement under any circumstances that would change the statement he gave the police."

Once more, Mason resumed his pacing of the floor, then he said, "Put men out to watch Staunton's house. As soon as the police let him get back into circulation, ask him one question."

"What question?" Drake wanted to know.

Mason said, "Last Wednesday Faulkner took these fish out to him and told him to telephone the pet store and ask for treatment. Find out what time the pet store sent out the treatment tank."

Drake showed surprise. "That's all?"

"That's all. There are other questions I'd like to ask him, but by the time the police get done with him, he won't answer. So just ask him that one question. Today's Saturday, and everything closes at noon. They'll probably keep Gridley and Staunton sewed up until it's too late to get any court orders. And the way things are now I don't dare to ask for a *habeas corpus* on Tom Gridley."

The telephone rang.

Della Street answered it, said, "It's for you, Paul," and handed the instrument over to Drake.

Drake said, "Hello . . . Okay, spill it . . . Right . . . You sure? . . . All right, give me everything you've got."

Drake listened for nearly two minutes while the receiver continued to give forth a continuous rattle of crackling, metallic sounds.

At the end of that time, Drake said, "Okay, I guess there's nothing much to do except keep a line on what's happening and let me know."

He hung up and turned to Perry Mason.

Mason took one look at the detective's face and asked, "Is it that bad, Paul?"

Drake nodded.

"What is it?" Della Street asked.

"You lose," Drake said.

"What?"

Drake said, "This is confidential, Perry. The police don't want it to leak out, but I've got it straight from one who knows. They took Sally Madison into custody. They found the gun and the roll of bills in her purse. They fingerprinted the gun and got some excellent latents. There were two fingerprints on top of the barrel, not complete fingerprints, but nevertheless enough to enable the police to make an identification. Tragg is nobody's fool. He closed up the room in the Kellinger Hotel, went to work on the bathroom mirrors and the doorknobs, got fingerprints of both Della Street and Sally Madison. Then he checked the prints on the gun. He found he had half a dozen fingerprints of Sally Madison, and two of Della Street. Then, after they'd photographed the gun, they turned it over to the ballistics department and fired a test bullet and compared that with the bullet they found in Faulkner's body. There's no question but what the gun they took from Sally Madison's purse was the weapon with which the murder was committed. And there's also no question but what that weapon belonged to Tom Gridley. It was a thirty-eight caliber revolver he'd purchased six years before when he was acting as messenger for a bank. The gun is registered with the police."

Della Street looked up at Perry Mason in dismay.

Mason said grimly, "All right, Paul. Put as many men on the job as are necessary to give it complete coverage. Find out where they've got Sally Madison held for inquiry if you can. Della, get out some blanks and fill out a writ of *habeas corpus* on behalf of Sally Madison."

Drake said, "It won't do you any good, Perry. They'll have wrung her dry by this time. There's no use trying to lock the stable after the horse has been stolen."

"To hell·with the stable," Mason said. "There's no time for that now. *I'm* going after the horse!"

12

∎

Paul Drake was back in Perry Mason's office within five minutes after he had left. He encountered the lawyer just leaving from the exit door of his private office.

"Where to?" Drake asked.

"Wilfred Dixon," Mason told him. "I'm going to check up on Dixon and on the affairs of the first Mrs. Faulkner. He is her lawyer. What's new? Anything important?"

Drake put his hand on Mason's arm, drew Mason back into the inner office and closed the door. "Sometime during the night," he said, "an attempt was made to get that goldfish tank out of the office. It sure looks as though you called the turn on that business, Perry."

"Just when was the attempt made?"

"Police don't know. For some reason or other, they never looked into the other side of the duplex house, but confined their investigations to Faulkner's residence. Then, this morning, when Alberta Stanley, the secretary, opened up the real-estate office, she found the place something of a wreck. There was a long rubber hose which had evidently been used to siphon the water out of the empty goldfish tank. That is, it was empty of goldfish."

Mason nodded.

"After the water was siphoned out, the goldfish tank had been tipped over on its side and all of the mud and gravel in the bottom had been scooped out and left in a pile on the floor."

Mason's eyes narrowed. "Has it occurred to the police as yet, that someone was looking for that bullet Faulkner carried into the office?"

"You can't tell, Perry. It hasn't occurred to Sergeant Dorset, but you never know what Lieutenant Tragg is working on. Dorset shoots off his mouth to the newspaper boys and tries to get publicity. Tragg is smooth as velvet. He kids the boys along and prefers results to publicity."

"Anything else?" Mason asked.

Drake said, "I hate to do this, Perry."

"Do what?"

"Be hanging crepe all over things, but it's one of those cases where every bit of information you get is the kind you don't want."

"Shoot," Mason told him.

"You remember Faulkner had a reputation of being a man who would skin the other fellow in a business deal. He kept within his own standards of honesty but he was completely ruthless."

Mason nodded.

128

"Well, it seems that Faulkner was really anxious to get hold of that formula that Tom Gridley had developed for the treatment of gill disease. You remember he bought out Rawlins' pet shop? That was the first move in his campaign. Then, it turns out that Tom Gridley had mixed up a batch of his paste which was to be painted on plastic panels that were to be introduced into fish tanks. The trouble with Gridley is that he gets so interested in what he's doing and . . . well, he's just like a doctor. He wants to effect cures and doesn't care too much about the financial end of things."

"Go ahead," Mason said.

"Well, it seems that yesterday evening, Faulkner, who had, of course, got the combination of the safe from Rawlins, went down to the pet store, opened the safe, took out the can of paste that Gridley had mixed up and sent it to a chemist to be analyzed. Rawlins was there and tried to stop him but it was no soap."

"Faulkner certainly was a heel," Mason said.

"According to the police, it furnishes a swell motivation for a murder."

Mason thought the matter over and nodded his head. "Academically it's bad. Practically it isn't so bad."

"You mean the way a jury will look at it?"

"Yes. It's one of those things that you can play up strong to a jury. While technically it's a motivation for murder, it's such a flagrant example of oppression by a man who has money and power, who's picking on a chap in his employ . . . No, Paul, that isn't at all bad. I presume the theory of the police is that when Gridley found out about it he became terribly angry, took his gun and went up to kill Faulkner."

"That's about the size of it."

Mason smiled and said, "I don't think Tragg will hold to that theory very long."

"Why not?"

"Because the evidence is against it."

"What do you mean? It's Gridley's gun, there's no question of that."

"Sure, it's Gridley's gun," Mason said. "But mind you this: If the circumstantial evidence means what the police think it means, Tom Gridley effected a settlement with Faulkner. He may have gone up there *intending* to kill him, but Faulkner gave him a check for a thousand dollars. Faulkner wouldn't have done that unless he had reached some sort of a settlement with Gridley. Gridley certainly couldn't have killed him *before* the check was made out, and would have had no reason to have killed him afterward."

"That's right," Drake said.

"The minute Faulkner died, that check, and also the five-thousand-dollar check that Sally Madison has, weren't worth the paper they were written on. You can't cash a check after a man dies. I have an idea, Paul, that you'll find Lieutenant Tragg begins to think this motive isn't as simple as it appears to be on the surface. Hang it, if it weren't for the evidence against Sally Madison and the fact that Della Street's fingerprints are on that gun, we'd sit tight and tell the police to go jump in the lake. As it is, I've got to find out all the facts and be the first one to get the correct interpretation."

"Suppose Sally Madison bumped him off?"

"Then," Mason said, "the police have a perfect case against Della Street and me as being accessories after the fact."

"Think they'll press it?"

"You know damn well they'll press it," Mason said. "They'd like nothing better."

"Well, of course," Drake pointed out, "you can't blame them. You certainly do skate on thin ice, Perry. You've been a thorn in the flesh of the police for a long time."

Mason nodded. "I've had it coming to me once or twice," he admitted, "but what makes me sore is to think that they'd really hang it on me in a case where we were

130

absolutely innocent and only trying to help a young fellow who had T.B. get enough money to take treatments that would cure him. Hang it, Paul, I'm really in a mess this time, and they've got Della roped into it. That's what comes of trusting a golddigger. Oh well, there's no use conducting post-mortems. By the time the police let me get in touch with Sally Madison she'll have been bled white. I'm getting out a writ of *habeas corpus* and that of course will force their hand. They'll have to put a charge against her. But by the time they do that, they'll have really put her through a clothes wringer. Keep working, Paul, and if you get anything new, let Della Street know. Work on this case as you've never worked on anything else in your life. We're working against time and we've got to find out not only the evidence, but we've got to interpret that evidence."

"Did the broken goldfish tank mean anything to you?"

"It means a lot," Mason said.

"How come?"

"Suppose Sally Madison isn't as dumb as she appears. Suppose back of that poker face of hers is a shrewd, calculating mind that isn't missing a bet."

"I'll go with you that far," Drake said.

"And suppose," Mason went on, "she reasoned out what had happened to the bullet that Faulkner had taken to the office. Suppose when Faulkner gave her the key there in the café at the time he made the deal with her and told her to get Tom Gridley and go out and treat his fish, Sally Madison went out instead and used the soup ladle to get the bullet out of the tank. Then suppose she very shrewdly sold that bullet to the highest bidder."

"Wait a minute," Drake said. "You've got something wrong there, Perry."

"What?"

"According to all the evidence, those goldfish must have been gone when Sally got there. Faulkner must have given her a complete double cross on that."

"All right, so what?"

"So when she went there to get the bullet, she would have known that the goldfish were gone."

"Not goldfish," Mason said, "a pair of Veiltail Moor Telescopes."

"Okay. They're goldfish to me."

"You won't think so after you've seen them," Mason said. "If Sally Madison went in there to get that bullet, the fact that the fish weren't there wouldn't have stopped her from getting what *she* was after."

"And then she went back and got Tom Gridley and came out the second time?"

"That's right."

"Well," Drake said, "it's a theory, Perry. You're giving that girl credit for an awful lot of sense."

Mason nodded.

"I think you're giving her too much credit," Drake said.

Mason said, "I didn't give her enough credit for awhile. Now I'm going to make my mistakes on the other side. That girl's batted around a bit, Paul. She knows some of the answers. She's in love with Tom Gridley. You take a woman of that type, when she falls for a man, it's usually a combination of a starved-mother instinct and a sex angle. My best guess is that that girl would stop at nothing. Anyway, I haven't time to stay here and talk it over now. I'm on my way to see Dixon."

"Be careful," Drake warned.

Mason said, "I'm going to be careful with everybody from now on, Paul, but it isn't going to slow me down any. I'm going to keep moving."

Mason drove to the address of Wilfred Dixon, found the house to be a rather imposing edifice of white stucco, red tile, landscaped grounds, a three-car garage and an atmosphere of quiet luxury.

Mason had no difficulty whatever in getting an immediate audience with Wilfred Dixon, who received him in a room on the southeast side of the house, a room which was something of a cross between a den and an office, with deep leather chairs, Venetian blinds, original oils, a huge flat-topped desk, a portable bar, and a leather davenport which seemed to invite an afternoon siesta. There were three telephones on the desk, but there were no filing cases in the room, no papers visible on the desk.

Wilfred Dixon was a short, chunky man with perfectly white hair, steel-gray eyes, and a face which was deeply tanned from the neck to the roots of the hair. His complexion indicated either considerable time spent on the golf links without a hat, or regular treatments under a quartz lamp.

"Won't you sit down, Mr. Mason," Dixon invited, after giving the lawyer a cordial grip with muscular fingers. "I've heard a great deal about you, and naturally it's a pleasure to meet you, although, of course, I can't understand why you should look *me* up. I presume it's connected in some rather remote way with the tragic death of Harrington Faulkner."

"It is," Mason said, giving Dixon a steady look.

Dixon met his eyes with calm assurance. "I have, of course, managed the affairs of Genevieve Faulkner for some years. She was the first wife, you know. But of course you *do* know."

And Dixon smiled, a disarming, magnetic smile.

"You knew Harrington Faulkner personally?" Mason asked.

"Oh yes," Dixon said, as though stating a fact which must have been well known and perfectly obvious.

"Talked with him occasionally?"

"Oh yes. You see, it was a little embarrassing for Genevieve to hold business conferences with her former husband. Yet the first Mrs. Faulkner—I'll call her Genevieve if you don't mind, Mr. Mason—was very much interested in the business transactions of the firm."

"That firm made money?" Mason asked.

133

"Ordinarily, Mr. Mason, I would consider that question involved Genevieve's private affairs. But inasmuch as an investigation in connection with the Faulkner Estate will make the whole matter public, I see no reason for placing you to the inconvenience of getting your information through more devious channels. The business was immensely profitable."

"Isn't it rather unusual for a real-estate business to make that much money under present conditions?"

"Not at all. It was more than a real-estate business. The business was diversified. It administered various other businesses which had been previously used as investment outlets. Harrington Faulkner was a very good businessman, a very good businessman, indeed. Of course, he was unpopular. Personally, I didn't approve of Mr. Faulkner's business methods. I wouldn't have employed them myself. I was representing Genevieve. I certainly was in no position to—well, shall we say, criticize the goose that was laying the golden eggs?"

"Faulkner was the money-maker?"

"Faulkner was the money-maker."

"What about Carson?"

"Carson was an associate," Dixon said suavely. "A man who had an equal interest in the business. One third of the stock was held by Faulkner, one third by Carson and one third by Genevieve."

"That still isn't telling me anything about Carson," Mason said.

With every simulation of candid surprise, Dixon raised his eyebrows. "Why, I thought that was telling you *everything* about Carson."

"You haven't said anything about his business ability."

"Frankly, Mr. Mason, my dealings were with Faulkner."

"If Faulkner was the mainspring of the business," Mason said, "it must have galled him to do the bulk of the work and furnish the bulk of the capital, and then receive only one third of the income."

"Well, of course, he and Carson had a salary—a salary that was fixed and approved by the court."

"And they couldn't raise those salaries?"

"Not without Genevieve's consent, no."

"And were the salaries ever raised?"

"No," Dixon said shortly.

"Was any request made to raise the salaries?"

Dixon's eyes twinkled. "Several times."

"Faulkner, I take it, didn't feel too friendly toward his first wife?"

"I'm sure I never asked him about that."

"I presume that originally Harrington Faulkner furnished most of the money which started the firm of Faulkner and Carson."

"I believe so."

"Carson was the younger man and Faulkner relied on him perhaps for an element of young blood in the business?"

"As to that, I couldn't say. I only represented Genevieve after the separation and during the divorce."

"You had known her before then?"

"No. I was acquainted with the attorney whom Genevieve employed. I'm a businessman, Mr. Mason, a business adviser, an investment counselor, if you wish. I try to be a good one. You really haven't stated the object of your visit."

Mason said, "Primarily, I'm interested in finding out what I can about Harrington Faulkner."

"So I gathered. But the reason for your interest is not apparent. Doubtless, many people would like to know something of the affairs of Mr. Faulkner. There's a difference between a casual curiosity, Mr. Mason, and a legitimate interest."

"You may rest assured I have a legitimate interest."

"Mr. Mason, I merely wanted to know what it was."

Mason smiled. "I will probably be the attorney for a claimant against the Faulkner Estate."

"Probably?" Dixon asked.

"I haven't as yet definitely accepted the case."

"That makes your interest rather—shall we say, nebulous?"

"I wouldn't say so," Mason said.

"Well, of course, I wouldn't have a difference of opinion with an attorney who has such an established reputation, Mr. Mason. So perhaps let us say you have your opinion and I will try to keep an entirely open mind. I'm perfectly willing to be convinced."

Mason said, "With two thirds of the stock and complete control of the corporation, Faulkner, I guess, controlled the corporation with an iron hand?"

"There's no law against guessing, Mr. Mason, none whatever. There are times when I find it a rather interesting occupation, although of course one hardly dares to reach a decision predicated solely upon a mere guess. One prefers to have facts to justify one's opinion."

"One does, indeed," Mason said. "Therefore, one asks questions."

"And receives answers," Dixon told him suavely.

Mason's eyes twinkled. "Not always the most definite answers that one would want."

"That's quite right, Mr. Mason. That's something I myself have found repeatedly in my business dealings. For instance, you'll remember I asked *you* about *your* interest in the unfortunate death of Harrington Faulkner. You stated, I believe, that you were considering representing a person who had a claim against the estate. May I ask the nature of that claim? I don't think you told me."

Mason said, "It involved a claim based upon a formula that was worked out for the cure of a fish disease."

"Oh, Tom Gridley's formula," Dixon said.

"You seem to know a good deal about the business, Mr. Dixon."

"As the person who represents a client whose financial eggs are virtually all in one basket, Mr. Mason, it behooves me to know a great deal about the details of the business."

"Now, to go back," Mason went on. "Faulkner was in the driver's seat until suddenly, and I presume out of a clear sky, Genevieve Faulkner sued him for divorce. Quite evidently she must have had the goods on him."

"The evidence in that case has all been introduced and a decision long since reached, Mr. Mason."

"That decision must have been gall and wormwood to Harrington Faulkner. In place of controlling the corporation he suddenly found that he was in the position of being a minority stockholder."

"Of course," Dixon pointed out somewhat smugly, "since under the laws of this state man and wife are presumed to be partners, if the marriage is dissolved it becomes necessary for some sort of a settlement to be made."

"And I presume," Mason went on, "that with the constant threat being held over Faulkner's head that you would go back into court and ask the judge to reopen the alimony settlement in the event of any failure on the part of Faulkner to accede to your wishes, you must have incurred Faulkner's enmity."

Once more the eyebrows went up. "I merely represent Genevieve's investments. Naturally, I represent her interests to the best of my ability."

"You talked with Faulkner occasionally?"

"Oh yes."

"He told you many of the details of the business?"

"Naturally."

"Did he come to you and tell you the details voluntarily, or did you ask him?"

"Well, of course, Mr. Mason, you'd hardly expect a man in Mr. Faulkner's position to run to me with every little detail about his business."

"But you were interested?"

137

"Quite naturally."

"Therefore, I take it you asked him?"

"About the things I wanted to know, yes."

"And that included virtually everything?"

"Really, Mr. Mason, I couldn't say as to that, because naturally I don't know how much I didn't know. I only know the things I did know."

And Dixon beamed at the lawyer with a manner that indicated he was trying his best to co-operate in giving Mason any information that was available.

"May I ask you when you last talked with Faulkner?" Mason asked.

Dixon's face became as a wooden mask.

"Of course," Mason said, "it's a question that the police will ask sooner or later."

Dixon carefully placed the tips of his fingers together, regarded his nails for a moment.

"I take it," Mason said, "that you talked with him sometime yesterday evening."

Dixon raised his eyes. "Really, Mr. Mason, what is the ground for that assumption?"

"Your hesitancy."

"I was deliberating."

Mason smiled. "The hesitancy may have been due to deliberation, but it was nevertheless a hesitation."

"A very good point, Mr. Mason. A good point, indeed. I'm frank to admit that I was deliberating and therefore hesitating. I don't know whether to answer your question or whether to reserve my answer until I am interrogated by the police."

"Any particular reason why you shouldn't tell me?"

"I was debating that with myself."

"Anything to conceal?"

"Certainly not."

"Then why conceal it?"

"I think that's unfair, Mr. Mason. I am not concealing

anything. I have answered your questions fully and frankly."

"When did you last talk with Faulkner?"

"Well, Mr. Mason, as you have so shrewdly deduced, it was yesterday."

"What time yesterday?"

"Now, do you mean when I talked with him personally, face to face?"

Mason said, "I want to know when you talked with him personally and I want to know when you talked with him over the telephone."

"What makes you think there was a telephone conversation?"

"The fact that you differentiate between a conversation with him face to face and another conversation."

Dixon said, "I'm afraid I'm no match for you, Mr. Mason. I'm afraid I'm in the hands of a very shrewd lawyer."

"I am," Mason said, "still waiting for an answer."

"You have, of course, no official right to ask that question."

"None whatever."

"Perhaps I wouldn't choose to answer it. What then?"

"Then," Mason said, "I would ring up my friend, Lieutenant Tragg, tell him that you had seen Harrington Faulkner on the day he was murdered, perhaps on the evening he was murdered; that you had apparently talked with him over the telephone. And then I would hang up, shake hands with you, tell you I appreciated your co-operation, and go away."

Once more, Dixon put his fingers together. Then he nodded his head, as though having reached some definite decision. But he still remained silent, a chubby figure with a masklike countenance, sitting behind a huge desk, slowly nodding his head in impressive acquiescence with himself.

Mason waited silently.

Dixon said at length, "You make a very powerful argument, Mr. Mason. You do indeed. You would make a good poker player. It would be hard to judge what was in your hand when you shoved your chips into the pot—very hard indeed."

Mason said nothing.

Dixon nodded his head a few more times, then went on to say, "I will, of course, be called on eventually by the police. In fact, I have debated with myself whether I should telephone the police and tell them exactly what I know. You will, of course, be able to get all this information sooner or later, else I wouldn't be talking to you. You still haven't told me your exact interest in finding out the facts."

Dixon looked up at Mason, his attitude that of a man who is courteously awaiting a reply to a routine question.

Mason sat absolutely silent.

Dixon drew his eyebrows together, looked down at his desk, then slowly shook his head in a gesture of negation, as though after giving the matter thoughtful consideration, Mason's refusal to be more frank had caused him to reverse his former decision.

Still Mason said nothing.

Suddenly the business counselor put both hands flat on the desk, palms down, the gesture of a man who has definitely reached a decision. "Mr. Faulkner conferred with me several times yesterday, Mr. Mason."

"In person?"

"Yes."

"What did he want?"

"That goes beyond the scope of your original question, Mr. Mason."

Mason said, "I am more concerned with the question than with the reason for asking it."

Dixon raised and lowered his hands, the palms making little patting noises on the desk. "Well, Mr. Mason, it's asking for a good deal, but, after all—Mr. Faulkner wanted to buy out Genevieve's interest."

"And you wanted to sell?"

"At a price, yes."

"The price was in dispute?"

"Oh, very much."

"Was there a wide difference?"

"Quite a wide range. You see, Mr. Faulkner had certain ideas as to the value of the stock. To be perfectly frank, Mr. Mason, he offered to sell his stock to us at a certain figure. Then he thought that in case we didn't want to accept that offer, we should be willing to sell our stock at the same figure."

"And you weren't?"

"Oh, definitely not."

"May I ask why?"

"It's rather elemental, Mr. Mason. Mr. Faulkner was operating the company on a very profitable basis. He was receiving a salary that had not been raised during the past five years. Nor had Mr. Carson's. If Genevieve had purchased Mr. Faulkner's stock, Mr. Faulkner would then have been at liberty to step out into the commercial world and capitalize upon his own very remarkable business qualifications. He could even have built himself up another business which might well have been competitive to ours.

"On the other hand, when it came to fixing a price for which Genevieve Faulkner would be willing to sell *her* stock, I was forced to adopt the position that the value of the stock, so far as she was concerned, was predicated upon the income she was receiving from it, and if she were to sell out, she would want to get a sum of money which would draw an equal return. And, of course, investments are not nearly as profitable as they once were, nor do they have the element of safety. That made a wide difference, a very, very wide difference, Mr. Mason, between our selling price and our buying price."

"I take it that made for some bad feeling?"

"Not bad feeling, Mr. Mason. Surely not bad feeling. It was merely a difference of opinion about a business transaction."

"And you held the whip hand?"

"I'd hardly say that, Mr. Mason. We were perfectly willing to let matters go on in status quo."

"But Faulkner found it very galling to be working for an inadequate salary . . ."

"Tut, tut, tut, Mr. Mason. The salary wasn't inadequate, it was the same salary he had been drawing when he owned a two-thirds interest in the corporation."

Mason's eyes twinkled. "A salary which he had fixed so that Carson wouldn't be in a position to ask for any salary increases."

"I certainly don't know what Mr. Faulkner had in mind. I only know that the arrangement which was made by all parties concerned when the divorce decree was granted by the court was that salaries could not be raised without Genevieve's consent unless the court was called in to reopen the whole business."

"I can imagine," Mason said, "you had Harrington Faulkner in a position that was very, very disagreeable to him."

"As I have stated several times before, Mr. Mason, I am not a mind reader, and I see no reason for speculating upon Mr. Faulkner's ideas."

"You saw him several times yesterday?"

"Yes."

"In other words, the situation was approaching a crisis?"

"Well, Mr. Faulkner definitely wanted to do something."

"Of course," Mason said, "if Faulkner had bought Genevieve's stock, he would then once more have been a two-thirds owner in the company. Faulkner would have been in a position to have got rid of Carson, and firing

Carson would have been a perfect answer to Carson's lawsuit."

"As a lawyer," Dixon purred, "you doubtless see possibilities which, as a layman, I would not see. My own interest in the matter was simply to get the best possible price for my client in the event a sale was to be made."

"You weren't interested in buying Faulkner's interest?"

"Frankly, we were not."

"Not at any price?"

"Well, I wouldn't go so far as to say that."

"In other words, what with Faulkner's quarrel with Carson, the various and sundry suits Carson had been filing, and the situation in which your client found herself, you were in a position to force Faulkner to buy at your price?"

Dixon said nothing.

"It was something in the nature of a legalized holdup," Mason went on, as though thinking out loud.

Dixon straightened in the chair as though Mason had struck him. "My dear Mr. Mason! I was merely representing the interests of my client. There was no longer the slightest affection between her and Mr. Faulkner. I mention that merely to show that there was no reason for any sentiment to be mixed with the business matter."

"All right. You saw Faulkner several times during the day. When was the last time you talked with him?"

"Over the telephone."

"About what time?"

"At approximately . . . well, sometime between eight and eight-fifteen. I can't fix the time any closer than that."

"Between eight and eight-fifteen?" Mason said, his voice showing his interest.

"That's right."

"And what did you tell him?"

"Well, I told him that in the event any sale was going

to be consummated, we wanted to have the matter disposed of at once; that if the matter wasn't terminated before midnight, we would consider that there was no use taking up further time with discussions."

"And what did Faulkner say?"

"Faulkner told me that he would be over to see me between ten and eleven; that he wanted to look in very briefly on a banquet of goldfish fanciers, after which he had an appointment. He said that when he saw me he would be in a position to make us a final offer. That if we didn't accept the proposition he'd make us at that time, he would consider the matter closed."

"Did he say anything about anyone else being there with him at the time you phoned?"

"No, sir. He did not."

"That conversation might have been as late as eight-fifteen?"

"Yes."

"Or as early as eight o'clock?"

"Yes."

"Earlier than eight o'clock?"

"I'm quite sure it wasn't, because I remember looking at my watch at eight and speculating whether I'd hear any more from Mr. Faulkner that evening."

"And you don't think it was later than eight-fifteen?"

"At eight-fifteen, Mr. Mason, I tuned in a radio program in which I was interested, so I'm quite certain of the time there."

"There's no question but what it was Harrington Faulkner with whom you were talking?"

"No question whatever."

"I take it Faulkner didn't keep his appointment with you?"

"No, he didn't."

"That caused you some concern?"

"Well, Mr. Mason," Dixon said, running his chunky, capable fingers through his white hair, "I see no reason why I shouldn't be frank with you. I was—disappointed."

"But you didn't call Mr. Faulkner back?"

"No indeed I did not. I was keeping myself in the position of—well, I didn't want to show any eagerness whatever. The deal which I had previously outlined to Mr. Faulkner would have been quite profitable if it had gone through."

"Can you remember exactly what Faulkner said over the telephone?"

"Yes, he said that he had planned on attending a rather important meeting that night and was just getting dressed to go out to it. That he would much prefer to attend that meeting, keep his appointment and conclude his deal with us some time today."

"What did you tell him?"

"I told him I didn't think that would be satisfactory to my client because today was Saturday. He then said he'd be here between ten and eleven."

"Would you mind telling me the amount of the price you had fixed?"

"I don't think that needs to enter into it, Mr. Mason."

"Or the price at which Faulkner was willing to sell?"

"Really, Mr. Mason, I'm quite certain it would have no bearing on the matter."

"How much of a difference was there between the two figures?"

"Oh, a very substantial amount."

"When was Faulkner here personally?"

"About three o'clock in the afternoon, I believe it was—the last time—for just a few minutes."

"You had already made Faulkner your proposition?"

"Yes."

"And he had made you his?"

"Yes."

"How long was the interview?"

"Not more than five minutes."

"Did Faulkner see his wife—I mean his former wife?"

"Not at that interview."

"Had he seen her at any other interview during the day?"

"I believe he did—the meeting was by chance. I think Mr. Faulkner called about eleven o'clock in the morning and, as I remember it, encountered his wife—that is, his former wife, on the porch."

"And they talked for awhile?"

"I believe so."

"Is it fair to ask what they talked about?"

"I'm quite certain, Mr. Mason, that's between Genevieve and her husband."

"And might I see Genevieve to ask her a few questions?"

"For a man whose interest in Faulkner's estate is as nebulous as yours, if you'll permit me to say so, Mr. Mason, you want to cover quite a bit of territory."

Mason said, "I want to see Genevieve Faulkner."

"Are you, by any chance, representing someone who is charged with the murder of Mr. Faulkner?"

"So far as I know, no one has been charged with the murder of Mr. Faulkner."

"You are, however, aware of the probability that someone *may* be charged with such murder?"

"Naturally."

"And that someone might become, or might even now be a client of yours?"

Mason smiled. "I might be tempted to represent some person who is charged with the murder of Mr. Faulkner."

Dixon said quite definitely, "I don't think I would like that."

Mason's silence was significant.

Dixon said, "Things which one would discuss without hesitation with a lawyer who was planning merely to represent a claim against the estate of Harrington Faulkner are hardly the same things which one would

146

discuss with a lawyer who was planning to represent a person who was going to be accused of the murder of Harrington Faulkner."

"Suppose that person were unjustly accused?" Mason suggested.

"That," Dixon said self-righteously, "is something that would be left to a jury."

"Let's leave it to the jury, then," Mason said, grinning. "I should like very much to see Genevieve Faulkner."

"I'm afraid that is impossible."

"I take it that she has no interest in the estate."

Dixon's eyes abruptly shifted to his desk. "Why do you ask that, Mr. Mason?"

"Does she?"

"I would say she had none—unless the will provided otherwise—which is very unlikely. Genevieve Faulkner has no interest whatever in the estate of Harrington Faulkner. In other words, she has no possible motive for murder."

Mason grinned. "That wasn't what I asked."

Dixon matched his smile. "That was, however, the answer I gave."

Knuckles tapped lightly and in a perfunctory manner upon the door, and a half second later, without waiting for any answer, that door was opened by a woman who entered the room with all the assurance of one who belonged there.

A frown of annoyance crossed Dixon's face. "I have no dictation today, Miss Smith," he said.

Mason turned to look at the woman who had entered. She was slender and very attractive, somewhere in that vaguely indefinite period which is between forty-five and fifty-five. And, for a brief instant, Mason caught the flicker of a puzzled expression on her face.

Mason was on his feet instantly. "Won't you sit down, Mrs. Faulkner?"

"No, thank you. I . . . I . . ."

Mason turned to Dixon. "You'll pardon me for reaching the obvious conclusion."

Dixon admitted somewhat dourly that the name "Smith" had perhaps been a bit unfortunate. "Genevieve, my dear, this is Perry Mason, an attorney, a very skillful, clever attorney who has called on me to secure information about Harrington Faulkner. He asked permission to see you and I told him that I saw no reason for granting an interview."

Mason said, "If she has anything to conceal, it's bound to come out sooner or later, Dixon, and . . ."

"She has nothing to conceal."

"Are you," Mason asked of Genevieve Faulkner, "interested in goldfish?"

Dixon said, "She is not interested in goldfish."

Mrs. Faulkner smiled serenely at Perry Mason and said, "It would seem that Mr. Mason is the one who is interested in fishing. And so, if you gentlemen will pardon me, I'll retire and return when Mr. Dixon isn't engaged."

"I'm leaving right now," Mason said, getting to his feet and bowing. "I wasn't aware that Mr. Faulkner had had such an attractive first wife."

"Neither was Mr. Faulkner," Dixon said dryly, and then stood rigidly erect and silent while Mason bowed himself out of the room.

13

∎

Mason called up his office from a drugstore that was within half a dozen blocks of Dixon's house. "Della," he said when he had Della Street on the line, "get hold of

Paul Drake at once. Tell him to look up all of the evidence in connection with Harrington Faulkner's divorce case. Somewhere around five years ago. I not only want all of the dope on the case, but I want a transcript of the evidence if we can get it, and I want to know what was actually behind it."

"Okay, Chief, anything else?"

"That's all. What's new?"

She said, "I'm glad you phoned. I filed the application for a writ of *habeas corpus* and Judge Downey issued a writ returnable next Tuesday. They've now booked Sally Madison on a charge of first-degree murder."

"I suppose they booked her as soon as they learned of the writ," Mason said.

"I guess so."

Mason said, "All right, I'm going up to the jail and demand an audience with her."

"As her attorney?"

"Sure."

"You're going on record as representing her without first knowing what she has to say?"

Mason said, "It doesn't make a damn bit of difference what she has to say. I'm going to represent her because I've got to. I have no other choice in the matter. What have they done with Tom Gridley?"

"No one knows. He's still buried somewhere. Do you want me to prepare an application for a writ of *habeas corpus* for him?"

"No," Mason said. "I don't *have* to represent him—at least not until after I see what Sally Madison has to say."

"Good luck to you, Chief," Della Street said. "Sorry I got you into this."

"You didn't. I got you into it."

"Well, don't pull any punches."

"I won't."

Mason hung up, jumped in his car and drove to the jail. The excessive politeness with which the officers greeted him and the celerity with which they arranged for an interview between Sally Madison and the lawyer as soon as Mason announced that he was going to represent her as her attorney, indicated that the police were quite well satisfied with the entire situation.

Mason seated himself at the long table, down the middle of which ran a heavy-meshed steel screen. And a few moments later, a matron ushered Sally Madison into the other side of the room.

"Hello, Sally," Mason said.

She looked very calm and self-possessed as she walked across to seat herself at the opposite side of the table, the heavy screen furnishing a partition between the prisoner and the visitor.

"I'm sorry I walked out on you, Mr. Mason."

Mason said, "That's only about half of what you need to be sorry for."

"What do you mean?"

"Going out with Della Street when you had that gun and money in your purse."

"I shouldn't have done that, I know."

"Where were you when Lieutenant Tragg picked you up?"

"I hadn't walked more than four blocks from the time I left you. Tragg picked me up and talked with me a little while. Then he left me in the custody of a couple of officers while he went on a tour of the restaurants, looking for you and Miss Street."

"Have you made any statement to the police?"

"Oh yes."

"What did you do that for?"

"Because," she said, "I had to tell them the truth."

"You didn't have to tell them a damn thing," Mason said.

"Well, I thought I'd better."

"All right," Mason said, "what's the truth?"

She said, "I held out on you, Mr. Mason."

"Good Lord," Mason groaned, "tell me something new—at least give *me* the same break you gave the officers."

"You won't be angry?"

"Of course I'm angry."

"Then you won't—won't help me out?"

Mason said, "I have no choice in the matter. I'm helping you out because I've got to help Della Street. I've got to try to get her out of a jam, and in order to do that I've got to try to get you out too."

"Have I made trouble for her?"

"For her and for me and for everyone. Go ahead. What's the story?"

She lowered her eyes. "I went out to see Mr. Faulkner last night."

"What time?"

"It was right around eight o'clock."

"Did you see him?"

"Yes."

"What was he doing?"

"He was shaving. He had his face all lathered and he had his coat and shirt off. He was in his undershirt. There was water running in the bathtub."

"The bathroom door was open?"

"Yes."

"His wife was there?"

"No."

"Who answered the door?"

"No one. The door was standing ajar, open an inch or two."

"The front door?"

"Yes."

"What did you do?"

"I walked in. I could hear him in the bathroom. I called to him."

"What did he do?"

"He came out."

"You're sure the water in the bathtub was running?"

"Yes."

"Hot or cold water?"

"Why—hot water."

"Are you certain?"

"Yes. I remember there was steam on the mirror."

"Was Faulkner angry at you?"

"Angry at me? Why?"

"For coming to see him that way."

"I guess he was. But everything worked out all right."

"Go ahead," Mason said wearily, his invitation almost in the tone of a groan. "Let's hear the rest of it."

"Mr. Faulkner said he didn't want to have any trouble with me; that he'd like very much to get things cleaned up. He knew that Tom would do exactly as I suggested, and he said that we might as well come to terms."

"What did you say?"

"I told him that if he'd give me two thousand dollars we'd call everything square. That Tom would continue to work for him for six weeks and then would take a six-months layoff and then would come back to work for the pet store again; that if Tom worked out any inventions during the six months he was resting, Mr. Faulkner could have a half interest in them; that he and Tom would own them equally; that Faulkner would put Tom's remedies on the market and he and Tom would split the net profits. They'd be sort of partners."

"And what did Faulkner say?"

"He gave me the two thousand dollars and I surrendered the five-thousand-dollar check I had, and told him I'd go and see Tom and that I was certain it would be all right."

"Are you aware of the fact that Tom went to see him at quarter past eight?"

"I don't think Tom did."

"I think there's pretty good evidence he did."

"Well, I don't know anything about that, but I'm quite

certain Tom didn't go, because Tom had no reason to go. Tom had told me he'd leave everything in my hands."

"And the two thousand dollars you got, you received in cash from Mr. Faulkner?"

"That's right."

Mason thought for a moment, then said, "All right, how about the gun?"

She said, "I'm sorry about the gun, Mr. Mason."

"You should be."

"It's Tom's gun."

"I know."

She said, "I have no idea how it got there, but when I went in the bedroom with Mrs. Faulkner—trying to comfort her, you know—I saw this gun on the dresser. I recognized it as Tom's and—well, you know, I wanted to protect Tom. That was my first thought, my first instinctive reaction, and I just picked up the gun and shoved it into my purse. Knowing that a man had killed himself . . ."

"Been murdered," Mason supplemented.

"Knowing a man had been murdered," she went on, accepting his correction without protest, "I didn't want Tom's gun to be found on the place. I knew that Tom couldn't have had anything to do with the murder, but I didn't know how the gun had got there."

"And that's all?" Mason asked.

"I cross my heart and hope to die, Mr. Mason, that's all."

Mason said, "You told this story to the officers?"

"Yes."

"What did they do?"

"They listened."

"Did they question you?"

"Not much. A little bit."

"Was there a shorthand reporter there?"

"Yes."

"He took down everything you said in shorthand?"

"Yes."

"Then what?"

"Then they asked me if I had any objection to signing the statement and I told them certainly not, provided it was written up just the way I'd said it. They wrote out the statement and I signed it."

"Did they tell you you didn't have to say anything?"

"Oh yes. They recited some rigmarole in a sing-song voice saying I didn't have to say anything if I didn't want to."

"And that's the way your story stands on paper?"

"Yes."

Mason said, with a voice that was bitter with venom, "You little fool!"

"Why, what do you mean, Mr. Mason?"

Mason said, "Your story is so improbable on the face of it that it isn't even a good fairy tale. It's obviously something you thought up on the spur of the moment to protect Tom. But the officers were too smart to try to get you to change it right at the start. They reduced it to writing and got you to sign it. Now they'll begin to bring pressure to bear on you so you'll have to change it, and then you'll be in a sweet mess."

"But I don't have to change it."

"Think not?"

"No."

"Where did this figure of two thousand dollars come from—the one that you submitted to Faulkner?"

"Why, I thought that was just about a fair price."

"You hadn't mentioned it to him before?"

"No."

"And Faulkner was shaving when you got there?"

"Yes."

"Preparing to take a bath?"

"Yes."

"He was in the bathroom?"

"Yes."

"He came out of the bathroom when you went in there—into the bedroom?"

"Well, yes."

"Careful now," Mason said. "Did he come out of the bathroom or did he receive you in the bathroom?"

"Well, sort of in the door of the bathroom."

"And gave you two thousand dollars in cash?"

"Yes."

Mason said, "You asked him for two thousand dollars?"

"Yes."

"And he had two thousand dollars?"

"Yes."

"Exactly two thousand dollars?"

"Well . . . I don't know . . . he may have had more, but he gave me the two thousand dollars."

"In cash?"

"Certainly. That's where the money came from that was in my purse."

"And you found that gun of Tom Gridley's at Faulkner's house?"

"Yes. And if you want to know something, Mr. Faulkner was the one who took the gun there in the first place. Tom was keeping it at the pet store, and then yesterday evening about seven-thirty, Mr. Faulkner was down there prowling around, taking inventory, and— well, *he* took the gun. Mr. Rawlins can swear to that. He saw Mr. Faulkner take it."

"Did you tell that to the police?"

"Yes."

"That's in your written statement?"

"Yes."

Mason sighed. "Let's look at it another way. When I left you with Sergeant Dorset, he said he was going to take you out to call on James Staunton."

"That's right."

"Did he do so?"

"Yes."

"How long were you there?"

"I don't know. Some little time."

"And Staunton still stuck to his story that Faulkner had brought the fish to him?"

"Yes. He produced a written authorization from Mr. Faulkner to keep the fish."

"Then what happened?"

"Then Sergeant Dorset went back to Faulkner's house and took me with him."

"Then what?"

"Then after an hour or so, he told me I could leave."

"So what did you do?"

"Well, one of the men—I think he was a photographer—said that he was going downtown to police headquarters to get some films developed and I could ride along with him if I wanted. You know, said he'd give me a lift."

"So you went with him?"

"Yes."

"And then what?"

"Then I telephoned Della Street."

"Where did you find a telephone?"

"In an all-night restaurant."

"Near where this photographer let you out?"

"Yes, within a block."

"Then what?"

"Then Miss Street told me to call her back inside of fifteen minutes."

"So what did you do?"

"Had a cup of coffee and some scrambled eggs and toast."

"Can you remember where this restaurant was?"

"Yes, of course I can, and I think the night man in the restaurant will remember me. He was a man with very dark hair and I remember he had a limp when he walked. I think one leg had been broken and was quite a bit shorter than the other."

"All right," Mason said, "that has the ring of truth. You went back to Faulkner's house with Dorset. He kept you there for awhile and then decided he didn't need you any more and this photographer gave you a lift downtown. Did you talk any with him in the automobile?"

"Yes, of course."

"Tell him what you knew about the murder?"

"No. We weren't talking about the murder."

"What were you talking about?"

"Me."

"Was he making passes at you?"

"He wanted my telephone number. He didn't seem to be interested in the murder. If he hadn't been in such a hurry he said he'd have gone to the restaurant with me. He asked me if I wouldn't wait there for an hour or so until after he'd developed his films."

"That sounds natural," Mason said. "You're giving out stuff that has the ring of truth now. How long were you in the restaurant?"

"Just about fifteen minutes. I called Miss Street as soon as I went in and then she told me to call back in fifteen minutes, and in fifteen minutes I called back and she told me to go to the Kellinger Hotel."

"Then what?"

"Then I got a taxi and went to the Kellinger Hotel."

"You told the police this?"

"Yes, all of this."

"It's in your written statement?"

"Yes."

"Were there any other customers in that all-night restaurant when you were there?"

"No. It's just a little place—just a little lunch counter. Sort of a hole in the wall with a night man who does the cooking and then serves the food at the counter."

"And you got a good look at this man behind the counter?"

"Oh, yes."

"And he got a good look at you?"

"Yes."

"And you called Della Street twice from that restaurant?"

"Yes."

"Now then," Mason asked, "did you make any other calls?"

She hesitated.

"Did you?"

"No."

"That *doesn't* have the ring of truth," Mason said.

Sally Madison was quiet.

Mason said, "You got a taxicab there?"

"Yes, right near there."

"And went directly to the Kellinger Hotel?"

"Yes."

Mason shook his head. "From your description of where you were, the taxi ride to the Kellinger Hotel shouldn't have taken over two or three minutes at that hour of the night, and the meter should have been considerably less than a dollar."

"Well, what's wrong with that?"

"Della Street got there first," Mason said. "She had a lot farther to go than you did."

"Well, I . . . It took me a little while to find a taxicab."

"You didn't have one come to the restaurant?"

"No. I went out to look for a taxi stand. The restaurant man told me there'd be one right around there somewhere."

Mason said, "When Della Street got to the Kellinger Hotel, she sat in the lobby waiting for you. She saw you when you drove up in the taxicab. She saw you pay off the driver. You didn't open your purse. You had a bill all ready in your hand."

"That's right."

"Why did you do that?"

"Because, Mr. Mason, I had that gun in my purse and that big roll of bills, and I was afraid the taxi driver might see—well, you know, might see the gun or the roll of bills, or both, and think perhaps I was a stick-up artist and . . . well, you know how it was?"

"No, I don't know. How was it?"

"Well, I didn't want anyone to see what was in the purse, so I took this bill out of the purse when we were three or four blocks from the hotel, and I knew how much the meter was going to be."

"What was it," Mason asked, "a one-dollar bill?"

She started to say something, then instead of speaking, simply nodded.

Mason said, "Della Street said the man looked at the bill in rather a strange way, then said something to you and laughed and put it in his pocket. I don't think he'd have done that if it had been a one-dollar bill."

"What do *you* think it was?"

"A two-dollar bill," Mason said.

She said, "It was a one-dollar bill."

"Did you make any statement to the police about that?"

"No."

"Did they ask you?"

"No."

Mason said, "I think it was a two-dollar bill. I think the meter didn't show the fifty or sixty cents that it should have shown if you'd gone from the restaurant near police headquarters to the Kellinger Hotel. I think the meter showed around a dollar and eighty cents. I think that means you took a side excursion, and I'm making one guess as to where that excursion would have been."

She looked up at him defiantly.

"To Tom Gridley's boardinghouse or apartment—or wherever he lives," Mason said.

She lowered her eyes.

"Don't you see," Mason went on patiently, "the officers are going to trace every step you made. They're going to locate the taxicab that took you to the Kellinger Hotel; they're going to find out everything you did. They'll comb the city with a fine tooth comb. They'll find the man that took you to the Kellinger Hotel. He'll remember the trip—particularly if you gave him a two-dollar bill, and he made some comment to you about a two-dollar bill being unlucky."

She bit her lip.

"So," Mason said, "you'd better at least come clean with *me*."

"All right," she said defiantly, "I went up to Tom's place."

"And got the gun," Mason said.

"No, Mr. Mason. Honestly I didn't. I had the gun in my purse all the time. I found it just where I told you I did."

"And Sergeant Dorset was taking you around all that time with a gun in your purse?"

"Yes."

"And why did you go to Tom's place?"

"Because I knew it was his gun. You see, Mr. Mason, when I went to the pet store last night, I got there very shortly after Mr. Faulkner had left. I found Mr. Rawlins terribly upset. He told me he'd lost his temper and told Mr. Faulkner just what he thought of him. He told me Mr. Faulkner had taken some things that belonged to Tom, but he said he wouldn't tell me about what they were until today, because he said he didn't want me to do anything rash, and he didn't think Tom should know about it while he was having one of his bad spells.

"Well, at the time I didn't know what those things were. It was afterward that I learned from the police it had been this gun of Tom's and the can of remedy that Tom had mixed up and put in the safe. If I'd known Mr.

Faulkner had taken the gun I wouldn't have been so frightened when I saw it there on the dresser in Mr. Faulkner's house. But the minute I saw it, I recognized it as Tom's gun. You see, he'd etched his initials on the barrel with some acid. I used to shoot the gun a lot. I'm a pretty darn good shot with a revolver, even if I do say it myself. Well, when I saw that gun there on the dresser, and saw it was Tom's gun, I was panic-stricken. I just scooped it into my purse while you were there in the bathroom looking at the body on the floor.

"Then, just as soon as I could get away from the police, which was when I went into that restaurant, I called Tom up. I did that right after I'd called Miss Street. I told Tom that I had to see him right away, and to be sure that the door of his apartment was unlocked so I could get in."

"So what did you do?"

"I had the taxi take me down there. I went in to see Tom. I told him what had happened. He was absolutely flabbergasted. Then I showed him the gun and asked him if he'd had any trouble with Faulkner and he—he told me the truth."

"What was the truth?"

"He told me that he'd been keeping the gun at the pet store for the last six months; that Rawlins had told him there'd been some stickups in the neighborhood and that he wished he had a gun but he couldn't get one, and Tom said he had one, and Rawlins got Tom to bring it to the store. Then late yesterday afternoon, when Faulkner went down and took an inventory of stock that was in the store, and took that batch of fish remedy Tom had mixed up, Faulkner must have seen the gun there and decided that he wanted it and took it home with him. That, of course, was just what happened. Rawlins has said so, and the police were fair with me. They told me about it before I made my statement to them."

Mason studied her thoughtfully, said, "When Tom

found out that Faulkner had been down there and taken the jar of stuff containing his formula and sent it out to be analyzed, he became angry. He went up to Faulkner's house to try and effect a settlement. Faulkner gave him a check for a thousand dollars. . . ."

"No he didn't, Mr. Mason. Tom didn't go out to Faulkner's house at all, and he didn't know a thing about Faulkner taking the remedy. I didn't know it myself until the police told me. You can prove that by asking Rawlins."

"You're certain?"

"Absolutely."

Mason shook his head and said, "That doesn't check. Faulkner had made out a check for a thousand dollars to Tom Gridley. He was filling in the check stub when he was shot."

"I know that's what the officers say, but Tom didn't go out there."

Mason thought for a moment, then said, "If Faulkner found the gun in the pet shop and took it out to the house with him, how does it happen that Faulkner's fingerprints aren't on it?"

She said, "I can't tell you that. Mr. Faulkner picked it up at the pet shop. I don't think there's any question about that. Even the police say that."

Mason's eyes narrowed. "Look here," he charged, "when you found that gun there on the dresser, you became panic-stricken. You thought Tom had gone out there to have a showdown with Faulkner and had lost his temper and killed Faulkner, didn't you?"

"Not exactly that, Mr. Mason. I just didn't think it was a good place for Tom's gun to be. I was all upset, and when I saw the gun there—well, I didn't think."

"You did too," Mason said. "You picked that gun up and wiped all the fingerprints off it, didn't you?"

"Honestly I didn't, Mr. Mason. I just picked up the gun and dropped it into my purse. I didn't think about fingerprints. I just wanted to get that gun out of the way. That's all I was thinking of."

Mason said, "All right. Now let's get back to the two thousand dollars. Faulkner had that two thousand dollars in the pocket of his trousers, didn't he?"

She hesitated a moment, then said, "Yes."

"Just the two thousand dollars?"

"Yes."

"In the pocket of his trousers?"

"Yes."

"And what time did you get there?"

"Around—somewhere between eight and half past eight. I don't know exactly when."

"And you found the door open and walked in?"

"Yes."

Mason said, "You're trying to cover up for Tom, and it won't work."

"No, I'm telling you the truth, Mr. Mason."

Mason said, "Look here, Sally, your story just doesn't sound probable. Now you've got to face the facts. I'm talking to you not only for your own good, but for Tom's. If you don't do exactly as I tell you, you're going to get Tom into a mess. He'll be held in jail for months. He may be tried for murder. He might be convicted. But even if he's just held in jail, you know what that will do to Tom's health."

She nodded.

"Now then," Mason said in a low voice, "you've got to do one thing. You've got to tell *me* the truth."

She met his eyes steadily. "I've told you the truth, Mr. Mason."

Mason sat for some thirty seconds, his face a mask of concentration, his fingertips drumming on the table. Behind the heavy wire screen, the girl regarded him thoughtfully.

Abruptly, Mason pushed back his chair. "You sit right there," he said, and, catching the eye of the matron, he explained, "I want to make a telephone call, then I'm coming back."

Mason crossed over to the telephone booth in a corner of the visitor's room and dialed Paul Drake's office. A few seconds later, he had the detective on the line.

"Perry Mason, Paul," the lawyer said. "Anything new on Staunton?"

"Where are you now, Perry?"

"I'm up at the visitor's room in the jail."

"Gosh, yes. I called Della a few minutes ago. She didn't know where to get in touch with you. The police have got a statement out of Staunton and have put him back into circulation. He won't talk about anything that's in the statement, but one of my operatives got hold of him and asked him the question you wanted to know, and he answered that."

"What was the answer?"

"On Wednesday night, after Faulkner had taken those fish out to Staunton's place, and Staunton had telephoned the pet shop, he said it was quite late before the pet shop came out with the treatment."

"Not early?"

"No. He said it was quite late. He doesn't remember the exact time, but it was quite late."

Mason heaved a sigh, said, "That's a break. Sit right where you are, Paul," and hung up the telephone.

The lawyer's eyes were glinting as he returned to face Sally Madison across the visitor's table. "All right, Sally," he said in a low voice, *"now* we'll talk turkey."

Her eyes regarded him with studied innocence. "But, Mr. Mason, I have been telling you the exact truth."

Mason said, "We'll think back to Wednesday night, Sally, when I first met you, when I came over and sat down at the table with you in the restaurant. Remember?"

She nodded.

Mason said, "Now, at that time, you reached an agreement with Harrington Faulkner. You'd been holding him up, but you'd been exerting sufficient pressure on him to make him pay the piper. His fish were dying and he knew it, and he would have paid a good deal to have saved their lives. He also knew that this treatment for gill disease Tom had worked out was valuable, and he was willing to pay something for that."

Again she nodded.

Mason said, "Faulkner gave you a check and a key to the office and told you to go out and treat the fish, didn't he?"

Again she nodded.

"Now then, where did you go?"

She said, "I went directly to the store to get Tom, but Tom was fixing up some treatment for some other fish that Mr. Rawlins had consented to treat. Rawlins was fixing up a treatment tank and he wanted Tom to finish getting some panels ready."

"That was the tank he took to Staunton's place?"

"Yes."

Mason said, "You've overlooked one thing, Sally. You didn't think anyone would ever bother to check up on that time element with Staunton. You're lying. Tom didn't fix up that tank for Rawlins to take to Staunton's until *after* he'd gone to Faulkner's place. You intended to rush right back to the pet store to fix up that other tank. But the fact that Faulkner's fish were gone and that he called the police delayed you materially. You didn't get back until quite late. And Rawlins, therefore, didn't deliver Staunton's tank until quite late. Staunton is positive about that."

"He's mistaken."

"Oh no he isn't," Mason said. "When Faulkner gave you the key to that office, it was the opportunity you'd been waiting for. You went out there with a homemade extension dipper consisting of a silver soup ladle to which had been tied a section of broomstick. You dredged something out of the bottom of that fish tank. Then you had to leave in a hurry because Tom tipped you off someone was coming. So you ran out, jumped in Tom's car, drove around the block, and then came driving up to the office again as though you'd just arrived from the pet store."

She shook her head in sullen, defiant negation.

Mason said, "All right, I'm telling you what's happened. You lied to me and you're sending Tom to his death. Do you still stick with your story?"

She nodded.

Mason pushed back his chair. "That settles it," he said. "When Tom dies, remember that you're responsible."

She let him take two steps before she called him back. Then she leaned forward so that her face was all but pressed against the heavy mesh. "It's true, Mr. Mason—everything you said."

Mason said, "That's better. Now suppose you tell me the truth. How did you know that bullet was in the tank?"

"How did you know it was a bullet?"

"Never mind," Mason said, "I'm asking you. How did you know it was in the tank?"

"Mrs. Faulkner told me."

"Oh, oh!" Mason said. "Now we're getting someplace. Go ahead."

"Mrs. Faulkner told me that she was satisfied I'd find a .38 caliber bullet somewhere in the bottom of that fish tank; that she knew Tom was going to be called on to treat those fish; that she wanted to have that bullet recovered, and she also wanted to be absolutely certain that she could prove where the bullet came from. She said that I must arrange it so that both Tom and I were present when the bullet was recovered. Well, that's about all there was to it, Mr. Mason. When Mr. Faulkner gave me the key, I got hold of Tom, and we intended to

166

recover the bullet first and then come back *after* Mr. Faulkner had arrived, and treat the fish. But when we got there and let ourselves into the office, the fish weren't there. For a minute or two, I didn't know what to do. But then I went ahead just as we'd planned. I took the dipper and we got the bullet out and just then we heard a car coming."

"You didn't leave Tom out in the car to watch?"

"No. We both had to go in there. That was the agreement. But we felt certain we had plenty of time. The house next door was dark and I knew that Mr. Faulkner would be at the café for some little time—at least I thought he would. But we heard this car coming and it frightened us and we dashed out in such a hurry that we didn't dare to take the ladle with us."

"Then what did you do?"

"Then we drove around the corner and waited until we saw you and Mr. Faulkner drive up. And then we came around there and acted as innocent as possible, pretending that we'd just come from the pet store."

"And then what did you do with the bullet?"

"I gave it to Mrs. Faulkner."

"When?"

"Not until last night?"

"Why not until last night?"

"I telephoned her and told her I had it, and she said that it would be all right; that I could have the money all right but that I'd have to wait until the coast was all clear."

"And then last night?"

"Then last night I took the bullet out to her."

"Tom was with you?"

"No, I went alone."

"There was some identification mark on that bullet?"

"Yes. Tom had given me an etching tool and we'd both etched our initials on the base of the bullet. Mrs. Faulkner was very insistent that we do it just that way, and told us to be very careful not to mar the sides of the bullet because she wanted to be able to prove what gun had fired the bullet."

"How much were you to get?"

"She said that if a certain deal went through, we'd get five hundred, and if another deal went through we'd get two thousand."

"And then last night you took the bullet out to her?"

"That's right."

"When?"

"About half past nine, I guess it was."

"Half past nine!" Mason exclaimed incredulously.

"That's right."

"And where was she?"

"At her house."

"And she paid you the two thousand dollars?"

"Yes."

"And that's where the two thousand came from?"

"That's right."

"And this story about Faulkner paying you two thousand was all poppycock?"

"Yes. I had to account for two thousand some way, and I thought that was the best way to account for it, because Mrs. Faulkner warned me that if I ever said anything about that two thousand dollars that she wouldn't back me up at all, and the taking of that bullet would be burglary, a breaking and entering, and that both Tom and I would go to jail."

Mason said, "Wait a minute. By half past nine Faulkner must have been dead."

"Yes, I guess so."

"Lying there in the bathroom."

"Yes."

"Then, when you took the bullet out to Mrs. Faulkner, where was she sitting? In the living room? She must have known her husband was dead by that time, if she was there in the house . . ."

"Not *that* Mrs. Faulkner," Sally Madison explained. "Don't you understand, Mr. Mason? It was the first Mrs. Faulkner, Mrs. Genevieve Faulkner."

For more than ten seconds, Mason sat in utter silence, his eyes level-lidded, his brows knitted together. "Sally, you're not lying to me?"

"Not now, Mr. Mason. I'm telling you the absolute truth."

"Tom will back you up in your story?"

"About recovering the bullet and identifying it. But he doesn't know the person who was going to pay me the money. Those dealings were all through me."

Mason said, "Sally, if you're lying to me now, you're going to the death chamber just as sure as you're sitting there, and Tom Gridley will die in jail."

"I'm telling you the truth, Mr. Mason."

"You got the two thousand dollars at nine-thirty last night?"

"That's right."

"But you did call on Mr. Faulkner?"

"Yes. Between eight and eight-thirty. It's just like I told you. The door was open just an inch or two. I walked in. There was no one home except Mr. Faulkner. He was telephoning—I guess he'd just finished shaving because there was still just a bit of lather on his face— where the razor had left marks. There was hot water running in the tub and he only had on his undershirt above his trousers. I guess the running water prevented him from hearing the chimes when I pushed the bell button. I walked in because I felt I just had to see him, and his car was parked out in front so I knew he was there."

"What happened?" Mason asked.

"He told me to get out. He told me that whenever he wanted to see me, he'd send for me, and he was very abusive. I tried to tell him that Mr. Rawlins had told me he'd taken something that belonged to Tom, and that that was just the same as stealing."

"And what did he do?"

"He told me to get out."

"Didn't he give you a check payable to Tom, and offer that as a settlement?"

"No."

"Just told you to get out?"

"That's right. He said if I didn't get out he'd throw me out."

"And what did you do?"

"I hesitated, and he actually pushed me out, Mr. Mason. I mean he came and put his hands right on my shoulders and pushed me out of the house."

"Then what did you do?"

"Then I telephoned his first wife and asked her when she wanted to see me, and she told me to telephone again in about half or three-quarters of an hour. I did so, and she told me to come right out; that I could have the money. I went out there and she gave me the two thousand dollars."

"Anyone else present?"

"No."

"Did you see a man by the name of Dixon?"

"No."

"Ever meet him?"

"No."

"Do you know a man named Dixon?"

"No."

"Mrs. Faulkner gave you the two thousand dollars. Then what did you do?"

"Then I went back to the pet store and got the panels to treat Staunton's fish the way I'd promised Mr. Rawlins I would, and—and well, you know the rest, Mr. Mason. I went out to Staunton's and then I telephoned you."

Mason said, "Sally, I'm going to take a chance on you

because I've got to take a chance on you. I want you to say three words for me."

"What are they?"

"See my lawyer."

She looked at him in puzzled perplexity.

"Say it," Mason said.

"See my lawyer," she repeated.

"You can remember that, all right?"

"Why yes, of course, Mr. Mason."

"Say it again," Mason said.

"See my lawyer," she said.

Mason said, "Sally, from now on those are the only three words you know. If you ever say anything to anybody else you're sunk. The police will be after you in an hour or so, brandishing that written statement of yours in front of you. They'll show you inconsistencies. They'll show you where it's wrong. They'll show you where you were lying. They'll prove this and they'll prove that and they'll prove the other. They'll ask you to explain why you lied about where you went in the taxicab, and they'll tell you that if you can explain so that the explanation satisfies them they'll turn you loose; that if you can't, the only thing that remains for them is to arrest Tom. Do you understand?"

She nodded.

"And what are you to say?" Mason asked her.

She met his eyes. "See my lawyer," she said.

"Now," Mason told her, "we're beginning to get some place. Those are the only three words in the English language that you know from now on. Can you remember that?"

She nodded.

"*Can* you remember that no matter what happens?"

Once more she nodded.

"And if they tell you Tom has confessed in order to save you and that you shouldn't let the man you love take the rap and go to the death-house because he's simply trying to save you, what are you going to say?"

"See my lawyer," she told him.

Mason nodded to the matron. "That's all," he said. "My interview is finished."

14

■

Genevieve Faulkner lived in a small bungalow that was within half a dozen blocks of the place where Wilfred Dixon maintained his sumptuous bachelor residence.

Mason parked his car, ran up the steps and impatiently rang the bell.

The door was opened after a few moments by Genevieve Faulkner herself.

Mason said, "You'll pardon me for disturbing you, Mrs. Faulkner, but there are one or two questions I must ask you."

She smiled and shook her head.

Mason said, "I'm not fishing now, Mrs. Faulkner. I'm hunting."

"Hunting?" she asked.

"For bear," Mason said, "and I'm loaded for bear."

"Oh! I'm sorry I can't invite you in, Mr. Mason. Mr. Dixon says I'm not to talk to you."

Mason said, "You paid Sally Madison two thousand dollars for a bullet. Why did you do that?"

"Who says I did that?"

"I can't tell you that, but I'm stating it as a fact."

"When am I supposed to have paid her that sum of money?"

"Last night."

Mrs. Faulkner thought for a moment, then said to Mason, "Come in."

Mason followed her into a tastefully furnished living room. She invited the lawyer to sit down, promptly picked up a telephone, dialed a number and said, "Can you come over here right away? Mr. Mason is here." Then she dropped the receiver into place.

"Well?" Mason asked.

"Smoke?" she inquired.

"Thank you, I have my own."

"A drink?"

"I'd like an answer to my question."

"In a few minutes."

She settled down in the chair opposite Mason, and the lawyer noticed the supple grace of her movements as she crossed her knees, calmly selected a cigarette from a humidor and struck a match.

"How long have you known Sally Madison?" Mason asked.

"Nice weather we're having, isn't it?"

"A little cool for this time of year," Mason said.

"I thought so, but then on the whole it's nice.—You're sure you don't want a scotch and soda?"

"No, thank you, I just want an answer to that one question, and I warn you, Mrs. Faulkner, that you aren't playing around with blackmail any more. You're mixed up in a murder case up to your ears and if you don't tell me the truth here and now, I'm really going to turn on the heat."

"There's been quite a bit of rain. It's really nice to see the hills as green as they are now. I suppose we'll have rather a warm summer. The old timers seem to expect it."

Mason said, "I'm a lawyer. You're evidently relying for advice on Wilfred Dixon. Take a tip from me and don't do it. Either tell me the truth or get a lawyer, someone who knows the ins and outs of law and the danger you're running if you suppress facts in a murder case."

"It was really unusually cold around the first of the year," she said calmly. "Some of the people who have studied weather tell me *that* doesn't mean anything, but that if it's unusually cold around the *middle* of January it invariably means a cold summer. Personally I can't see any sense to that. I . . ."

Brakes sounded as a car slid to a stop out in front of the house. Mrs. Faulkner smiled benignly at Mason, said, "Excuse me, please," and crossed the room to open the door.

Wilfred Dixon came hurrying in.

"Really, Mr. Mason," Dixon said, "I had hardly thought that you would stoop to this."

"Stoop to what?" Mason asked.

"After I told you that I didn't care to have you interview my client . . ."

"To hell with you," Mason told him. "You're not a lawyer. You're a self-styled business counselor or investment broker or whatever you want to call yourself. But this woman is mixed up to her ears in a murder case. She isn't any client of yours as far as murder is concerned and you have no right to practice law. You go sticking your neck out and I'll push it back."

Dixon seemed completely nonplussed at Mason's belligerence.

"Now then," Mason went on, "Mrs. Faulkner bribed my client, Sally Madison, to get into the office of Faulkner and Carson and extract a bullet from a fish tank. Last night she gave Sally Madison two thousand dollars in cash for that bullet. I want to know why."

Dixon said, "Really, Mr. Mason, these statements of yours are *most* reckless."

"Play around with fire," Mason told him, "and you're going to get your fingers burned."

"But, Mr. Mason, surely you aren't making these accusations on the unsupported word of your client."

"I'm not making any accusations," Mason said. "I'm stating facts and I'm giving you just about ten seconds to come clean."

"But, Mr. Mason, your statement is absolutely unfounded. It's utterly ridiculous."

Mason said, "There's the telephone. Want me to call Lieutenant Tragg and let him ask the questions?"

Wilfred Dixon met his eyes calmly. "Please do, Mr. Mason," he said.

There was a moment of silence.

Mason said at length, "I've given this woman some advice. I'm going to give you the same advice. You're mixed up in a murder case. See a lawyer. See a good one, and see him immediately. Then, decide whether you're going to tell the truth or whether you want me to call Lieutenant Tragg."

Dixon indicated the telephone. "As you have so aptly remarked, Mr. Mason, there's the telephone. I can assure you that you're at liberty to use it. You talk about calling Lieutenant Tragg. I think we would be *very* glad to have you call him."

Mason said, "You can't monkey with the facts in a murder case. If you paid Sally Madison two thousand dollars for that bullet, that fact is going to come out. I'll drag it out if I have to spend a million dollars for detective fees."

"A million dollars is a lot of money," Dixon said calmly. "You were speaking of telephoning Mr. Tragg, Mr. Mason, or I believe *Lieutenant* Tragg is the title. If he's connected with the police I think it would be a good thing to call him. You see, *we* have nothing to conceal. I'm not, of course, certain about you."

Mason hesitated.

There was just a glint of triumph in Wilfred Dixon's eyes. "You see, Mr. Mason, I play a little poker myself."

175

Without a word, Mason got up, crossed to the telephone, dialed Operator, said, "Give me police headquarters," then he asked for Homicide and inquired, "is Lieutenant Tragg in? Perry Mason speaking."

After a few seconds, Tragg's voice sounded on the wire. "Hello, Mason. I'm glad you called. I wanted to talk with you about your client, Sally Madison. She seems to have adopted an unfortunate position. There are certain minor discrepancies in a written statement which she gave us, and when we asked her to explain those, she assumed a very truculent attitude and said, 'See my lawyer.'"

"I have nothing to add to that," Mason said.

There was genuine regret in Tragg's voice. "I'm really sorry, Mason."

"I can imagine you are, Tragg. I'm out at the residence of Genevieve Faulkner. She's Faulkner's first wife."

"Yes, yes. I had intended to interview her as soon as I could get around to it. I'm somewhat sorry you beat me to it, Mason. Finding out anything?"

Mason said, "I think you'd better question her at some length about whether or not she saw Sally Madison last night."

"Well, well," Tragg said, his voice showing surprise. "Does Sally Madison claim that she saw Mrs. Faulkner?"

"Any statements my client may have made to me are, of course, confidential," Mason said. "This is just a tip I'm giving you."

"Thank you very much, Counselor, I'll get in touch with her."

"At once, I would suggest," Mason said.

"At my earliest convenience," Tragg amended. "Goodby, Mason."

"Good-by," Mason said, and hung up. He turned to Wilfred Dixon and said, "That's the way I play poker."

Dixon beamed at him. "Very well done, Mason, very well done, indeed. But, of course, as you pointed out to

Lieutenant Tragg, you can hardly repeat to him any statements that your client made to you, and as I understand it, your client has already stated she received the two thousand dollars that was in her purse from Harrington Faulkner. It would be rather unfortunate if she should be forced to change her statement."

"How did you know she had made such a statement?" Mason asked.

Dixon's eyes twinkled. "Oh, I get around a bit, Mason. After all, you know, while I am not a lawyer, I have to represent the interests of my client—her business interests, you know."

Mason said, "Don't ever underestimate Tragg. Tragg will get a written statement out of you and you'll swear to it. And sooner or later, the true facts are going to come out."

"We'd be only too glad to have them come out," Dixon said. "You see, Mr. Mason, as it happens, Genevieve makes no moves without my advice, none whatever. I tell her what to do, but I don't bother her with details. She knows very little about the firm of Faulkner and Carson. She leaves that to me. She wouldn't have even seen this client of yours without me. I'm quite certain that this Lieutenant Tragg, whoever he is, will be only too glad to accept our statement, particularly in view of the fact that you are in no position even to suggest that the two thousand dollars held by your client was received from anyone other than Harrington Faulkner. And if you'll let me give you a little advice, Mr. Mason, it is that you should never put too much confidence in the word of a young woman of Miss Madison's type. I think if you'll investigate her past reputation you'll find that she's had considerable experience. A young woman who has from time to time been something of an opportunist. I won't say a blackmailer, Mr. Mason, but an opportunist."

"You seem to know a good deal about her," Mason said dryly.

"I do," Dixon told him. "I'm afraid, Mr. Mason, that to try and extricate herself and her friend from a very dangerous situation, she has given you some false information."

Mason got to his feet. "All right," he said, "I've told you."

"You certainly have, Mr. Mason. Unfortunately for you, as I have pointed out, you are in no position to make any direct accusation, and even if you were, Mrs. Faulkner's denial, supported by my corroborating statement, would effectually disprove the charges of this Sally Madison."

Mason said, "I don't give a damn what her past has been. I think she's on the square now, and I think she's genuinely in love with Tom Gridley."

"I'm satisfied she is."

"And," Mason said, "when she told me she got the two thousand dollars from Genevieve Faulkner, her statement had the ring of truth."

Dixon shook his head. "It's impossible, Mr. Mason. It couldn't have been done without my knowledge, and I assure you that it wasn't done."

Mason stood looking at the muscular figure of the chunky man, who met his eyes with such childlike candor. "Dixon," he said, "I'm a bad man to monkey with."

"I'm certain you are, Mr. Mason."

"If you and Genevieve Faulkner are lying about this, I'm likely to find it out sooner or later."

"But, Mr. Mason, why should we lie about it? What possible motive would we have? And why on earth should we want to pay two thousand dollars for—what did you say it was, a bullet?"

"A bullet," Mason said.

Dixon shook his head sadly. "I'm sorry for Miss Madison. I really am, Mason."

Mason asked abruptly, "And just how does it happen you know so much about her?"

"Mr. Faulkner bought an interest in a pet shop," Dixon said. "He used funds of the corporation. Naturally, I investigated the purchase, and, in investigating the purchase, I investigated the personnel."

"*After* he'd made the purchase?" Mason inquired.

"Well, during the time negotiations were pending. After all, Mr. Mason, my client is interested in the corporation and I like to know what's going on—and I have my own way of knowing every move that's made."

Mason thought that over. "Oh yes," he said, "Alberta Stanley, the stenographer—I begin to see a lot now."

Dixon hastily cleared his throat.

"Thanks for telling me," Mason said.

Dixon looked up, met the lawyer's eyes. "Not at all, Mason, not at all. It was a pleasure to be of assistance to you—but you can't pin that two thousand dollars on us. We didn't pay it and we won't be lied about. *Good*-day."

Mason started for the door. Mrs. Faulkner and Wilfred Dixon stood watching him in silence. With his hand on the doorknob, Mason turned. "Dixon," he said, "you're a damn good poker player."

"Thank you."

Mason said grimly, "You're smart enough to know that I can't make any definite accusation that the two thousand dollars came from Mrs. Faulkner. I'm a good enough sport to admit that I made a bluff and you called it."

A frosty smile twitched at the corners of Dixon's mouth.

Mason said, "And I think it's only fair that you should know where I'm going now."

Dixon raised his eyebrows. "Where?" he asked.

"Out after another stack of chips," Mason said, and pulled the door shut behind him.

15

■

Mason's face was as grim as that of a football player backed up against his team's goal line, as he entered Paul Drake's office.

"Hello, Perry," Drake said. "Did that information on Staunton do you any good?"

"Some," Mason said.

"It's just about the only question Staunton will answer. The police have sewed him up on a written statement, and he isn't giving out any information whatever upon matters that are contained in that statement. As far as anything that transpired the night of the murder is concerned, Staunton is an absolute clam. And the same holds true of all the details concerning the delivery of the fish."

Mason nodded. "I rather expected that.—Look here, Paul, I want you to do something for me."

"Shoot."

"I want you to find out whether or not Sally Madison saw the first Mrs. Faulkner yesterday night. I want you to find out whether Mrs. Faulkner made any substantial withdrawal from her bank in the form of cash. I particularly want to find out whether she or Wilfred Dixon withdrew any cash from a bank in the form of fifty-dollar bills."

Drake nodded.

"That isn't going to be easy," Mason said, "and I don't expect it to be easy. I'll pay you any amount of money that you need to get that information, Paul. Damn it, I started playing verbal poker with Wilfred Dixon. I made a bluff and he called it so cold and so hard that I feel like a spanked kid. Damn him, I'm going to back that bird in a corner if I have to spend every cent I've got in order to do it."

"Dixon was there when you got there?" Drake asked.

"No. Why?"

Drake said, "I'm having him shadowed, not that it will do any good, but I'm working on every angle of the case. My man picked him up about eight o'clock this morning as he was coming from breakfast."

"Where did he eat, Paul?"

"At the corner drug store. He must be an early riser. He'd been there since seven o'clock."

"That's fine, Paul. Keep it up."

"He walked down there for his breakfast, then came right back, arriving home at eight-ten. I've got men watching the house. It's about all there is to do."

Mason glanced at the detective.

"What's the matter, Paul? You seem to be stalling around. What's the trouble?"

Paul Drake picked up a pencil, twisted it in his fingers. "Perry," he said quietly, "Sally Madison's past reputation isn't too good."

Mason flushed. "That's the second time today I've heard that. All right, so what?" Mason asked.

Drake said, "If Sally Madison told you she got that two thousand dollars from Genevieve Faulkner she's lying."

"I didn't say she told me that, Paul."

"You didn't *say* so, no."

"What makes you think she'd be lying if she had told me that?" Mason asked.

Drake said, "My men have just uncovered some new evidence.—That is, they didn't uncover it, they picked it up from a friendly newspaper reporter who, in turn, got it from the police."

"What is it?"

"Yesterday afternoon Harrington Faulkner went to his bank and drew out twenty-five thousand dollars in cold, hard cash. He went to the bank personally. He insisted on having the money in the form of cash and from the way he acted, the bank teller thought that perhaps he was being blackmailed. He wanted the money in thousand-dollar bills and hundred-dollar bills and in fifty-dollar bills. The teller made an excuse that it would take him a little while to get the cash together in just that form, and kept Faulkner waiting for a few minutes while he and an assistant stepped back into the vault and hurriedly took down the numbers of the bills, just in case something should turn up later. The two thousand dollars that Sally Madison had in her purse is money that was given her by Harrington Faulkner, and by no one else. And there's another twenty-three thousand dollars that she has cached away somewhere."

Mason said, "You're sure, Paul?"

"Not dead sure, Perry, but I have the information pretty straight and I'm passing it on to you just the way I got it. I think you'll find that it checks."

Mason's mouth was hard.

"Now then," Drake went on, "there's some news on the credit side of the ledger. That gun is Tom Gridley's gun, all right, but I guess there's no question Gridley took it to the pet shop and Faulkner picked it up there. The police have pretty well reconstructed Faulkner's day from the time he left the bank until the time he was murdered."

"I already know about the gun. What time did he leave the bank, Paul?"

"It was well after banking hours. Pretty close to five o'clock. He'd telephoned and they'd let him in the side door. He put the money in a satchel. He left the bank and picked up a taxicab at the hotel right across the street from the place where he banks. He drove to the pet store, got hold of Rawlins and started taking an inventory. While he was taking the inventory he found Gridley's gun and slipped it in his pocket. Rawlins told him that it belonged to Gridley but Faulkner didn't say anything. Of course, in the light of what we know now and knowing that Faulkner had twenty-five thousand dollars in cash in that satchel, it's only reasonable to suppose that he might have been interested in having a gun for his own protection."

Mason nodded.

"Anyway, he put the gun in his hip pocket. Then he went over and opened the safe. Remember, he had the combination from Rawlins."

"And what happened then?"

"There was a can of paste in there, and Faulkner wanted to know what that was."

"What was it, the fish remedy?"

"That's right. It was some of that compound that Rawlins had talked Tom Gridley into mixing up, because Rawlins had some fish of his own that had gill disease and he wanted to treat them. He'd had some difficulty getting Tom to do it, but had finally persuaded Tom by promising him that he wouldn't let anyone know about it."

"Where was Tom that afternoon?"

"Tom was in bed at home. He was having a bad spell, running a fever and coughing, and Rawlins had told him to go home."

"What did Rawlins do when Faulkner opened the safe?"

"Rawlins had a fit when he saw what Faulkner was up to. Faulkner took the can of paste, and right there in the store, telephoned to a consulting chemist whom he knew. It was after office hours—getting along toward seven-thirty by that time—and Faulkner telephoned this chemist at his home, told him he had something that he wanted analyzed; that he was coming right out with it."

Mason said under his breath, "The dirty so-and-so."

"I know it," Drake said, "but what I'm giving you now, Perry, is evidence. This is the thing you're going to have to fight in court. They'll account for every minute of Faulkner's time right from five o'clock in the afternoon to the time he was killed."

"Go ahead," Mason told him.

Drake said, "When Rawlins saw what was happening he had a fit. He almost took the can away from Faulkner by force. He told Faulkner that he had given Tom Gridley his own personal word that the can would only be used to treat some fish that were suffering from gill disease there in the pet shop."

"What did Faulkner do?"

"He told Rawlins that Rawlins was working for him, and that he didn't want to hear any criticism. So Rawlins then proceeded to quit his job and tell Faulkner just what he thought of him."

"What did Faulkner do?"

"He didn't even get mad. He picked up the telephone and asked to have a taxicab sent around to the pet shop. Rawlins raved and sputtered, called Faulkner just about everything he could lay his tongue to, but Faulkner just waited until the taxicab came, then picked up his satchel, tucked the can of medicated paste under his arm and walked out, with the revolver still in his hip pocket."

"I suppose police have located the cab driver?"

Drake nodded, said, "The cab driver took Faulkner to the residence of the consulting chemist. Faulkner told him to wait. He was in there about fifteen minutes, then Faulkner drove to his house. It was then just a little after eight o'clock. Apparently, Faulkner immediately started to undress, take a bath, shave and get ready to go to that meeting at eight-thirty."

"No dinner?" Mason asked.

"That meeting of the fish experts was a dinner," Drake said. "They were having a little banquet and some talks afterward by some experts on fish breeding. That ties together, Perry. It ties right up to the time that someone entered the house, apparently without knocking, and the chap to whom Faulkner was telephoning heard Faulkner tell that party to get out. At first the police thought it was Tom Gridley, but Tom's come pretty clean with them. He's satisfied the police. The police know now that it was Sally Madison. No one will ever know exactly what happened there. Sally Madison entered, Faulkner tried to put her out, that much is certain. Sally admits it. Remember that Faulkner had a satchel containing twenty-five thousand dollars, which was probably in the bedroom. He also had Tom Gridley's gun. It must have been lying on the bed or on the dresser. Faulkner's coat, tie and shirt were spread over a chair where he had peeled out of them in a hurry. The gun had been in his hip pocket. Naturally, he took it out and put it somewhere."

Mason nodded thoughtfully.

"Put yourself in Sally Madison's place," Drake went on. "Faulkner had robbed the man she loved. He had been guilty of despicable business practices. Sally was fighting mad and she was desperate. Faulkner was pushing her out when she saw the gun lying there. She grabbed it. Faulkner was frightened, he ran back to the bathroom and tried to close the door. Sally pulled the trigger—then probably, for the first time, she realized the enormity of what she had done. She looked around. She saw the satchel on the bed. She opened it. There was twenty-five thousand dollars in it. That meant a lot to her. It meant an opportunity to escape. It meant an opportunity to cure Tom Gridley of tuberculosis. She took two thousand dollars in fifties for get-by money. The big bills she hid somewhere because she was afraid to try to monkey with those big bills while the heat was on."

"It's a pretty theory," Mason said, "but that's all it is—a theory. Plausible, but just a theory."

Drake shook his head. "I'm not telling you the worst of it, Perry. Not yet."

"Well, get on," Mason demanded irritably.

"Police found the empty satchel under the bed. The satchel which the bank teller identifies as the one that held the twenty-five thousand dollars. Of course, when the police first found it last night, they didn't know that it had any particular significance, but they were grabbing fingerprints off of everything, and so they dusted the handle of that satchel. They found three latent prints on it. Two of them were prints of Harrington Faulkner's right hand. The third one was the right middle finger of Sally Madison's hand. That's the story, Perry. That's the story in a nutshell. I have a tip that the district attorney is going to give you a chance to let Sally Madison plead guilty to second-degree murder or perhaps manslaughter. He recognizes the fact that Faulkner had been a first-class heel and that there'd been a lot of provocation for the crime. Furthermore, now that he knows Faulkner was the one who took Tom Gridley's gun from the pet shop, he knows that Sally must have seen the gun lying on the bed and acted on the spur of the moment. So there you are, Perry. There's the thing in a nutshell. I'm no lawyer, but if you can cop a plea for manslaughter, you'd better jump at it."

Mason said, "If Sally's fingerprint was on that satchel, we're licked—that is if the satchel was *under* the bed."

"Are you going to try and get a plea?" Drake asked anxiously.

"I don't think so," Mason said.

"Why not, Perry? It's the best thing you can do for your client."

Mason said, "It puts me in something of a spot, Paul. The minute she pleads guilty to manslaughter, or to second-degree murder, Della Street and I are hooked. We then automatically become accessories after the fact, and it doesn't make a great deal of difference whether we're accessories after the fact to manslaughter or to second-degree murder. *We* can't afford to take the rap."

"I hadn't thought of that!" Drake exclaimed.

"On the other hand," Mason told him, "I can't let my personal feelings influence my duty to my client. If I think a jury might stick her with a verdict of first-degree murder, I'll have to make a compromise if it looks as though I can serve her interests better by a compromise."

"She isn't worth it, Perry," Drake said earnestly. "She's two-timed you all the way along the line. I wouldn't consider her interests for a minute."

Mason said, "You can't blame a client for lying, any more than you can blame a cat for catching canaries. When a person of a certain temperament finds himself or herself in a jam, the natural tendency is to try and lie out of it. The trouble with Sally Madison was she thought she could get away with it. If she had, I probably wouldn't have condemned her too much."

"What are you going to do, Perry?"

Mason said, "We'll get all the facts we can, which probably won't be many, because the police have all the witnesses sewed up tight. We'll walk into court on the preliminary examination and turn everything wrongside out. We'll look around and see if we can't get a break."

"And if you can't?" Drake asked.

Mason said grimly, "If we can't, we'll do the best we can for our client."

"You mean you'll let her plead guilty to manslaughter?"

Mason nodded.

Drake said, "I hadn't realized before where that would leave you, Perry. *Please* don't do it. Think of Della, if you won't think of yourself . . ."

Mason said, "I'm thinking of Della. I'm thinking of her to beat hell, Paul, but Della and I are playing this thing together. We've played things together for a good many years. We've taken the sweet, and we'll take the bitter. She wouldn't want me to throw over a client, and by God I'm not going to."

16

There were only a few scattered spectators in the courtroom as Judge Summerville ascended the bench, seated himself, and the bailiff called the court to order.

Sally Madison, somewhat subdued, but with her face still giving no clue to her thoughts, sat directly behind Perry Mason, apparently completely detached from the tense, dramatic conflict of the trial itself. Unlike most clients, she didn't bother to whisper comments to her lawyer, and might as well have been a piece of beautiful furniture so far as taking any active part in her defense was concerned.

Judge Summerville said, "Time and place heretofore fixed for the preliminary hearing of The People versus Sally Madison. Are you ready, gentlemen?"

"Ready for the prosecution," Ray Medford said.

"Ready for the defense," Mason announced calmly.

The district attorney's office was quite apparently trying to sneak up on Mason's blind side.

So far, Tragg had said nothing about those incriminating fingerprints of Della Street's on the murder weapon. Ray Medford, one of the shrewdest men on the prosecutor's staff of trial deputies, was taking no chances with Perry Mason. He knew too much about the lawyer's ingenuity to overlook a single bet. But, on the other hand, he was very careful to treat the case merely as a routine procedure, one where the judge would bind the defendant over to answer, and the main contest would be made before a jury in the Superior Court.

"Mrs. Jane Faulkner will be my first witness," Medford said.

Mrs. Faulkner, clothed in black, took the witness stand, related in a low voice how she had returned from "visiting friends" and had found Perry Mason and Sally Madison, the defendant, waiting in front of the house. She had admitted them to the house, explained to them that her husband wasn't home, then gone to the bathroom and found her husband's body on the floor.

"Your husband was dead?" Medford asked.

"Yes."

"You are sure that the body was that of Harrington Faulkner, your husband?"

"Quite certain."

"I think that's all," Medford said, and then added with a disarming aside to Perry Mason, "Just to prove the *corpus delicti,* Counselor."

Mason bowed. "You had been with friends, Mrs. Faulkner?"

She met his eyes calmly, steadily. "Yes, I had been with my friend, Adele Fairbanks during the entire evening."

"At her apartment?"

"No. We had been to a movie."

"Adele Fairbanks was the friend to whom you telephoned after you had discovered your husband had been murdered?"

"Yes. I felt that I couldn't stay in the house alone. I wanted her to be with me."

"Thank you," Mason said. "That is all."

John Nelson was next called to the stand. He gave his occupation as a banker, stated that he had known Harrington Faulkner in his lifetime; that on the afternoon of the day on which Faulkner was murdered he had been at the bank when Mr. Faulkner had telephoned, stating that he desired rather a large sum of money in cash; that shortly after the telephone call had been received, Faulkner had shown up, had been admitted to the bank through the side door, and had asked for twenty-five thousand dollars in cash, which he had withdrawn from his checking account. It was, he explained, his individual account, not the account of Faulkner and Carson, Incorporated. The withdrawal had left Mr. Faulkner with less than five thousand dollars to his credit in his personal account.

Nelson had decided it would be a good plan to take the numbers of the bills, inasmuch as Faulkner had asked for twenty thousand dollars in one-thousand-dollar bills, for two thousand dollars in one-hundred-dollar bills, and for three thousand dollars in fifty-dollar bills. Nelson testified that he had called one of the assistant tellers, and, together, they had managed to list all of the numbers on the bills while they kept Mr. Faulkner waiting. Then the money had been turned over to Mr. Faulkner and he had placed it in a satchel.

Quite calmly and casually, Medford called for the list of numbers on the bills and that list was received in evidence. Then Medford produced a leather satchel and asked Nelson if he had ever seen it before.

"I have," Nelson said.

"When?"

"At the time and place I have referred to. That was the satchel which Mr. Faulkner carried with him to the bank."

"The satchel in which the twenty-five thousand dollars in cash was placed?"

"That's right."

"Are you certain that is the identical satchel?"

"Quite certain."

"You may cross-examine," Medford said to Mason.

"How do you know it's the same satchel?" Mason asked.

"I noticed it particularly when I put the money in it."

"You put the money in it?"

"Yes. Mr. Faulkner raised it to the little shelf in front of the cashier's window. I unlocked the wicket, swung it back on its hinges and personally placed the twenty-five thousand dollars in the satchel. And at that time, I noticed a peculiar tear in the leather pocket on the inside lining of the satchel. If you'll notice, Mr. Mason, you'll see for yourself that that tear is still there. It's a rather peculiar, jagged, irregular tear."

"And you identify the satchel from that?" Mason asked.

"I do."

"That's all," Mason said.

Sergeant Dorset was the next man on the witness stand. He testified to the conditions he had found at Faulkner's house when he arrived, the position of the body, the discovery of the satchel under the bed in the bedroom, the place where Faulkner's coat, shirt and tie had been found tossed carelessly on a chair, the safety razor on the shelf, still uncleaned, with the lather and hairs still adhering to the blade. The lather was partially dry, which, in his opinion, indicated that it had been "some three or four hours" since the razor had been used. The face of the corpse was smooth-shaven.

Medford desired to know whether Sergeant Dorset had seen the defendant there.

"I did, yes, sir."

"Did you talk with her?"

"I did."

"Did she accompany you upon any trip?"

"Yes, sir."

"Where did she go?"

"To the residence of one James L. Staunton."

"That was at your request?"

"It was."

"Did she make any objection?"

"No, sir."

"Was there a fingerprint expert present in the Faulkner house?"

"There was."

"What was his name?"

"Detective Louis C. Corning."

"Did he examine certain articles for fingerprints under your direction and supervision and in accordance with your instructions?"

"He did."

"You may take the witness," Medford said to Perry Mason.

"Just how did Mr. Corning examine the fingerprints?"

"Why, through a magnifying glass, I presume."

"No. That isn't what I meant. What method did he use in perpetuating the evidence? Were the fingerprints developed and then photographed?"

"No. We used the lifting method."

"Just what do you mean by that?"

"We dusted certain objects to develop latent fingerprints, and then placed adhesive over the fingerprints, lifting the entire fingerprints from the object, then covering the adhesive with a transparent substance so that the fingerprints could be perpetuated and examined in detail."

"Who has the custody of those fingerprints?"

"Mr. Corning."

"And he has had such custody ever since the night of the murder?"

"To the best of my belief, he has. However, I understand he's going to be a witness, and you can ask him about that."

"The method of perpetuating the fingerprints was suggested by you?"

"It was."

"Don't you consider that rather a poor method to use?"

"What other method would you have preferred, Mr. Mason?"

"*I* wouldn't have preferred any method," Mason said. "But I have always understood that it was more efficient and better practice to develop the latents and then photograph them in their position on the object, and, if the fingerprints seemed to be important, to bring the object into court."

"I'm sorry that we can't accommodate you," Sergeant Dorset said sarcastically, "but it happens that in this particular case the fingerprints were all over the bathroom of a dwelling house which was in use. We were hardly in a position to dispossess the tenants, and keep all fingerprints intact. We used the lifting method, which I believe is infinitely preferable to the other where the circumstances justify it."

"What circumstances justify it?" Mason asked.

"Circumstances such as these, where you are dealing with objects that can't readily be brought into court."

"Now what means did you use to identify the places from which the fingerprints had been taken?"

"I didn't use any, personally. That is entirely within the province of Mr. Corning, and you will have to ask him those questions. I believe, however, he prepared envelopes on which the exact location from which each print had been lifted were printed and kept the prints straight by that method."

"I see. Now, did you have occasion that night to look into the other side of the duplex house—the side which was, I believe, utilized as an office for the real-estate corporation of Faulkner and Carson?"

"Not that night, no."

"You did the next morning?"

"I did."

"What did you find?"

"An oblong glass tank, which had been apparently used as an aquarium or fish tank, had been drained of water, apparently by means of a section of long, flexible rubber tubing of an inside diameter of approximately one-half inch. The glass tank had then been turned over on its side and the mud and gravel in the bottom of the tank had been dumped out on the floor of the office."

"Did you make any attempt to get fingerprints from that tank?"

"No, sir. I didn't take any fingerprints from the glass tank."

"Did you try to take any?"

"I didn't personally, no sir."

"Did you suggest that anyone else do so?"

"No, sir."

"As far as you know, none of the police made any attempt to develop fingerprints from that tank?"

"No, sir."

"May I ask why?"

"For the simple reason that I didn't consider the overturned tank had any connection whatever with the murder of Harrington Faulkner."

"It may have?"

"I don't see how it could have."

"It is quite conceivable that the same person who murdered Harrington Faulkner might have drained that tank and overturned it?"

"I don't think so."

"In other words, because you, yourself, personally didn't see how there could have been any connection between the two crimes, you let this evidence be destroyed?"

"I'll put it this way, Mr. Mason. In my capacity as an officer on the police force, it is necessary for me to make certain decisions. I take the responsibility for those decisions. Obviously, we can't go around fingerprinting everything. We have to stop somewhere."

"And this was your stopping place?"

"That's right."

"You usually take fingerprints in case of a burglary, don't you?"

"Yes, sir."

"Yet you didn't in connection with this one?"

"It wasn't a burglary."

Mason raised his eyebrows.

"Nothing was taken."

"How do you know?"

"Nothing was missing."

"How do you know?"

"I know," Dorset said angrily, "because no one made any complaint that anything was missing."

"The tank had been installed there by Harrington Faulkner?"

"So I understand."

"Therefore," Mason said, "the only person who could have made any complaint was dead."

"I don't consider anything was taken."

"You made an examination of the contents of the tank before it was upset?"

"No."

"Then, when you say you don't consider anything was taken, you're using a telepathic, intuitive . . ."

"I'm using my judgment," Dorset all but shouted.

Judge Summerville said placidly, "Is this overturned fish tank important, gentlemen? In other words, does the prosecution or the defense intend to connect it up?"

"The prosecution doesn't," Medford said promptly.

"The defense hopes to," Mason said.

"Well," Judge Summerville ruled, "I'll permit a very wide latitude so far as questions are concerned."

"We are not making any objection," Medford hastened to assure the judge. "We want to give the defendant every opportunity to establish any facts which may tend to clarify the case."

"When you entered the bathroom of Faulkner's house," Mason asked, "you found some goldfish in the bathtub, Sergeant?"

"I did, yes."

"Two goldfish?"

"Two goldfish."

"What was done with them?"

"We took them out of the tub."

"Then what was done with them?"

"There seemed to be no place where we could keep them, so we simply swept them out with the other goldfish."

"By the other goldfish, you mean the ones on the floor?"

"That's right."

"You didn't make any attempt to identify the two goldfish that were in the bathtub?"

"I didn't ask them their names," Sergeant Dorset said sarcastically.

"That will do," Judge Summerville rebuked the witness sharply. "The witness will answer counsel's questions."

"No, sir. I simply made note of the fact that two live goldfish were in the bathtub and let it go at that."

"There were goldfish on the floor?"

"Yes."

"How many?"

"I'm certain I couldn't say. I think the photograph will show the number."

"As many as a dozen?"

"I would say somewhere around that number."

"There was a shaving brush and a razor on the glass shelf above the wash stand?"

"Yes. I have already testified to that."

"What else was there?"

"There were, I believe, two sixteen-ounce bottles of peroxide of hydrogen. One of them was almost empty."

"Anything else?"

"No, sir."

"Now, what did you notice on the floor?"

"There were pieces of broken glass."

"Did you make an examination of those pieces of broken glass to determine if they had any pattern or if they had been originally a part of some glass object?"

"I didn't personally. I believe at a later date Lieutenant Tragg caused all of those pieces to be assembled and had them fitted together so that they formed a rather large curved goldfish bowl."

"You say that there was a checkbook on the floor?"

"There was."

"Near the body of the murdered man?"

"Quite near."

"Can you describe its appearance?"

Medford said, "Your Honor, I intended to introduce this checkbook in evidence by another witness, but if counsel wants to examine this witness about it, I'll introduce it right now."

Medford produced the checkbook, Sergeant Dorset identified it, and it was received in evidence.

"Calling your attention," Medford said to Judge Summerville, "to the fact that the last check stub in the book—that is the last one from which the corresponding check has been torn away along the perforated line, is a check stub bearing the same date as the day of the murder, with an amount of one thousand dollars written in the upper right-hand corner, and in the body of the stub a portion of a name has been written. The first name is completely written and the last name has been unfinished. Only the first three letters of that name appear. They are '-G-r-i.' "

Judge Summerville examined the check stub with keen interest.

"Very well, this will be received in evidence."

"Were any of the goldfish on the floor alive when you entered the room?" Mason asked Sergeant Dorset.

"No."

Mason said, "For your information, Sergeant, I will state that I noticed motion on the part of one of the goldfish when I entered the room—and I was, I believe, in the room some ten or fifteen minutes before the police arrived. I placed that goldfish in the bathtub and apparently it resumed life."

"That, of course, was something you had no right to do," Sergeant Dorset said.

"You made no test to ascertain whether there was some life on the part of any of the other goldfish?"

"I didn't apply a stethoscope to them," Dorset said sarcastically.

"Now then, you have stated that you asked the defendant to accompany you to the home of James L. Staunton?"

"I did, yes, sir."

"You had some conversation with Mr. Staunton there?"

"Yes."

"And Mr. Staunton gave you a statement purporting to bear the signature of Harrington Faulkner, the deceased?"

"He did."

Medford said, "Your Honor, I don't want to seem technical, but after all, this is a preliminary examination. The purpose of it is to determine whether there is reasonable ground to believe the defendant murdered Harrington Faulkner. If there is, the Court should bind her over to answer. If there isn't, the Court should dismiss her. I think that we have plenty of evidence to establish our case without carrying the inquiry far afield. These matters are entirely extraneous. They have nothing whatever to do with the murder."

"How do you know they have nothing to do with the murder?" Mason asked.

"Well, I will put it this way," Medford said. "They

have nothing to do with our case. We can establish our case by an irrefutable chain of evidence without dragging in all of this extraneous stuff."

Mason said, "Your Honor, I understand the law and I know the Court does, but I submit to the Court that under the circumstances of this case and in view of the very apparent mystery which surrounds the case, I should be permitted to show *all* of the surrounding circumstances which *I* contend played an important part in connection with the murder of Harrington Faulkner. I know that the Court doesn't want to hold this young woman over for trial if she is in fact innocent, regardless of the fact that it might be possible for the prosecution to establish a technical case. I also know that the Court is anxious to see that the real murderer is apprehended in the event this young woman should actually be innocent. Therefore, I submit to your Honor that it is better at this time, in view of the peculiar circumstances of this case, to let all of the facts come into the record."

"We don't have to put in all of the facts," Medford said angrily. "We only have to show enough of our hand to convince the Court that there is a reasonable cause to believe this defendant is guilty."

"That's just the trouble with the entire situation, your Honor," Mason retorted. "It is the attitude of the prosecution that it's playing some sort of a game; that it only needs to introduce a certain amount of evidence; that it can hold back the rest of its evidence as a miser hoards his gold, so that the defendant can be surprised when confronted with that evidence in the Superior Court. Now, that may be the way to secure a large number of convictions and to make a good showing for efficiency on the part of the district attorney's office, but I submit, your Honor, that it is hardly the way to clear up a rather puzzling and baffling mystery."

"It isn't a mystery to the police," Medford snapped.

"Certainly not. Because, as your Honor has just seen

from the attitude of Sergeant Dorset, he collected the evidence which he thought would result in a conviction of this defendant. Any evidence which tended to point to the guilt of some other person was disregarded. The police didn't think this other crime had any connection with the murder of Harrington Faulkner simply because it didn't involve this defendant."

Judge Summerville said, "I know it's somewhat irregular, but I'd like to hear from counsel just what the general surrounding facts of the case are."

"I protest that it's irregular," Medford said.

"I'm only asking counsel to make a general statement of his position," Judge Summerville ruled placidly. "I certainly have a right to know what is in counsel's mind before I rule on an objection the prosecution has made."

Mason said, "Your Honor, Harrington Faulkner had a pair of rather valuable fish, fish which were vastly more valuable to him personally than they would be on the market, but fish which were, nevertheless, of a rare strain. Harrington Faulkner rented one side of a duplex dwelling from the corporation which owned it. The other side was where the corporation had its office. Faulkner had installed a fish tank in the office and placed these two very valuable fish in that tank. He and Elmer Carson, the other active member of the corporation, quite apparently became mortal enemies. The fish in the tank were suffering from a fish disease that is nearly always fatal. Tom Gridley, whose name has been brought into the case, had a cure for that disease. The decedent tried, by various and sundry means, to get control of the formula by which young Gridley was able to cure the fish. Sometime prior to the murder, Elmer Carson had filed suit and secured a temporary restraining order preventing Harrington Faulkner from moving the fish tank from the real-estate office on the ground that it had been so affixed to the building that it had become a fixture. Before the hearing on the temporary restraining order and order to show cause, I understand Harrington Faulkner removed the fish without disturbing the tank, and took those fish to the residence of James Staunton. Now then, your Honor, in view of the peculiar circumstances, and in view of the fact that the defendant in this case was concededly what is known colloquially as the girl friend of Tom Gridley, and active in the store where Tom Gridley worked, a store which Harrington Faulkner subsequently bought in order to get control of Gridley's formula, I claim that *all* of these things are an integral part of the case."

Judge Summerville nodded his head. "So it would seem."

"Well, I submit that we are entitled to stay within our legal rights," Medford said angrily. "We didn't make the law, and I notice that learned counsel for the defense never hesitates to grab at any technicality which will advance *his* case. We have a law on the statute books. Let's conform to it."

"Quite right," Judge Summerville said. "I was about to make that statement when counsel interposed his comments."

"I beg the Court's pardon," Medford said stiffly.

"I was about to say," Judge Summerville ruled, "that under the law, the prosecution only needs to put on sufficient evidence to show that a crime has been committed and that there is reasonable ground to believe the defendant is the one who committed that crime. But, I want to go on record at this time as stating that under the circumstances of this case, and in view of the peculiar and rather mysterious incidents which seem to have surrounded it, after the prosecution has rested its case, the Court is going to permit the defendant to call witnesses and ask them any questions the defendant wants which may bring out the facts which counsel for the defense has just outlined to the Court."

Medford said, "The effect of that, if the Court please,

is to accomplish the same result. All of the extraneous facts will be dragged into this case."

"If they have a bearing on the question before the Court, I want to hear all of the things which you refer to as 'the extraneous facts.' "

"But the point I am making is that the effect is just the same as though they were brought in at this time."

"Why object to them then?" Judge Summerville asked urbanely.

Mason said, "I was only calling for a document which is in the possession of the police. I can, if I have to, subsequently put Sergeant Dorset on the stand as my witness and ask that the document be produced."

"But what earthly bearing does that document have on the murder of Harrington Faulkner?" Medford asked.

Mason smiled. "Perhaps a few more questions to Sergeant Dorset will clear up that part of the case."

"Ask him the questions," Medford said. "Ask him if the document has any bearing on the case. I defy you to ask him that question, Mr. Mason."

Mason said, "I prefer to ask my questions in my own way, Counselor." He turned to the witness and said, "Sergeant, after you discovered the body of Harrington Faulkner, you proceeded to investigate the murder, did you not?"

"I did."

"You investigated every angle of it?"

"Naturally."

"And during the course of the evening you questioned the defendant and also me about an interview we had had with James Staunton, and about whether the fish which Mr. Staunton had in his possession were actually the two fish which had been delivered to him by Mr. Faulkner, and which had been taken from the tank which was in the real-estate office, didn't you?"

"I asked questions, yes."

"And insisted upon answers?"

202

"I felt that I was entitled to answers."

"Because you thought that matter might throw some light upon who murdered Harrington Faulkner?"

"I thought so at the time."

"What has caused you to change your opinion?"

"I don't know that I have changed it."

"Then you *still* think that the circumstances you investigated in connection with James Staunton had some bearing on the murder of Harrington Faulkner?"

"No."

"Then you have changed your opinion."

"Well, I've changed my opinion because I know now who committed the murder."

"You know who you *think* committed the murder."

"I know who committed the murder, and if you'll quit throwing legal monkey wrenches in the machinery, we'll prove it."

"That will do," Judge Summerville ruled. "Counsel is questioning the witness for the purpose, I take it, of showing bias."

"That is right, your Honor."

"Proceed with your questioning."

"You demanded that the defendant accompany you out to the residence of James L. Staunton?"

"I did."

"At that time you had been advised by both Miss Madison and by me of all the facts which we had learned in connection with the possession of the fish by Staunton?"

"I suppose so. You said they were all the facts you had."

"Exactly. And, at the time those facts seemed sufficiently significant so you went out to verify them?"

"At the time, yes."

"What has caused you to change your mind?"

"I haven't changed my mind."

"You took from the possession of James L. Staunton a written statement signed by Harrington Faulkner?"

"I did."

Mason said, "I want that statement introduced in evidence."

"I object," Medford said. "It is not proper cross-examination. It's no part of the case. It's incompetent, irrelevant and immaterial."

"It's not proper cross-examination," Judge Summerville ruled calmly. "The objection will be sustained on that ground."

"That is all," Mason said.

Judge Summerville smiled. "And now, Mr. Mason, do you want Sergeant Dorset to remain in Court as a witness on the part of the defense?"

"I do."

Judge Summerville said, "The witness will remain in Court, and if the witness has in his possession any paper which he received from James L. Staunton relating to the fish which had belonged to Harrington Faulkner in his lifetime, the witness will have the statement ready to produce when he is called as a witness by the defense."

"This is going all the way around our elbow to get to our thumb," Medford said with some feeling.

"Apparently you object to reaching the thumb by any shorter route," Judge Summerville pointed out. "The Court doesn't want to be unduly harsh in its ruling so far as the prosecution is concerned, but it has always been the attitude of this Court that if any defendant in a preliminary hearing has any evidence to introduce which will tend to clarify the issues or throw any light upon a crime which has been committed, this Court wants to hear it. And that is going to continue to be the attitude of the Court. Call your next witness."

Somewhat sullenly, and with poor grace, Medford called the photographer who had taken the photographs showing the position of the body and the surroundings.

One by one, those photographs were introduced, and as they were introduced, they were carefully studied by Judge Summerville.

It was eleven-thirty when Medford said to Mason, "You may cross-examine."

"These photographs were all taken by you on the premises and all show the condition of the premises as they were at the time you arrived on the scene, is that right?"

"That's right?"

"Now you not only acted as photographer, but you also saw the things you photographed?"

"Naturally."

"And, therefore, are a witness to the things you saw?"

"Yes, sir, I so consider myself."

"These photographs, then, may be used to refresh your memory as to what you found at the scene of the crime."

"Yes, sir."

"I direct your attention to this photograph," Mason said, handing the witness one of the photographs, "and ask you if you noticed a granitewear container in the bathtub. I believe this photograph shows it."

"I did, yes, sir. It was a two-quart container and was lying submerged in the bathtub."

"There were two goldfish in the bathtub?"

"Yes, sir."

"On the floor were three magazines—I believe they are shown in this photograph?"

"Yes, sir."

"Did you notice the dates on those magazines?"

"I did not, no, sir."

Medford said, "As a matter of fact, your Honor, those magazines were carefully marked for identification and are in the possession of the prosecution, but I certainly hope that counsel is not seriously contending that those magazines have any bearing on the murder of Harrington Faulkner."

Mason said gravely, "I think, your Honor, those magazines will prove a very interesting and perhaps a vital link in the evidence."

"Well, we won't waste time arguing about them. We'll produce them," Medford said.

"Do you know which magazine was on top?" Mason asked.

"I'm sure *I* don't," Medford said. "And I don't know which goldfish was lying with his head facing south and which one was lying with his head facing south-southeast. As far as I am concerned, the police investigated the important angles of the case, and as a result of that investigation, reached a conclusion which is so logical it can't be questioned. That's all I know and that's all I want to know."

"So it would seem," Mason said dryly.

Medford flushed.

Judge Summerville said to Mason, "Do you contend that the position of the magazine is significant?"

"Very," Perry Mason said. "And I think if counsel will produce those magazines, we can examine the photographs with a magnifying glass and tell the relative position of those magazines. We can certainly tell which one was on top. This photograph which I hold in my hand shows that rather plainly."

"All right," Medford said, "we'll produce the magazines."

"Do you have them in court?"

"No, your Honor, but I can produce them after lunch, if the Court wishes to take its noon recess at this time."

"Very well," Judge Summerville ruled. "The Court will take a recess until two o'clock this afternoon."

Spectators, arising from the court benches, made the usual confused sounds of shuffling steps and low voiced comments. Sally Madison, without a word to Perry Mason, arose from her chair and stood waiting calmly for the officers to escort her from the courtroom.

206

17

■

Mason, Della Street and Paul Drake sat at lunch in a little restaurant near the courthouse where they ate frequently when trials were in progress. The proprietor knew them and kept reserved for them a small private dining room.

Paul Drake said, "You're doing okay, Perry. You've got Judge Summerville interested."

"It's a break for us that we drew Judge Summerville," Mason admitted. "Some judges like to get preliminary hearings over with as quickly as possible. They adopt the position that there's nothing very much to worry about because the defendant is going to have a trial before a jury anyway, so go ahead and bind 'em over and let it go at that. Judge Summerville has different ideas. He realizes that the function of the courts is to protect the rights of citizens at all stages of the proceedings, and believes that the function of the police is to investigate and perpetuate evidence while it's fresh. I happen to know from talking with him off the bench, and in casual conversation, that he is fully aware of the habit the police have of investigating a case until they pick on some person as the guilty one, and then disregard any evidence that doesn't coincide with their own opinions."

"Just what can you do?" Della Street asked. "Do you dare to put on all of this evidence, calling these witnesses as your own witnesses?"

"I don't dare to do anything else," Mason said.

"Well," Drake observed, "as I get the sketch, Sally Madison is lying. Her written statement contains falsehoods. She's lied to the police and she's lied to you and she's still lying to you."

Mason said, "Clients are all human—even the innocent ones."

"But that's no reason why they should be permitted to double-cross their own lawyers," Drake said with feeling. "Personally, I wouldn't have nearly such a broadminded attitude toward her."

Mason said, "I'm trying to keep an open mind, Paul. I'm trying to visualize what must have happened."

"Well, she's lying about one thing. She didn't get that money from Genevieve Faulkner."

"I didn't say that she said she did," Mason observed, his eyes twinkling.

"Well, you didn't need to say so, for me to draw my own conclusions," Drake observed dryly. "She got that money from that satchel, and there's another twenty-three thousand dollars salted away somewhere."

Mason said, "While we're looking at discrepancies, let's look at some of the other discrepancies. I can't imagine why Mrs. Jane Faulkner waited in her automobile for Sally Madison and me to show up unless she had been tipped off that we were coming. And no one could have tipped her off we were coming except Staunton. As a matter of fact, Paul, I'm well pleased with the way things are going. Medford played right into my hands. He's fixed it now so that I can put Staunton or any of these other hostile witnesses on the stand as my witnesses, and ask them leading questions, and Judge Summerville will permit it. That's going to give me a chance to examine Staunton about that phone call."

Drake said, "Well, even if you could prove that Jane Faulkner had been in the house before, discovered the body, and then had gone out and sat in her automobile and waited for you to come, so that she could go through all the motions of being surprised and hysterical, I still don't see that you're going to get anywhere."

Mason said, "If I get the opportunity to crucify her, I'm going to do it. You know as well as I do she's lying about having spent the evening with Adele Fairbanks. She pulled the wool over Sergeant Dorset's eyes there. She pretended to be ill and suffering *so* greatly from shock she simply had to have a girl friend come down to stay with her. She summoned the girl friend whom she knew she could depend upon to back her up in anything she said. And while Dorset was chasing around to Staunton's place with Sally Madison, Jane Faulkner and Adele Fairbanks were hatching up their cute little alibi about having been together and having gone to a movie. Lieutenant Tragg would certainly never have let Mrs. Faulkner slip one over on him like that."

"I'll say he wouldn't," Drake said. "That certainly was a raw deal."

Mason said, "Of course, Paul, *someone* must have been in that room with that corpse at least two or three hours after the murder was committed."

"On account of the one live goldfish?" Drake asked.

"On account of the one live goldfish," Mason said.

"It might have been one that happened to light in a low place in the bathroom floor where the water would collect in a little puddle and give him an opportunity to get just a little oxygen out of the water—just enough to keep him alive."

"It could have been," Mason said, and then added, "I consider the chances of that about one thousand to one."

"So do I."

"You take the fact that someone must have been in that room, coupled with the fact that we know Jane Faulkner was waiting around the corner where she could see us drive up to the house, and there's only one answer."

"I don't see what good it's going to do if you could prove that she was lying about having been in the room with the body," Drake said. "In any event, her husband must have been dead at that time."

Mason said, "They're pinning a murder on my client simply because she told a few fibs. I'd like to prove someone else was telling lies as well. It all gets back to Staunton and the fact that he must have telephoned Mrs. Faulkner we were coming."

Drake said, "I've got someone working on that, Perry. I won't burden you with details, but it occurred to me there was only one way to check Staunton's phone call."

"How was that?"

"Through his wife. And in doing that I found out a few incidental facts."

"Go ahead," Mason said. "What did you find and how did you do it?"

"There was only one way of going at it," Drake said. "That was to plant some good operative in the house who would take the part of a servant and who could pump Mrs. Staunton. I've got an operative right there in the house who's checking up on things. Mrs. Staunton is tickled to death. She thinks this girl is the best all-around maid she ever had." Drake grinned and went on, "What Mrs. Staunton doesn't realize is that she's getting maid service from a twelve-dollar-a-day detective and that the minute this girl gets the information she wants, she'll dust out of there, leaving Mrs. Staunton with a sink full of dirty dishes."

"Any reports on the phone call?" Mason asked.

"Nothing on that as yet," Drake said.

"Keep after it," Mason told him. "That's an important angle in the case."

Drake looked at his watch, said, "I think I'll give her a ring right now, Perry. I'm supposed to be her boy friend. Naturally, Mrs. Staunton is so tickled with the service she's getting, she makes no objection whatever when the maid's boy friend rings up. Of course, this girl may not be able to talk with me, but I have an idea she may be there all alone today. Staunton is hanging around, waiting to be a witness in this case, and there's a pretty good chance Mrs. Staunton is out. Let me give her a ring."

Drake pushed back his chair and went out into the main part of the restaurant where there was a phone booth.

Mason said to Della Street, "You know, Della, if it weren't for the time element in this case, we could bust it wide open."

"What do you mean?"

"The way the district attorney follows every move Faulkner made up to the time of his death. They pick him up at five o'clock when he went to the bank, and carry him right on through from there. From the bank to the pet shop, from the pet shop to the consulting chemist, from the consulting chemist to his home, and leave him just time enough to get his coat and shirt off when the call to the man at the banquet place is put through, and then Faulkner is heard ordering Sally Madison out. At that time, he's in a hurry to get dressed and shaved, and go to that banquet. He's evidently been in that house not over five or six minutes. He's partially undressed, turned hot water in the bathtub, has lathered his face, shaved and put the razor on the shelf. Hang it, Della, if it weren't for that fingerprint on the satchel. How I would like to prove that someone entered that house right after Sally Madison went out and pulled the trigger on that gun!"

Della Street asked abruptly, "Do you suppose Sally really got that bullet?"

"She must have. I had doped that out even before I talked with her in jail. I felt certain that she must have been the one who dredged that bullet out of the fish tank."

"You don't think she got it for Carson?"

"No."

"Why?"

"Because Carson didn't know that anyone had taken the bullet out of there."

"What makes you think that?"

"Because," Mason said, "Carson *must* have been the one who made that final desperate attempt to recover the bullet by siphoning the water out of the tank and turning the tank upside down. And he must have done that on the night Faulkner was murdered. Hang it, Della, let's go at this thing in an orderly way. Let's quit letting ourselves be confused simply because we're representing a client who is lying to us and who has got us into a jackpot. Let's quit being exasperated and use our brains as reasoning machines."

"No matter how you reason," Della Street said, "you always come back to the same focal point in the case that no matter how much others may have been mixed up in it, Sally Madison was the one who opened that satchel and took out the money, the one who threw the empty satchel under the bed, the one who was found in possession of a part of the money."

Mason started drumming with the tips of his fingers on the white tablecloth.

Paul Drake pushed open the door to enter the private dining room.

"Anything new, Paul?" Mason asked.

"This operative of mine is alone in the house, just as I thought. She's been there all by herself ever since nine o'clock. Naturally, she's been busy!"

"Prowling around?"

"That's right. She's stumbled across some interesting sidelights but nothing particularly startling."

"What are the sidelights?"

"Apparently Faulkner had been financing Staunton in some sort of a mining activity."

Mason nodded. "I had assumed all along that

Faulkner must have had some hold on Staunton; otherwise he wouldn't have taken the fish out there and told Staunton what to do—you know the fact that Staunton handled insurance business for the real-estate corporation isn't anything that would give Faulkner such a leverage. Of course, Staunton might have mentioned that when I was talking with him, but he probably thought it was none of my business and simply mentioned the insurance matter."

Drake said, "One thing my operative told me has me stumped."

"What?"

"Talking with Mrs. Staunton last night, she found out that on the night of the murder the telephone in the house had been out of order. Only the telephone in Staunton's study was working."

"Is she sure, Paul?"

"That's what Mrs. Staunton told her. Mrs. Staunton said she had to go to the study that night when she wanted to telephone. She mentioned it because she doesn't like the fish and didn't like to go in the room where the fish were. She said they gave her the creeps, staring at her with those queer, protruding eyes. But that her telephone had been out of order all afternoon and that the company didn't get it fixed until the next day; that the one in the study was a separate line and was working."

Mason said, "Hang it, Paul, do you suppose Staunton was smart enough to know what I was doing when I casually walked over and pulled the drapes back and stood looking out of the window?"

"I don't know," Drake said. "How long did you watch outside of the house after you went out, Perry?"

"It must have been four or five minutes. Staunton came back and stood looking at the fish. He seemed to be thinking of something—turning it over in his mind. Then he went back and switched out the light. We waited there a few minutes after he'd turned out the light. Of course, he *could* have deliberately fooled us. I felt certain that if he had been going to telephone somebody, he'd have done the telephoning right then."

Drake said, "Well, we know that Mrs. Faulkner was out there watching. And you must be pretty certain that she upset that bowl of goldfish within, say, ten or fifteen minutes of the time you got there."

Mason said, "Of course, the other goldfish were dead, Paul. Only the one that I picked up had just a little life in him."

"All right, have it any way you want," Drake said. "The one goldfish was alive. Someone must have put that one goldfish on the floor."

Mason said thoughtfully, "There was a curved segment of the broken fish bowl that still had a little water left in it. I remember noticing that at the time, and I noticed it on one of the photographs this morning. Now, I'm wondering if that one fish couldn't have been in that segment that had a little water in it, and then flopped out."

"That, of course, would mean that the goldfish bowl *could* have been knocked over a long time before," Drake said. "Perhaps when Faulkner was murdered, right around eight-fifteen or eight-twenty."

"I wonder if a goldfish could live that long in such a small amount of water."

"Darned if I know," Drake said. "Want me to get a goldfish and try it?"

"I have an idea you'd better," Mason said.

"Okay. I'll phone my office and ask them to make the goldfish experiment."

Perry Mason looked at his wrist watch, said, "Well, I guess we've got to go back and take it on the chin some more. Lieutenant Tragg will probably be on the stand this afternoon, and Tragg is a smooth worker. How much of a mining deal was it that Staunton had with Faulkner, Paul?"

"I don't know, Perry," Paul Drake said, holding open the door of the dining room. "I may get a little more information later on in the afternoon."

"I don't imagine I'd have cared to have Faulkner as a partner in a mining deal," Della Street said.

"Or in anything else," Drake observed fervently.

They walked slowly back to the courthouse, and as Judge Summerville reconvened court at two o'clock, Ray Medford, with every indication of smug virtue, said, "I want the record to show that at this time we are turning over to counsel for the defense, for his inspection, three magazines which were found on the floor of the bathroom where the murder was committed. By carefully observing photographs which were taken and using a magnifying glass to bring out details, we are able to state that the magazines as now handed to counsel for the defense are in the order in which they were found on the floor."

Mason took the proffered magazines and said, "Calling the attention of the Court to the fact that the magazine which was on top, and which bears a peculiar semicircular ink smear, is a current issue, while the bottom two are older numbers."

"Do you think there's some significance in that?" Medford asked curiously.

"I do," Mason said.

Medford started to ask some question, then caught himself in time and regarded Mason with thoughtful speculation as the attorney opened the magazine and riffled the pages.

"Our next witness will be Lieutenant Tragg," Medford said, "and . . ."

"Just a moment," Mason interrupted. "I call the attention of Court and counsel to a check which I have just discovered in the pages of this magazine which was on the top of the pile, a blank check which has not been filled in in any way, a check bearing the imprint of the Seaboard Mechanics National Bank."

215

Judge Summerville showed his interest. "That blank check was in the magazine, Mr. Mason?"

"Yes, your Honor."

Judge Summerville looked at Medford. "You have noticed the check, Counselor?"

Medford said, casually, "I think somebody did mention something about a book mark in one of the magazines."

"A book mark?" Mason asked.

"If. it is a book mark," Judge Summerville said, "it might be interesting to note the place in the magazine where it was found."

"On page seventy-eight," Mason said, "which seems to be a continuation of a romantic story."

"I'm quite certain it has no significance," Medford said easily. "It was simply a blank check which had been used as a book mark."

"Just a moment," Mason said. "Has any attempt been made to get fingerprints from this check?"

"Certainly not."

"Your Honor, I want this check tested for latent fingerprints," Mason said.

"Go ahead and test it, then," Medford snapped.

Mason's eyes showed that he was excited, but with the ring generalship which had been learned from many courtroom battles, his voice showed no trace of emotion, only that clear resonance which enabled him to hold a courtroom completely spellbound without seeming to raise his voice.

"I call your Honor's attention," he went on, "to the fact that in the lower left-hand corner of this check there is a peculiar triangular point of paper adhering to the body of the check. In other words, the check was torn out of a checkbook along a line of perforations, but at the extreme bottom of the check the line of cleavage left the perforations, and a small triangular tongue of paper is adhering to the check."

Medford said sarcastically, "That happens about half

of the time when *I* tear checks out of a book. It merely means that the check was torn out in a hurry and . . ."

"I think counsel doesn't get the significance," Mason interrupted. "If the Court will notice the checkbook which has been introduced in evidence, and which has the stub showing an amount of one thousand dollars, and the name 'Tom' and then the three letters 'G-r-i', the Court will notice that in the lower *right*-hand corner of that stub, there is a little triangular piece of paper missing. It occurs to me that it might be well to compare this check with that stub and see *if this isn't the check which was torn from that stub.*"

Medford's face showed consternation.

"Let's see that check," Judge Summerville said abruptly.

Mason said, "May I suggest, your Honor, that the check be handled very carefully and only by one corner so that if there *are* any fingerprints remaining . . ."

"Quite right. Quite right," Judge Summerville said.

Mason, holding the check by one corner carried it up to Judge Summerville's desk. Judge Summerville took the checkbook which had been introduced in evidence from the clerk of the court, and while Medford and Mason leaned over his shoulders, the judge carefully placed the check against the perforations of the checkbook. There was no mistaking the keen interest on the judge's face.

"It fits," he said in a tone of finality. "That's the check."

"Of course," Medford started to protest, "that merely means . . ."

"It means that there is less than one chance in ten million that the jagged, irregular lines of that torn piece of paper would coincide with the place which was torn from the check stub unless that was the check that was torn from the book," Judge Summerville said sharply.

"Therefore," Mason interposed, "we are faced with a situation where the decedent evidently started to fill out the stub of a check showing a payment made to Tom Gridley of one thousand dollars, but tore the check which was attached to that stub out of the book and placed it within the leaves of this magazine. It is, therefore, quite apparent that the decedent never intended to fill out the check, but only to fill out a check stub, leaving it to appear that he had made a check to Tom Gridley."

"What would be the object in doing that?" Judge Summerville asked Mason.

Mason smiled. "At the moment, your Honor, the prosecution is putting on its case, and I will therefore leave the answering of that question to the prosecution. When the defendant puts on her case, she will endeavor to explain any evidence that she introduces. And in the meantime, I suggest that the prosecution explain the evidence it introduces."

"I haven't introduced it," Medford said testily.

"Well, you should have," Judge Summerville told him sharply, "and the evidence is going to be introduced if the Court has to do it on its own motion. But first we're going to turn that over to a fingerprint expert and see whether any latent fingerprints can be developed."

"I would suggest," Mason said, "that the Court appoint its own expert. Not that the police are at all incapable, but they may be somewhat biased."

"The Court *will* appoint its own expert," Judge Summerville announced. "The Court will take an adjournment for ten minutes, during which time the Court will get in communication with an expert criminologist and see what fingerprints can be developed on this check. In the meantime, the clerk will keep this check in his custody. I suggest that we run a pin through this corner and that the check be handled in such a way that any fingerprints *which may remain* on it will not be disturbed."

There was just enough accent on the words "which may remain" to make it apparent that Judge Summerville was expressing judicial irritation that the evidence had not been given proper consideration by the police at a time when there would have been a chance of developing latent fingerprints.

Judge Summerville retired with dignity to his chambers and left Medford free to engage in a whispered conference with Sergeant Dorset and Lieutenant Tragg. Dorset, quite plainly, was angry and irritated. But Tragg was puzzled and cautious.

Della Street and Paul Drake came up to stand beside Mason.

"Looks like a break, Perry," Drake said.

"It's about time," Mason told him. "It certainly has been a hoodooed case."

"But what does it mean, Perry?"

"Frankly," Mason said, "I'll be darned if I know. I guess there's no question but what that was Faulkner's handwriting on the check stub."

"I understand there's a handwriting expert who will swear to it," Drake said.

"A good one?"

"Yes."

"What I can't understand," Della Street said, "is why the man should write out the stub of a check and then tear the check out. Of course, Faulkner was equal to anything, and he may have intended to have it appear he had given Tom Gridley a thousand-dollar check."

"But it wouldn't make any difference if his books *had* shown he'd given Gridley twenty one-thousand-dollar checks. Not until Gridley cashed the check would there be any actual payment of money. There's something a lot deeper here than appears on the surface. And I've really overlooked a bet."

Paul Drake said, "I've just found out something, Perry. I don't know whether it will help or not, but somewhere around eight-thirty, the night of the murder, someone rang up Tom Gridley. He said he wanted to talk a little business, but wouldn't give his name. He said he wanted

219

to ask just one or two simple questions. He then went on to say that he understood Gridley was having a dispute over some money matters with Harrington Faulkner and that Faulkner had offered Gridley seven hundred and fifty dollars for a settlement."

Mason's eyes were alert with concentration. "Go on, Paul. What did Gridley say to that?"

"Said he didn't know why he should discuss his affairs with a stranger, and the man's voice said he wanted to do Tom a favor, that he'd like to know if Tom would settle for a thousand."

"Then what?"

"Then Tom, being sick and irritable, said that if Faulkner had a check for one thousand dollars in his hands before noon of the next day he'd settle, if it meant anything to anyone, and slammed up the phone and went back to bed."

"To whom has he told this?" Mason asked.

"Apparently to the police. He hasn't held anything back with the police and they're giving him what breaks they can. They tried for a while to fit that conversation in with the thousand-dollar check stub. Their best guess was that someone was acting as intermediary and had already got the thousand-dollar check from Faulkner and was trying to clean things up."

"But why?" Mason asked.

"Search me."

"And that conversation was around eight-thirty?"

"There we run into a snag. Tom Gridley had been in bed with fever. He was terribly nervous and all worked up over his dealings with Faulkner, and Faulkner buying the pet store and all that stuff. He had been just dozing off, and he didn't notice the time. A while later, after he'd thought things over a bit, he looked at his watch, and it was then around nine ten. He thinks the call was around a little more than half an hour before he looked at his watch. . . . That's a poor way to fix time. It might have been right around eight-twenty, or it may have been quite a bit later. The point is that Gridley swears it wasn't before eight-fifteen because he'd looked at his watch at eight o'clock and then had been awake for several minutes before he dozed into a light slumber.

"That's the story, Perry. The police didn't think much of it after they found they couldn't tie it in with the check for one thousand dollars, and particularly since Tom wasn't certain of the time."

"It wasn't Faulkner, Paul?"

"Apparently not. Tom said it was a strange voice, the voice of a stranger to him. The man seemed rather authoritative, as though he knew what he was doing, and Tom had thought it might have been some lawyer Faulkner had consulted."

"It could have been, at that," Mason said. "Faulkner had those lawsuits which demanded attention. But why wouldn't any lawyer have come forward? Hang it, Paul, the conversation must have taken place right about the time Faulkner was murdered."

Drake nodded, said, "On the other hand, it may have been someone who thought he had a chance to settle things, someone whom the wife had consulted, or perhaps someone Carson had asked to get things straightened out."

"I prefer the wife," Mason said thoughtfully. "It sounds like her. By George, Paul, it *must* have been someone the wife consulted! I'd certainly like to know where she *really* was the night of the murder."

Drake said, "I've had men nosing around, but we can't find a thing. Sergeant Dorset gave her the chance to frame that alibi, and the police are taking it at its face value."

"I'll bet Tragg smells a rat," Mason said.

"If he does, he's keeping his nostrils from quivering even the least bit," Drake replied. "He isn't going to stir up any stink in the department merely because Sergeant Dorset let a woman pull the line that she was going to have hysterics and so get a chance for a frame-up. You know, Perry, if Mrs. Faulkner had said she wanted to go out and *see* her girl friend before Dorset questioned her, they'd have given her the merry ha-ha, and then really given her a third degree. But she says she feels ill, goes out to the back porch, goes through the motions of being sick, and then starts having hysterics, and Dorset is so anxious to get her out of the way until he's finished his investigation that when she says she wanted to have one of her girl friends come over and stay with her, Dorset practically jumps down her throat telling her to go ahead."

Mason nodded, said, "I'm beginning to get an idea, Paul. I think that . . . Here's the judge coming back to the bench. Looks as though he had really taken things into his own hands . . . Bet *he's* going to give us the breaks from now on. He's certainly mad enough at the cops."

Judge Summerville returned to the bench, once more called court into session and said, "Gentlemen, the Court has arranged over the telephone with one of the best consulting criminologists in the city to take charge of that check and see what can be done toward developing latent fingerprints on it. Now do you gentlemen wish to go on with the case? I am frank to state that in view of the peculiar development, the Court will be inclined to give the defense an adjournment in case the defendant wishes it."

"I think not," Mason said, "not at the moment, anyway. Perhaps as the evidence progresses . . ."

"I don't think I'd like that," Medford interrupted. "In other words, the counsel for the defense is adopting the position that we've got to go on putting on our case and showing our hand and then, at any moment, when the defendant wants to, the defendant can call for an adjournment. I think if there's any question about it, we should

222

adjourn the case until after the fingerprints have been developed on that check."

Judge Summerville said crisply, "The Court's offer was made to the defense. I don't think that the prosecution is entitled to ask for an adjournment when a valuable piece of evidence, I may say a most valuable piece of evidence, has been permitted to all but slip through its fingers, and would have gone entirely unnoticed if it hadn't been for counsel for the defense. Proceed with your case, Mr. Medford."

Medford took the court's rebuke with the best grace he could muster. "Of course, your Honor," he said, "I am merely presenting the case as developed by the police. It is not the function of my office to . . ."

"I understand, I understand," Judge Summerville interrupted, "the fault undoubtedly lies with the police, but on the other hand, gentlemen, it is quite evident that it is not the function of the attorney for the defendant to come into court and point out evidence, the significance of which has been entirely overlooked, both by the police and the prosecution. However, that is neither here nor there. Mr. Mason says that he does not care for an adjournment at this time. The Court will state frankly that it will be inclined to give Mr. Mason a reasonable adjournment whenever it is made to appear that it would prejudice the defendant's case to go on with the examination before all of the evidence is in on that check. Call your next witness, Mr. Medford."

"Lieutenant Tragg," Medford said.

Tragg had never been in better form than when he got on the witness stand. In the manner of an impartial, skillful police officer who is only doing his duty and has no personal interest or animosity in the matter, he began to weave a net of circumstantial evidence around Sally Madison, and then, when he testified to the occasion of picking up Sally Madison on the street and finding the gun and the two thousand dollars in bills in her purse, he sprang the bombshell which Ray Medford had been so carefully preparing.

"Now then, Lieutenant Tragg," Medford said, "did you examine that weapon for the purpose of developing any latent fingerprints?"

"Certainly," Tragg said.

"And what did you find?"

"I found several latent fingerprints which retained sufficiently distinct characteristics so that they could be positively identified."

"And whose fingerprints were they?"

"Four fingerprints were those of the defendant."

"And the others?" Medford asked in a voice that held just a note of conscious triumph.

"The other two fingerprints," Lieutenant Tragg said, "were those of Miss Della Street, the secretary of Mr. Perry Mason, and the one who, at the request of Perry Mason, had taken Miss Sally Madison to the Kellinger Hotel in an attempt to keep her from being questioned."

Medford glanced quickly at Mason, not knowing that Paul Drake's detectives had already tipped Mason off to this point in the evidence, and thinking that he would encounter some expression of dismay.

Mason merely glanced casually at the clock, then looked inquiringly over at Medford.

"Have you finished with the witness?" he asked.

"Cross-examine," Medford snapped.

Judge Summerville held up his hand. "Just a moment," he said. "I want to ask your witness a question. Lieutenant Tragg, are you quite certain that the fingerprints you found on that weapon were actually those of Miss Della Street?"

"Yes, your Honor."

"Showing that she had touched that weapon?"

"That is quite right, your Honor."

"Very well," Judge Summerville said in a voice that

showed his appreciation of the gravity of the situation, "you may cross-examine, Mr. Mason."

Mason said, "You'll pardon me, Lieutenant Tragg, if I perhaps review some of your testimony, but as I understand it, you have made a very thorough check of the movements of Harrington Faulkner on the afternoon of the day he met his death?"

"From five o'clock on," Tragg said. "In fact, we can account for *every* move he made from five o'clock until the time of his death."

"And he went to the Rawlins pet store sometime after five o'clock?"

"Yes. He went to the bank, got the money and then went to the Rawlins pet store."

"And he was there some time taking inventory?"

"Around an hour and forty-five minutes."

"And while he was there he noticed this revolver?"

"That's right."

"And put it in his pocket?"

"Yes."

"And then, according to your theory of the case, when he went to his home he took the gun out of his pocket and put it down—perhaps on the bed?"

Tragg said, "The gun was in his hip pocket. He went home, took off his coat and shirt and started to shave. It's only natural to suppose that he took the gun out of his pocket."

"Then," Mason said suavely, "how does it happen that you didn't find any of Mr. Faulkner's fingerprints on the gun?"

Tragg hesitated a moment, said, "The murderer must have wiped all fingerprints off the gun."

"Why?"

"Obviously," Tragg said, smiling slightly, "to remove incriminating evidence."

"Therefore," Mason said, "if the defendant had been the one who committed the murder and had thought

225

enough of the problem of fingerprints to have wiped all fingerprints off the gun she would hardly have gone ahead after that and left her own fingerprints on it, would she?"

Tragg was obviously jarred by the question. He said, "Of course, you're assuming something there, Mr. Mason."

"What am I assuming?"

"You're assuming that I know something of what was in the defendant's mind."

"You've already testified to what was in the mind of the murderer," Mason said. "You have testified that the murderer wiped the fingerprints off the weapon to remove incriminating evidence. Now then, I am asking you if that theory is consistent with the theory that Sally Madison committed the murder."

Lieutenant Tragg obviously realized the force of Mason's suggestion. He shifted his position uncomfortably.

"Isn't it far more likely that she is telling the truth, and that she picked up the gun in order to remove it from the scene of the crime, knowing that it was Tom Gridley's gun?"

"I'll leave that up to the court," Tragg said.

"Thank you," Mason announced, smiling. "And now, I want to ask you a couple of other questions, Lieutenant Tragg. It is the theory of the police, I believe, that Harrington Faulkner was writing this check stub and was about to write the name Tom Gridley in the check stub when he was shot?"

"That's right."

"The fact that he had written only the first three letters of the last name, and the fact that the checkbook was found where it had fallen on the floor, are the things on which you predicate your conclusion?"

"That, plus the fact that the fountain pen also fell on the floor."

226

"Don't you think that something else might have interrupted the deceased?"

"Such as what?" Tragg asked. "I'd be glad to have you mention something that would cause a man to stop writing in the middle of a name that way."

"Perhaps the ringing of a telephone?" Mason asked.

"Not a chance in the world," Tragg said. ". . . that is, if you want my opinion."

"I'm asking for it," Mason said.

"If the telephone had rung, the decedent would certainly have finished the name 'Gridley' before he answered the telephone. And he wouldn't have dropped the checkbook on the floor and wouldn't have dropped the fountain pen on the floor."

"Therefore," Mason said, "the thing that prevented the decedent from finishing writing the name 'Gridley' was the fatal shot?"

"I think there's no other conclusion."

"You have talked with a gentleman named Charles Menlo?"

"Yes."

"And, without anticipating Mr. Menlo's testimony, I believe you know that Mr. Menlo will state that he was talking with the decedent on the telephone at the time when someone, apparently the defendant, entered the house and was ordered out by Mr. Faulkner?"

"This, of course, is very irregular," Medford interposed.

"I think counsel is simply trying to save time," Judge Summerville said. "Do you want to object to the question?"

"No, I think not. There's no question about Mr. Menlo's testimony."

"That's right," Lieutenant Tragg said.

"Therefore," Mason went on, "if it had been the defendant who entered the house at that time . . ."

"She admits that she did," Tragg said. "Her own written statement covers that point."

"Exactly," Mason went on. "And if she found the door open and entered, encountered Harrington Faulkner in the bedroom, talking on the telephone, and if Faulkner then tried to eject her and she snatched up the gun and shot him, she could hardly have shot him while he was writing a check stub in the bathroom, could she?"

"Wait a minute. How's that again?" Tragg asked.

Mason said, "It's quite obvious, Lieutenant. The police theory is that Faulkner was telephoning when Sally Madison came into the room. Faulkner still had some lather on his face. He was running water in the bathtub. He ordered the defendant out. There was a struggle. She saw the gun lying on the bed and picked it up and shot him. Now then, if she had shot him while he was struggling with her in the bedroom, she couldn't have shot him while he was writing that check stub in the bathroom, could she?"

Tragg said, "No," and then after a moment added, "I'm glad you brought up that point, Mr. Mason, because it makes the murder a deliberate, cold-blooded murder instead of one committed in the heat of rage."

"Just how do you reason that out?" Mason asked.

"Because Faulkner must have gone back to the bathroom and picked up the checkbook and started writing the check stub when she shot him."

"That's your theory now?" Mason asked.

Tragg said, smiling, "It's *your* theory, Mr. Mason, and I'm now beginning to think it's a good one."

"And when Faulkner fell as the result of that shot, did he upset the table containing the bowl in which the goldfish were swimming?"

"He did."

"But," Mason said, "there was a graniteware container and one goldfish in the bathtub. How do you account for those?"

"I think one of the fish must have fallen into the bathtub."

Mason smiled, "Remembering, Lieutenant, that at that time Faulkner was drawing *hot* water for a bath. How long do you think the fish would have lived in *hot* bath water and how do you think the graniteware container got in the bathtub?"

Tragg frowned, thought for a few seconds, then said, "I'm not a mind reader."

Mason smiled courteously. "Thank you, Lieutenant, for that concession. I was afraid that you *had* been trying to qualify as such. Particularly in regard to your comments as to the fingerprints of Della Street on the gun. For all you know, those prints might have been put on the gun before the murder."

"Not the way *you've* explained it," Tragg said. "The murderer must have wiped all fingerprints off the gun."

"Then, the murderer could hardly have been Sally Madison."

Tragg frowned. "I want to think that over a bit," he said.

Mason bowed to Judge Summerville. "And that, your Honor, is the point at which I will terminate my cross-examination. I would *like* to let Lieutenant Tragg think it over a little bit—think it over a whole lot."

Judge Summerville said to Medford, "Call your next witness."

"Louis C. Corning," Medford announced. "Please come forward, Mr. Corning."

Corning, the fingerprint expert who had lifted the fingerprints from the various objects in Faulkner's house, testified in detail as to the fingerprints he had found, and paid particular attention to a fingerprint of Sally Madison which had been found on the handle of the satchel under the bed—a fingerprint which was introduced in evidence and marked, "F. P. No. 10."

"Cross-examine," Medford said to Perry Mason, as

soon as the witness had positively identified that particular fingerprint.

"Why," Mason asked on cross-examination, "did you use the so-called lifting method?"

"Because," the witness answered defiantly, "that was the only method to use."

"You mean that you couldn't have used any other?"

"I mean that it wouldn't have been practical."

"What do you mean by that?"

The witness said, "Attorneys for the defense always try to hold a field day with an expert who has lifted fingerprints. But when you're called on to investigate a crime of that sort, you have to lift the fingerprints, and that's all there is to it. Lifting enables you to make a complete examination and a careful examination, and to avoid the mistakes which are sometimes made by the use of too much haste—such as when a person is trying to examine and classify a lot of latent fingerprints in a short time."

"It took you some time after you had lifted these prints to examine them?"

"I worked on them for a good many hours, yes."

"You found a fingerprint of the defendant—the one that has been introduced as the People's Exhibit F. P. No. 10—on the handle of the satchel, which has also been introduced in evidence?"

"I did."

"How do you know you found that fingerprint there?"

"How do I know anything?"

Mason smiled.

Judge Summerville said, "Answer the question."

"Well, I knew it because I took an envelope, wrote on the outside of it, 'Fingerprints taken from satchel,' and I then proceeded to dust the satchel and wherever I found a latent I pulled it off and dropped it into this envelope."

"And what did you then do with the envelopes?"

"I put them in my briefcase."

"And what did you do with your briefcase?"

230

"I took it home that night."

"And what did you do with it then?"

"I worked on some of the fingerprints."

"Did you find F. P. No. 10 that night?"

"No, I didn't find that until late the next morning."

"Where were you when you found it?"

"At my office."

"Did you go directly from your house to your office?"

"I did not."

"Where did you go?"

"At the request of Lieutenant Tragg, I went out to the residence of James L. Staunton."

"What did you do there?"

"I took some fingerprints from a fish tank."

"By the lifting method?"

"By the lifting method."

Mason said, "And what did you do with *those* fingerprints?"

"I put them in an envelope marked 'Prints lifted from fish tank at residence of James L. Staunton.'"

"And that envelope was also put in your briefcase?"

"Yes."

"Is it possible that you made a mistake and that one of the fingerprints of the defendant which was actually lifted from this tank was placed inadvertently in this envelope labeled 'Fingerprints taken from satchel'?"

"Don't be silly," the witness said scornfully.

"I'm not being silly," Mason said. "I'm asking you a question."

"The answer is an unequivocal, absolute, final and emphatic *no*."

"Who was present when you were taking these fingerprints?"

"No one except the gentleman who had admitted me."

"Mr. Staunton?"

"That's right."

"How long did it take?"

"I would say not over twenty to thirty minutes."

"Then you went back to your office?"

"That's right."

"And how soon after that did you finish checking the fingerprints and find this exhibit F. P. 10?"

"I would say about three hours afterwards."

Mason said, "That's all."

As the witness left the stand, Mason said, "Now, you Honor, I think I would like to request that recess which the Court has previously suggested might be in order. would prefer to know the result of the examination o that blank check for fingerprints before I go on with th cross-examination of witnesses."

"The Court will adjourn until tomorrow morning at te o'clock," Judge Summerville said promptly. "And, for th benefit of counsel, it will be noted that the Court ha advised the criminologist who is examining the blan check for fingerprints to notify both counsel immediatel upon the completion of his examination. Until tomorro morning at ten o'clock."

Sally Madison, without the slightest change of her fa cial expression, said in a low voice to Perry Mason "Thank you." Her voice was as calmly impersonal a though she had been expressing her gratitude for th lighting of a cigarette or some similar service. Nor did sh wait for the lawyer to make any reply, but instead aros and stood waiting to be escorted from the courtroom.

18

■

Late afternoon sunlight was throwing somewhat vague shadows from the palm trees on the lawn against the stuccoed side of the residence of Wilfred Dixon when Mason parked his car, walked up the steps to the porch and calmly rang the bell.

Wilfred Dixon opened the door, said rather formally, "Good afternoon, Mr. Mason."

Mason said, "I'm back."

"I'm engaged at the moment."

"I have," Mason announced, "more chips. I want to sit in the game again."

"I'll be glad to accommodate you some time this evening. Perhaps around eight o'clock, Mr. Mason?"

"That," Mason announced, "won't be satisfactory. I want to see you now."

Dixon shook his head. "I'm sorry, Mr. Mason."

Mason said, "The last time I saw you I made a bluff and you called it. This time I've got more chips and I think I have better cards."

"Indeed."

Mason said, "Thinking back on your conversation, I am impressed by the very skillful way in which you led me to believe that you never for a moment considered *buying* Faulkner's interest in the company, but only selling Genevieve's interest to him."

"Well?" Dixon asked, acting as though he were on the point of closing the door.

Mason said, "It was a rather clever piece of work, but the only reason you would have had for being interested in the bullet which Carson had concealed in the fish tank would have been because you wanted to have some definite hold on Carson, and the only reason that I can think of for wanting to have such a hold would be either because you or Genevieve had fired the shot, or because you intended to buy out Faulkner, and when you bought him out wanted to have a strangle-hold on Carson so you could freeze him out without his being able to fight back."

"I'm afraid, Mr. Mason, that your reasoning is entirely fallacious. However, I'll be glad to discuss it with you this evening."

"And," Mason said, "so that the deal would look better for income tax purposes, you arranged to give Faulkner a check for twenty-five thousand *more* than the price that was actually agreed upon and have Faulkner bring you twenty-five thousand dollars in cash."

Wilfred Dixon's eyes closed and opened three times, as though they might have been regulated by clockwork. "Come in," he invited. "Mrs. Genevieve Faulkner is with me at the moment. I saw no reason to disturb her, but perhaps we'd better get this over with once and for all."

"Perhaps we had," Mason said.

Mason followed Dixon into the room, shook hands with Genevieve Faulkner, calmly seated himself, lit a cigarette and said, "So, of course, having received the twenty-five thousand dollars from Faulkner in a deal which was completely fraudulent because it had for its primary purpose an attempt to defraud the Collector of Internal Revenue, you inadvertently paid Sally Madison two thousand dollars in cash from the twenty-five thousand which Faulkner had previously delivered to you. Now, that means that you must have seen Faulkner

234

either at his house or at some other place, subsequent to the time Sally Madison left Faulkner's residence, and *before* you paid the money over to Sally Madison out here."

Dixon smiled and shook his head at Genevieve Faulkner. "I don't know just what he's driving at, Genevieve," he said calmly. "Apparently it's some last-minute theory he's using to try and get his client acquitted. I thought perhaps you'd better hear it."

"The man seems to be crazy," Genevieve Faulkner said.

"Let's go back and look at the evidence," Mason said. "Faulkner was very anxious to attend a banquet where some goldfish experts were to talk and where he was to mingle with some other goldfish collectors. He was in such a hurry that he wouldn't even discuss matters with Sally Madison. He rushed her out of the house. He had drawn the water for his bath. He had shaved but part of his face, still had lather on it. It's reasonable to suppose that after he put Sally Madison out, he washed his face. Then, before he had had a chance to clean his razor, before he had had a chance to take off his clothes and hastily jump into his hot bath, the telephone rang.

"Whatever was said over the telephone was something that was of the greatest importance to Harrington Faulkner. It was something that caused him to forego his bath, to put on his shirt, tie and coat and go dashing out to meet the person who had telephoned. That person must have been either you, Genevieve, or both. He paid over the twenty-five thousand dollars, and then returned to his house. By that time it was too late to attend the banquet. The water, which had been hot in the bathtub when he had drawn it some time before, had now become cold.

"Harrington Faulkner had another appointment he didn't care to miss. But he had an hour or so before that appointment. He decided that he'd treat a fish that had tail rot, and then segregate that fish from the others. The treatment for tail rot is to immerse the fish in equal parts of hydrogen peroxide and water. So Faulkner once more took off his coat and shirt, went to the kitchen, got a graniteware pot, put equal parts of hydrogen peroxide and water in it, immersed the fish in that water, and then, when the treatment was finished, put that fish in the bathtub.

"At that point, Faulkner remembered that he had given a thousand-dollar check payable to Tom Gridley, which he hadn't entered on the stub of his checkbook and therefore hadn't deducted from his bank account. In view of the twenty-five-thousand-dollar withdrawal, the balance in his checking account had been diminished materially, and he wanted to be certain that he kept right up to date on it. So he got his checkbook, took his fountain pen from the pocket of his coat, and picked up a magazine to use as a backer so he could write. He found that one magazine wasn't enough, so at random, he picked up two old magazines. There was some reason why he remained in the bathroom to write that check stub. It probably had to do with the exact timing of his fish treatment. He was writing on the stub of that check when he was killed."

Dixon yawned and politely stifled the yawn with his forefinger. "I'm afraid, Mr. Mason, you're not getting anywhere with that theory."

Mason said, "Perhaps not, but my own idea is that once the police start questioning Mrs. Genevieve Faulkner along the lines of that theory of mine, they'll either force her to disgorge that other twenty-three thousand dollars and make a statement which will clarify the situation, or they'll start searching the place and find the twenty-three thousand dollars."

With elaborate courtesy, Dixon moved over toward the phone. "Would you like to have me call the police and suggest that to them?"

236

Mason looked him squarely in the eyes. "Yes," he said, "and when you make the call, ask for Lieutenant Tragg."

Dixon shook his head sadly. "I'm afraid, Mason, that you want us to play into your hands. On second thought, I've decided that I'm simply not going to have anything to do with this."

Mason grinned. "You made a bluff, just as I did yesterday, and this time *I'm* calling it. When you called me, I actually telephoned Tragg. Now go ahead and be as good a sport as I was."

"You're too anxious," Dixon said, and walked back to his chair.

Mason said, "All right, if you won't do it, I'll do it."

"Go right ahead."

Mason moved over to the telephone, turned back over his shoulder and said, "That one-thousand dollar check to Tom Gridley is the payoff. You didn't want to buy the business and have any possible claims outstanding that might involve litigation. So you telephoned Tom Gridley and asked him if he'd accept a thousand dollars by way of a complete settlement. Gridley said he would. So you had Faulkner sign a check for that amount right here, which you mailed to Gridley. But when you learned Faulkner had been murdered, you had to get that check back. At the time you didn't realize you were gambling with Sally Madison's life. You only knew that if you could keep it from becoming known that Faulkner had rushed out here, you would be in a position to keep twenty-three thousand dollars in cold, hard cash, and still have plenty of opportunity to buy the business at your own price from Faulkner's estate."

Dixon said, "Come, come, Mr. Mason. This is being said in the presence of a witness. Tomorrow I shall sue you for defamation of character. You must have *something* on which to pin such a fantastic story."

Mason said, "I have the word of my client."

Dixon smiled. "For a veteran lawyer, you're *most* susceptible to feminine charm."

Mason said, "And I also have some shrewd deduction. You got up this morning and went to the corner drug store for breakfast. You were there an hour. That's a long time to eat a light breakfast at a corner drug store. When I drove up, I looked the drug store over. There's a mail box in front of it. The hour of the first mail collection in the morning is seven forty-five. I think the mailman who collects the mail will be able to testify that when he opened the box you were there with a plausible story and a bribe. You had inadvertently mailed a letter to Thomas Gridley. It had a check in it, but there was a mistake on the check. You wanted to rectify it. You convinced the man of your identity, of the fact that you had mailed the letter. . . . That is a hunch, but when I play poker, I play hunches. And now I'm going to call Lieutenant Tragg."

Mason picked up the telephone receiver, dialed Operator, and said, "Get me the police. This is an emergency."

For a moment the room was completely silent, then suddenly a chair overturned. Mason looked back over his shoulder to see the squat, athletic form of Wilfred Dixon coming at him with a rush.

The lawyer dropped the receiver, swung in a body pivot, and at the same time jerked his head to one side.

Dixon's punch missed Mason's chin, went harmlessly over Mason's shoulder. Mason's right hand sank into the pit of Dixon's stomach. Then, as the business counselor folded up, Mason jerked back his arm, raised his shoulder, and caught the man a terrific uppercut.

Dixon dropped to the floor with a thud that was as inanimate as the sound of a flour sack falling to the floor.

Mrs. Genevieve Faulkner sat very calmly, her knees crossed, eyes slightly narrowed, an expression of concentration on her face. She said, "You're a rough player, Mr Mason—but I always did like men who could take care of

238

themselves. Perhaps you and I could talk a little business."

Mason didn't even bother to answer. He picked up the dangling receiver, said, "Police headquarters? Get me Lieutenant Tragg of Homicide, and get him in a hurry."

19

It was after seven o'clock when Lieutenant Tragg entered Mason's office.

"Some people are born lucky," Tragg said, grinning. "Others achieve luck, and others have luck thrust upon them."

Mason nodded. "I did have to put it on a silver platter and dump it in your lap, didn't I?"

Tragg's grin faded. "I was referring to you. I'd really have hated to have done it to you, Mason, but you've slipped it over on us so often, that when you left yourself wide open, I wouldn't have had any other choice. I was going to put the skids under you."

"I know," Mason said, "I don't blame you. Sit down."

Tragg nodded to Della Street. "No hard feelings, Della. It was all in the line of duty." He sat down and said, "How about one of your cigarettes, Mason?"

The lawyer gave Tragg a cigarette.

"Well," Tragg said, "we've got most of it in the bag. We're going to turn your golddigger loose. I wondered if you wanted to be on hand for the ceremony."

"Of course I do."

"I don't blame you. It'll be impressive. The deuce of it is I haven't got a really good case as yet."

"Suppose you tell me just what you've found out."

Tragg said, "I'd like it a lot better if you'd tell me how you knew what had happened."

"We held out a little evidence on you, Lieutenant."

"Such as what?"

Mason said, "I deduced that Carson must have picked up that bullet from Faulkner's desk and tossed it over his shoulder into the fish tank. Now, the only reason he would have done that would have been because he wanted to protect the person who fired the shot."

"Meaning that he fired it?"

Mason said, "No. Meaning that someone else had, and he wanted to protect that person."

"Who?"

Mason said, "When we went to Faulkner's house the night of the murder, Mrs. Faulkner came tearing up in an automobile. She seemed in the devil of a hurry, but the way the exhaust smelled, I thought the choke must be nearly all the way out. That meant she'd been running with a cold motor, and that in turn meant she hadn't come very far. So Paul Drake examined the car and found that the ash tray was empty. As he pointed out, a nervous person will almost invariably empty the ash tray of a car if there's a long wait under tension."

Tragg nodded and said, "I've done it myself."

"Drake found the place where the ash tray had been emptied. It was a place from where you could see the front of the Faulkner house."

"You mean Mrs. Faulkner was waiting for you to drive up?"

"That's what I thought at the time," Mason said, "and I damn near got a client convicted because the true solution didn't occur to me."

"What was it?"

"I was right in deducing that she had only come a short distance," Mason said. "Her car had been parked earlier that evening at the spot where the ash tray had been emptied. I made the mistake of picking on the obvious and jumping at the wrong conclusion. It had been much earlier in the evening. It had been between five and seven instead of around the hour Sally Madison and I arrived."

"And why should she have parked there at that time?"

"Because her husband had gone out, and Elmer Carson had taken advantage of his absence to go into the real estate office and start looking for that bullet. And Jane Faulkner, who had fired the shot at her husband in an attempt to get him out of the way, had been sitting there in her car, where she could see the entrance to the house, and blow her horn and warn Carson in the event Faulkner returned unexpectedly. In that event, Carson would have slipped out of the back door, gone through the alley, joined Mrs. Faulkner in her automobile, and been whisked away."

Tragg's eyes narrowed. "You think Mrs. Faulkner took that shot at her husband?"

"I'm satisfied she did. She pulled that sleep medicine stuff as a species of alibi. She'd managed to plant herself where she knew her husband was going to be driving his automobile. She planned to fire the shot, jump into her own car, take a dose of quick acting sedative, drive back to the house, undress, and go to bed. She fired the shot at her husband, all right, but she hadn't realized the difficulty of shooting at a man in a moving automobile. She missed him by inches. The evidence shows that the only possible explanation of what happened is that Carson was protecting the person who tried to commit the murder. Obviously, Carson didn't do it. Therefore, who was the person who had made the attempt, and whom Carson was trying to protect? I should have known when Mrs. Faulkner came driving up in her automobile in a terrific hurry and with the motor almost cold. She was trying to get home before her husband returned from that banquet, and her car was cold, not because she had been parked around there watching the house, but because she had been spending the evening in the arms of Elmer Carson, who lived, you will remember, within four blocks of Faulkner's house."

Tragg stared steadily at the pattern of the carpet as he correlated these points in his mind.

"That doesn't make sense, Mason."

"What doesn't?"

"That elaborate attempt at getting the bullet earlier in the evening when they knew that Faulkner was going to be out after eight-thirty. They'd have waited until then."

"No they wouldn't," Mason said. "They knew that he was going to be at the pet store while there were still some minutes of daylight. They wanted to drain that fish tank and try and find the bullet, which seemed to have eluded them, while they still had daylight. If Faulkner had driven up and found the lights on in the office, it would have been a give away. And you'll remember that since the duplex side of the building was to be used as an office, there were no curtains on the windows, merely Venetian blinds on the south and west windows."

"Well," Tragg admitted, "you called the turn on Dixon. They telephoned Faulkner, told him they'd make the deal promptly at eight-thirty, but that he had to be there with the twenty-five thousand dollars; that if he wasn't there at that exact moment, they wouldn't make the deal.

"What I can't figure out, though, is why Faulkner paid out twenty-five thousand in cash and trusted to Dixon's good faith to go through with the deal."

"He had no alternative," Mason said. "Besides, he knew Dixon *wanted* to buy his interest in the company."

"Well, anyway, Faulkner dropped everything to rush out there. When he got out there, they raised the point about Tom Gridley. They weren't buying any lawsuits. So Dixon called up Tom Gridley, and reached a deal with him over the phone by which Faulkner was to mail him a check for a thousand dollars. But how did Dixon and

242

Genevieve Faulkner know all about that bullet business? I neglected to get that cleared up."

Mason said, "How did they know everything else that went on in the company? There's only one answer. Alberta Stanley, the secretary for the company, was in Dixon's employ. When she told him about the bullet, he deduced what must have happened—just as I did when I heard of it."

Tragg nodded. "Of course. The Stanley girl is the answer to lots of things."

"What became of the check?" Mason asked.

Tragg grinned. "Just as you deduced, that was the one weak spot in Dixon's armor. The postman was talked and bribed into giving the letter back to Dixon when the mail was collected. But I'm still a long way from pinning the murder on Wilfred Dixon."

"Pinning the murder on *him!*" Mason exclaimed.

"Why, yes."

"You can't pin it on *him,*" Mason told the officer. "Use your head. The person who killed Faulkner went to Faulkner's house. He found Faulkner treating a goldfish for tail rot. He got Faulkner to stop his treatment of the goldfish and go get his fountain pen so that he could write some document, or sign some document. And then, after that document had been signed, and while Faulkner still had his fountain pen in his hand, Faulkner remembered about that check to Gridley and decided he'd make a stub that would cover the amount of the check. So he tore the check out of the book, started making out the stub, and was shot in cold blood by a man who had started to leave the house, but who saw Gridley's gun lying on the bed, and couldn't resist the temptation to use it.

"Faulkner fell down dead. When he fell, he upset the bowl of goldfish that was on the table in the bathroom. The bowl broke. One segment of the bowl contained a little water. One of the fish lived in there until he had exhausted the oxygen in the water, and then in his strug-

gles, flopped out onto the floor. Taking the evidence o
that goldfish, I'd say that the crime must have bee
committed somewhere around nine-thirty, and you'
remember Faulkner said that he had an appointment a
around that time.

"Wilfred Dixon and Genevieve Faulkner weren'
above rigging their books so that they had a twenty-fiv
thousand dollar profit that wouldn't show on their incom
tax. They weren't above throwing the hooks int
Faulkner and forcing him to sell out. They weren't abov
getting the bullet Carson had tossed into the fish tank
proving that Carson must have put it there, and black
mailing Carson into letting go of his own holdings for a
fraction of their value; but they weren't the type tha
deliberately kill a man without any motive. Once they'
got Faulkner's twenty-five thousand dollars, they certain
ly had no interest in bumping him off. They didn't realiz
that keeping silent would doom Sally Madison—not a
first. By the time they did, they were in so deep they ha
to carry on. Dixon couldn't tell the truth without implicat
ing himself and Genevieve Faulkner in a fraudulen
transaction. So they decided to keep quiet. But the
certainly weren't the ones who followed Faulkner hom
and murdered him."

"Then who the devil did?" Tragg asked.

"Use your head," Mason told him. "Remember there'
a blot on the magazine, an ink smear. What makes an in
smear? A fountain pen that's almost empty. And Jame
L. Staunton had a written release from Faulkner whic
he showed you when you started crowding him, bu
which he didn't show to me when I questioned him. Wh
didn't he produce it sooner? Why didn't he show it to me
Because the ink was hardly dry on it, and probabl
because a portion of the blot that had fallen from th
almost empty fountain pen when Faulkner took it out o
his pocket had stained one edge of the document."

Tragg abruptly got up and reached for his hat. "Thanks, Mason."

"Did that written statement have a blot on it?" Mason asked.

"Yes, on one edge. And like a damn fool I didn't have the ink analyzed. I could have done it when I first saw the statement, and it would have shown that it had been written the night before, instead of at the time Faulkner brought the goldfish. I'm afraid, Mason, I've been so hypnotized by the fact that I was dealing with a girl who happened to have the murder gun in her purse, that I closed my eyes to everything else."

"That's the big trouble with being an officer," Mason agreed. "You have the responsibility of getting the evidence which will support a conviction. Once you make an arrest, you have to put in all of your energies getting evidence which will insure the conviction of the arrested person. Otherwise you're in bad with the D. A."

Tragg nodded, then half way to the door turned and said, "How about that fingerprint—that F. P. No. 10?"

Mason said, "That fingerprint shows the danger of the lifting method. Every bit of evidence shows that Staunton was a shrewd man and a cunning man. Sergeant Dorset must have let it drop while he was out there with Sally Madison that they were lifting fingerprints at the scene of the murder. After they had left, Staunton, whom you will probably find knows something about fingerprinting, himself, knew that Sally Madison's fingerprints would be on the glass tank where she had handled it while treating his goldfish. He simply lifted one of her fingerprints off of that tank and had it all ready, looking for a chance to slip it into the collection of lifted fingerprints. When Louis Corning came out to Staunton's house to fingerprint the tank, it gave Staunton the opportunity he'd been anticipating. While Corning was taking fingerprints from the fish tank and completely absorbed in what he was doing, Staunton saw the collection of envelopes which Corning had so obligingly taken from his briefcase, and slipped Sally's fingerprint in where he thought it would do the most good."

"I don't believe he could have done that," Tragg said.

"Ask him," Mason said, grinning. "And when you ask him, tell him that you've found his fingerprint on the lif that carries Exhibit F. P. 10."

"Why did Staunton kill him?" Tragg asked after he had thought over Mason's suggestion for a second or two

Mason said wearily, "Go find out. Good Lord, do you want me to do *everything* for you? Faulkner and Staunton had been secret partners in a mining deal. I'll bet you ten to one that Faulkner had Staunton over the barrel Faulkner had just been forced by Dixon to sell out hi business for less than it was worth, and you'll probably find that Faulkner was passing the bite on to Staunton Hell, I don't know, and I'm not paid to think about it My job was to get Sally Madison out of jail and I'm getting her out of jail. Della Street and I are going out o the town. We're going to eat. Maybe we're even going t drink!"

"More power to you," Tragg said. "Where will yo be?"

Mason wrote the names of three night clubs on a sli of paper, handed it to Lieutenant Tragg. "We'll be a one of those three places, but don't try to reach us t report anything except a confession from Staunton an the time at which you're going to release Sally Madiso from jail. We don't want to be disturbed over mino matters."

20

■

The orchestra was playing one of the old-time waltzes. [l]ights had been turned down and blue spotlights shin[i]ng on the dome above the dance floor gave the place [th]e appearance of summer moonlight, showing the forms [o]f couples waltzing slowly.

Mason's lips brushed Della Street's cheek. "Happy?" [h]e asked.

"Yes, darling," she said softly. "And it's lovely not to [b]e going to jail!"

A waiter came hurrying toward them, caught Mason's [e]ye, made frantic signals.

Mason guided Della Street over toward him, then, on [th]e edge of the dance floor they ceased moving their feet [b]ut kept swaying to the rhythm of the music. "What is [it]?" Mason asked.

"A Lieutenant Tragg has called up. Says he's from [H]omicide and to convey the message to you that you win [al]l the way along the line, and that Sally Madison is to be [r]eleased at midnight. He wants to know if you care to [ta]lk to him?"

Mason grinned. "He's on the line?"

"Yes."

Mason said, "Kindly give him my thanks—tell him [th]at I'll be there in time for the ceremonies, and that I'm [t]oo agreeably engaged at the moment to talk with anyone [e]xcept my partner."

The waiter turned away. Mason guided Della Stre
back toward the center of the dance floor.

"Poor Sally Madison," Mason said, "she was willing
take a chance on the death chamber in order to save t
man she loved."

Della Street looked up at him. "You can't blame h
for that. It's . . . it's feminine nature."

Mason said, "It surprises some people, Della, to thi
you find as much loyalty in the Sally Madisons of t
world as you do in women who have followed all t
rules."

Della Street lowered her eyes. "It's the way a woma
made, Chief. She'll do anything for the man she loves-
anything." Then she added hastily, "What time is
Chief? We don't want to be late getting to the jail."

"We won't," Mason assured her, circling her waist wi
his arm, as the music ended. "I even think," he added
the lights blazed into brilliance and they started ba
toward their table, "that Lieutenant Tragg might
grateful enough to delay things a few minutes for us. A
the next time you go places with a golddigger, Della, ta
a look in the purse first."

Della Street laughed. "I probably won't," she sai
"You and I learn everything from our adventures exce
prudence."

"That's the way I like to have it," Mason said, grinni
at her.